perfect liars

perfect.

liars

kimberly reid

TU BOOKS
AN IMPRINT OF LEE & LOW BOOKS INC.
NEW YORK

Copyright © 2016 by Kimberly Reid
Jacket photo copyright © by wundervisuals/Getty Images

TU BOOKS, an imprint of LEE & LOW BOOKS Inc., 95 Madison Avenue, New York, NY 10016
leeandlow.com

Manufactured in the United States of America by Worzalla Publishing Company, May 2016

Book design by Elizabeth Casal
Book production by The Kids at Our House
The text is set in Granjon

10 9 8 7 6 5 4 3 2 1
First Edition

Cataloging-in-Publication Data is on file with the Library of Congress

To the readers. Thank you for loving books.

last summer

1

When Drea pulled up to the house, she was surprised to find the iron gate wide open. The huge magnolias standing guard on either side of the gate and the scent of the rose garden on the other side of the ivy-covered, six-foot brick walls that the gate joined together may have appeared as welcoming as Southern hospitality itself, but the place was a fortress worthy of a federal mint. The open gate was the kind of thing that ought to have made Drea suspicious, but she drove through anyway.

She didn't get very far. The turnoff leading to the circular drive in front of the house had a barricade—if that was what one considered two brass stanchions linked by a red velvet rope, which Drea didn't. She shifted her car into park, but kept the engine idling while she got out and moved the sorry excuse for a barricade, ignoring the hand-calligraphied sign instructing her to "Please follow the drive to the back of the house, where additional parking is available."

Just as she was getting back into her car, she noticed a stranger jogging up the drive from the direction of the additional parking around back. Considering the open gate and all, it was the second thing that should have made her jump back in the car and leave the way she came, but she didn't, because of the velvet ropes, the fine calligraphy on heavy-weight stock, and the fact that the man was wearing a white shirt, black pants, and a bow tie. There must be a party in the works. As the man came closer, she realized he wasn't actually a man. Not yet anyway. He was probably her age. He was definitely good-looking.

"I'm sorry, but you may not park here," he instructed. "You must park around back."

Drea detected a French accent, which she loved, especially when delivered by a guy with such great cheekbones and full lips. Yummy. No. *Délicieux*. He distracted her so much she just stood there saying nothing, and now the yummy-sounding *garçon* stared at Drea as though he worried she was deaf. But she didn't mind because it gave her a chance to really notice how expressive his eyes were, a warm brown that—

"*Mademoiselle*, did you hear me?"

"What, um, why are you—I mean . . . who says I can't park here?"

When she finally spoke, it went nothing like the way she'd planned, which was, *You're way too hot to be giving instructions. You should be taking orders. From me. And who the hell are you, anyway, cute French boy?*

"The owner, and she pays me to make it so. I am the valet. Either I park your car or you may drive it around back yourself, but you cannot park in front of the house."

Drea had visited France many times and French was one of several languages she spoke. Something was not quite right about his accent, even if his embossed name tag read Xavier. She ran down a mental list of Asian countries that were once part of the French empire: Laos, Cambodia, and Vietnam were the obvious choices. She'd never visited any of them because her parents believed Europe was the only place worth traveling to—and maybe South Africa when they were in an adventurous mood, or the South Pacific when they were feeling tropical—but if the pushy valet was from any of those places, he still shouldn't have a French accent since it wouldn't be his first language. Drea decided he was from Montreal, one of her favorite cities, with its hodgepodge of people and continental feel, but without the hella-long plane ride.

"*Allô*...anyone home?" He looked past Drea, giving her car a good once-over, before adding, "Are you sure you're even supposed to be here? I'd like to see your invitation."

Drea actually knew the owner—quite well in fact—even if she knew nothing about the open gate, blocked-off driveway, and the cute, if somewhat rude, valet. Not only was he rude, but the way he ran his eyes over her as though he had some claim on her made Drea nervous, mostly because she didn't hate it. He was all swagger. She was all aflutter. Drea didn't like the way this stranger could throw her off her game so easily. The proprietress had once taught her an important lesson, but the boy's scrutiny had almost made her forget it. *If you can't*

3

be the part, play the part. Even if you don't believe it, make sure everyone else does. That lesson had served her well so far, so she played the part of a confident girl who owned the world and was completely unfazed by that accent and those eyes.

"As a matter of fact, I *am* home," she said with the confidence that had eluded her a minute ago when she was only playing herself.

"Driving that?"

The way he said it, you'd have thought Drea was driving a go-cart. In fact, her sweet-sixteen gift was only a month old, custom-painted in an understated shade of magenta, and pretty darn cute in Drea's opinion.

"What one drives has little to do with who one is or how much they have in the bank. Or where they live, for that matter."

He looked at Drea as though she'd just announced the world was flat. "Whoever told you that story lied. The car is *everything.*"

"No, the planet is everything. Small cars get excellent gas mileage, and I'm more interested in protecting the environment than looking good." In truth, Drea had never really considered her adorable car's green factor, but who was he to mock it, or her?

"Well, you still manage to do that despite your ride," he said more softly, and almost smiled before going back to being obnoxious. "Look, I've seen the cars these people own and the least expensive one is worth five of what you're driving. If there was an enviro-freak in this family, they'd be driving a Tesla. Like hell you live here." His accent was suddenly gone, replaced by a regular old Georgia drawl, Southside Atlanta edition.

"Are you the valet or the bouncer? And where'd your accent go? I rather liked it."

"Only tipping customers get the accent. Makes 'em feel like they're going someplace swanky. I get the feeling you don't plan on tipping me."

"Take a look around," Drea said, waving her arm slowly, as though she were a showroom model. "It's one of my mother's parties. Believe me, they really are going someplace swanky, with or without your accent, which wasn't all that great, anyway."

Drea said it dismissively, even turning back toward her car, but she knew she wasn't going anywhere.

"Worked on you, didn't it?"

Apparently, he knew it too. She decided to turn the tables—after all, he was on her turf despite seeming to believe he was the one with the advantage. "How do I know you're who you say you are?" She moved to the other side of her open door, suddenly feeling the need to put metal and glass between them. "My mother didn't tell me anything about a party today, you're the most brutish valet I've ever met, and you've already lied about your accent. For all I know, I'll hand you my keys and never see my car again."

"That thing?" he said, flicking his hand at her car as though it were an annoying insect. "Believe me—nobody wants your little hamster car. And I could ask you the same thing. Shouldn't you know if there's some big party going on at your own house?"

"Look, I've had a long day of exams and now I just want—"

His expression changed, and for the first time since she'd arrived, he didn't seem to be on the offensive. "Summer school? Yeah, that sucks. Bad grades last year, huh?"

"Hardly. I have better than a five-point-oh GPA."

"Five? The highest you can get is a four, so stop making stuff up."

"It's a weighted GPA. Have you never heard of AP and honors classes?" she asked, trying hard to sound as though she didn't really care whether he had or not.

"Nah, we don't need all that at my school. Every kid is an honors student."

Now who was making stuff up? Drea wanted to knock that smug look off his face, except it only made him cuter, which pissed her off more.

"Hathaway isn't that kind of summer school. It's the exact opposite, in fact—college-level courses for accelerated learners," Drea said, wondering why she was standing here telling her business to a stranger.

"Never heard of it."

Drea summoned as much contempt as she could muster, though she was beginning to grow tired of playing the role. "I don't doubt it." She'd been in character all summer, and now she only wanted to slip into the house undiscovered so she could just hide out in her room and avoid whatever her mom was up to today.

"Where is it?"

"You ask too many questions," she said, unable to stop herself from answering them. "If you must know, it's near Lookout Mountain and quite prestigious, by the way."

"That's a helluva commute."

"I don't commute. I board there."

"Like a kennel? One time, we had to board our dogs in a kennel overnight when my foster parents took me to Disney—"

"No, it is nothing at all like a kennel," Drea interrupted before she realized he was just messing with her and knew exactly what she meant. "Don't you have some cars to park or something?"

He moved closer, but remained on the other side of the car door. Still, he was close enough for Drea to smell the starch in his crisp white shirt. She wondered how he managed to seem so cool when it was ninety degrees and beyond humid. Her tank top had already begun to cling to her back just minutes outside her air-conditioned car, but Drea only now noticed how warm she felt.

"That's what I been trying to do, but my first customer keeps giving me a hard time."

Though it was the least significant thing about this strange conversation with a random boy who used fake accents to trick people into thinking he was something he clearly wasn't, Drea had to resist the urge to correct his grammar. As he moved further away from that elegant, accented boy she'd met a few minutes earlier, she grew more intrigued to learn his real story, and more annoyed that he made her want to.

Now he stepped away and circled her car, looking through the passenger-side windows, leaning close and cupping his hands around his eyes to block out the sun's glare.

"You don't travel light, do you?" he asked.

"You don't have any boundaries, do you?"

He ignored Drea and moved to check the backseat. "You're driving a fifteen-thousand-dollar tin can, but your purse on the front seat is a Louis Vuitton. Same for the luggage. The whole set probably costs more than the car. I suppose your story about living here could be true."

"Look, I am not going to stand here being questioned by the help." Drea immediately wished she could take it back, even though he'd been asking for it. But that comment was totally something her mother would say. She'd gone too far playing the part.

He looked as though he was about to tell her off, so he surprised her when all he said was, "Your keys, *mademoiselle?*" The mild playfulness that had crept into his voice a few minutes ago was gone, replaced by the faux accent.

After Drea grabbed her purse and dragged three pieces of wheeled-luggage from the car, refusing the help he offered her, she removed the car key from the key fob—trying to hide that it, too, was from the Vuitton collection—and dropped it into his open hand. What she'd said to him was ugly, but Drea wasn't stupid. She'd been ripped off by a valet more than once—twenty dollars from the center console, a very expensive pair of sunglasses, even her lucky rabbit's foot that once dangled from the rearview mirror. She wasn't giving him her house key.

"Enjoy the party, *mademoiselle*," the boy said, getting into her car.

"Stop calling me that, and using the fake accent." Whatever game this boy was playing, cute or not, it was annoying. "I told you I live here. I'm not some party guest."

"Of course you do, Andrea Faraday."

She'd never told him her name, and it wasn't visible from the luggage tags. From the minute he found her moving the velvet-rope barricade, he'd known she lived here. By the time Drea realized the game he'd been playing was flirtation, he was already halfway down the drive.

2

Drea's plan to sneak into the house undetected fell apart the moment she walked through the back entrance into the kitchen. With a party about to be thrown, she should have known that's where her mother would be, micromanaging the caterers even though she always used the same company because they were the best in town. Only her mom knew the best way to garnish the appetizer platters or place the floral arrangements. She felt sorry for the caterers, but could also sympathize with her mother, from whom she had inherited the perfection gene.

At least Drea was a nice control freak, always softening a critique with a compliment—though she hadn't been especially nice to the valet, even if it was partly his fault. Maybe later she'd take some food to him as a peace offering. Not that she'd probably ever see him again after today. But she couldn't have him going around telling stories of the grade-A bitch he met while working a Faraday party.

"Good, you're here," her mother said after chastising a server for having an infinitesimally small stain on her shirt and sending her off to the laundry room to remove it.

"Can we pretend I'm not, Mom? You guys should still be in New York for another two days, and I wasn't even supposed to be home until tomorrow. I skipped out early just so I could avoid having to deal with all the end-of-summer festivities at Hathaway."

"But this party is for you, really. And your friends."

"I have no idea what you're talking about," Drea said as she pulled the last of her bags through the back door.

"Of course you do. My annual Woodruff School fund-raiser?"

"Since when was that ever a thing?"

"Since today. And who better to pry open all those fat wallets than the class valedictorian?" She stopped a passing florist to make adjustments to the vase of flowers he was carrying.

"You've never had any problem getting money out of people, Mom."

"True, I'm a natural-born fund-raiser, but I could really use another hostess to help me work the room."

"When have I ever been good at working a room? I'm sure you and Dad will do fine without me. I just want to crash." Drea began heading for the back stairs that led to up her room before stopping to add, "Wait. When you say work the room, how—"

"You know what I always say. If you can't *be* the part... well, I need you to play the part."

A pang of guilt shot through Drea as she recalled how she'd just played the part a little too well. She'd definitely take that plate out to the valet as soon as she got the chance. She stood there for a minute trying to decide which would take the most effort—arguing with her mom for ten minutes before she could escape to her room, or playing the perfect hostess to a bunch of wealthy stuck-ups for two hours. She decided arguing would be a waste of energy—she'd never win. Linnea Faraday was a force, the way a Category-5 hurricane was a force. You couldn't fight it, so it was best to just hunker down and hope you made it out the other side in one piece.

"Can't I chill for a minute?" Drea asked, hoping for at least a small concession. "I've been driving for two hours, and now I'm all sweaty after standing around out there dealing with that rude valet."

"What's that about the valet?" her mom asked, turning her full attention to Drea for the first time since she'd arrived home.

"Nothing...I just meant it's so hot today. I'm kinda funky," Drea said, changing her tone. Xavier could have been a little more professional, but she didn't want him fired or anything.

"I know. This was supposed to be an outdoor party, but I'm forced to bring it inside. Unfortunately, I didn't have enough time to straighten up, so I'll need your assistance—at least for the first hour until the extra help I hired arrives."

A housekeeper came five times a week—her parents were too private to hire a live-in—so the house was always immaculate, but Drea knew what her mother was really saying even if the catering staff overhearing them didn't have a clue.

Your assistance: She needed Drea to help watch the room.

Extra help: A well-paid, undercover security team was on the way.

Straighten up: Replace all the valuables with fakes.

After twenty years in the fine-antiques business, Drea's parents had amassed a fortune in furniture, jewelry, and art, though it was just a fraction of what they'd sold. Everyone in town knew their house was a gold mine, which is why her parents rarely invited people inside, instead holding garden parties in spring and fall when the Georgia weather was most cooperative. The closest that most people came to seeing any of the Faraday collection was in the guesthouse on the other side of the backyard, from which caterers usually operated and where people could use the facilities. They displayed their least valuable collectibles there, if for no other reason than to keep up appearances.

On the rare occasions they actually let people into their home, they switched out the rarest, most valuable items with replicas. It didn't matter that their guest lists only included the wealthy. The Faradays knew better than anyone that people aren't always what they seem. That was why they preferred not to invite people over at all. But being leaders in the community, they had to occasionally interact with it, or else people might get ideas.

Drea picked up two of her bags, finally accepting her fate as a people greeter/security guard, and started for the stairs. "I'll come back for that last one in a minute."

"Leave the bags there. I'll have your brother take them up when he gets here to help out with . . . things. You go get ready. Check your closet—I just brought back a Stella McCartney dress that would be perfect."

Of course it would be. Everything had to be perfect.

Drea was regretting her decision to go along to get along by the time she got upstairs and opened the door to her room—where she found the server her mom had just reprimanded.

"Excuse me, but what are you doing in here?" Though it was pretty clear what she was doing here. The girl was holding a dress—the very one Linnea had told Drea to wear to the party—against herself as she twirled around in front of the full-length mirror.

"Your mom asked me to bring this dress up here."

"Really? I heard her tell you to go see about that stain on your shirt."

"Oh, yeah. Guess I got a little lost looking for the laundry room."

"You mean the room she pointed to down the hall from the kitchen? On the first floor?"

"Is *that* what she meant? I'm so geographically challenged, I need a map just to find my way out the door in the morning."

Drea wanted to say, *My foot on your ass could help you find your way out*, but responded more civilly, even if it was total BS. She'd already been rude to the valet. She didn't want word to get around that she was undeserving of last year's "Sweetest Sophomore" award. "Honest mistake. But you might want to go clean your shirt. I'm sure my mother is looking for you."

"Right," the girl said, laying the dress on the bed. "I swear, going through your closet is like flipping through the pages of *Vogue*. Did you know they showed this dress at Fashion Week? I couldn't resist having a look."

"I bet you couldn't." And if Drea hadn't walked in when she did, no doubt the waiter would have taken more than a look.

"You won't mention this to your mom, will you? Like you said, it was an honest mistake, and this job is *really* important to me."

Drea knew this girl's kind all too well. She scanned her room—which was immaculate like the rest of the house and everything in it arranged just so—looking for anything out of place. She'd know at first glance whether a drawer from her Louis XVI commode had been left slightly open or if the nineteenth-century chinoiserie jewelry box on top of it had been moved half an inch. Nothing seemed amiss, but Drea knew better.

"Depends," Drea said, watching the girl's reaction. "Is there anything else you need to return?"

"What? I *told* you I was just looking. I can't believe you're suggesting—"

"I'm not suggesting." Drea stared her down so hard the girl had no choice but to come clean.

The girl pulled a ruby-encrusted comb from her mass of dark hair. "How did you know?" Her hair was so thick and lush, she could have hidden the contents of Drea's jewelry box in there.

"Wild guess."

"No, you were certain. But how? You couldn't *possibly* have known it was missing just from looking around the room. I was careful to—"

"Are you sure you need this job?" Drea asked. "It doesn't sound as though you do."

"I wasn't stealing it, just trying it on."

"It sounds as though I should fire you right now and have you escorted out," Drea said, ignoring the girl's protests.

"You're overreacting. All I did was—"

"Overreacting?" Drea was this close to going off on the thief. Screw her Sweetest Sophomore status or her manners. "You should be glad I'm not calling the police."

Something about the girl's demeanor changed after Drea's threat, like she'd gone off the defensive and had taken up the offense. She flipped her hair over her shoulder, put a hand on one hip, and cocked her head slightly as she stared Drea down, giving as good as she'd gotten. She reached down the front of her shirt, pulled out the black-pearl ring Drea's father had brought back from a trip to Tahiti last year, and threw it on the bed before heading toward the door.

"You wouldn't do that, now would you?" The girl brushed past Drea, knocking her in the shoulder before she left the room.

16

Even after Drea was showered, dressed, and downstairs with her mother greeting their first guests, she was still feeling unnerved by the waiter. Considering how much the girl claimed she needed the job, you'd think she'd have apologized, or at least have shown a little remorse. But somehow, maybe it was that parting comment of hers, she'd made Drea feel as if she were the guilty party. Granted, it never took much to guilt Drea—it was so easy, in fact, a stranger could do it. Two of them, if you counted the valet. But this guilt felt very specific, though Drea couldn't put her finger on exactly why.

Rather than try to figure it out, she spent the next hour flashing a game show-model smile and schmoozing the pillars of Peachland's society, checking off the arrivals from the RSVP list her mother had given her. Much like sending Drea's sense of guilt into overdrive, it didn't take much effort to join this club, only a seven-figure bank account, and that was pretty much everyone in Peachland. The pillars weren't so much about the community as they were the economy, and Drea's mother had gathered them for a shakedown in the name of her school.

Woodruff, along with the entire hamlet of Peachland, had been created years ago by people who'd made a ton of money in the earliest days of the dot-com era and had begun to think Atlanta was great for making money, but not for raising kids. At first they moved to the northern suburb of Magnolia, but the crime and poverty—which was hardly any compared to the big city they were fleeing—was still enough to keep it from being called idyllic, so they created their own little town from scratch. They had the kind of cash that allowed them to buy up farms just outside Magnolia and thirty miles from Atlanta. They built mansions, a country club, and a K-12 private school worthy of their kids, because the county system wouldn't do. The parents made the daily commute for work while pretending they were from old money.

But when the Great Recession hit twenty years later, it became obvious that most of them were also living a charade. Many lost their big tech jobs and had to send their kids back to public school. Some had left Peachland altogether. Those who remained, mostly the owners of the tech businesses, became even richer when they sold off their companies to big corporations. Those were the Peachlanders who'd made the Faradays' invitation list.

By her estimate, there were about fifty people at the party, and Drea recognized them all except for the man who had her father cornered against a Childe Hassam painting on the other side of the gallery. Given the pained look on her father's usually calm face, she guessed the stranger had crashed the party to conduct his own personal shakedown. The only thing that ever unnerved Ellis Faraday was anyone trying to get a hand in his pocket, and it wouldn't be a Faraday party without a crasher looking for a donation for this cause or that one. Drea wanted to go rescue her dad, but by the time she'd escaped a conversation with her next-door neighbor, Mr. Hansen, by promising she'd join his Habitat for Humanity building team again in the fall, the stranger and her father had disappeared. Maybe this one had managed to break her father down, and just like Mr. Hansen, the only way to get rid of him was to promise him something. In the stranger's case, that probably meant her dad had gone to write him a check.

Once everyone on the guest list had arrived and her mother had pointed out the addition of two burly, intimidating waiters to the hired staff, Drea broke away from her duties as greeter/security guard and escaped upstairs, where she found her brother leaning over the hallway banister and looking down at the party.

"It's like shooting fish in a barrel," he said when Drea joined him at the railing.

"You're supposed to be watching the guests, not casing them."

"Old habits die hard. Besides, you're the good one, not me."

Drea felt the familiar knot in her stomach she got whenever people called her "good." She worked so hard to earn that praise, yet it gave her a sense of doom every time she received it, like waiting for the final clue that revealed that the least likely suspect was actually the guilty party.

"How did the interview go?" she asked, shifting the conversation back to Damon. "Did they give you that last-minute slot?"

"Of course. You know how convincing I can be."

It was true. Damon was a natural at charming people— seducing them really—just like his and Drea's parents. Physically, they'd both inherited the best of their parents' DNA.

Their father claimed to be the great-great-great-grandson of a Nigerian prince, her mother, the descendant of some long-ago Nordic king, a mix of dark and fair that gave Damon and Drea the kind of beauty people called exotic. Complete strangers asked them stupid questions like, *Where are you from?* When what they really wanted to know is what box they checked on a census form. Or their mom's favorite when their dad wasn't around: *Are your kids adopted?* Their looks not only confused people, but also made it is easy to convince them of just about anything.

But the seduction gene had somehow missed Drea, who was always saying the wrong thing—if she managed to say anything at all. Being charming was something she had to work at. Hard.

"We'll both be going back to school this fall, though they would kick me out—and then some—if they knew about this." He opened his hand to reveal a gaudy, if genuine, gold-and-diamond cuff link.

"Damon, no, you didn't."

"That's what he gets for wearing them to an afternoon garden party. People from old money would never be so flashy."

"None of these people are from old money." Including her family, no matter how well they sold the story. "When did you do it? I never saw you down there."

"Got him before he even came into the house, when I pulled in behind the guy at the valet stand."

"Was that valet pushy or what?" Drea asked, looking for confirmation that the valet also had deserved the way she'd treated him, and there was no need for her to offer an apology for her rudeness in the form of rumaki and caviar blintzes.

"Yeah, now you mention it. But I didn't feel like arguing with him, so I let the kid park my car. Cuff-link Guy comes over and shakes my hand like we know each other. Taking this off him was a reflex, like muscle memory."

" 'Cuff-link Guy?' " Drea recalled the party crasher who was probably in her father's office right now getting a check to make him go away. "You didn't recognize him?"

"I would have restrained myself with someone I knew, and I only did it to see if I still could." Drea must not have looked convinced because Damon added, "Don't worry, I'll put it back. But you can see why I've been questioning my new career path."

"Well, don't. It's a good choice. You just need to stop working as hard to prove you're a bad guy as I do at trying to prove . . . Look, just promise to put it back where it belongs. No harm, no foul."

"No harm, plenty of foul." Damon was quiet for a minute, staring down at the party. "Who's that girl? I saw her come out of your room earlier. Well, only the back of her, but that was enough."

Drea followed his gaze and landed on the glossy mane of the black-pearl ring thief. When she wasn't busy stealing, the girl could earn a living as a model in those spray-on tan ads where their dark bronzy glow "looks so natural" because they were actually born with it. She and her tray of prosciutto-wrapped shrimp were surrounded. One thing Drea had learned after too many of her mother's parties: People lost their minds over free shrimp, even rich people. It caused the perfect distraction for a girl like that—not that she needed any help since she was distraction enough on her own—to do the real job she'd probably come to do. Drea had noticed the girl flirting with several of the party guests as she served amuse-bouches, and now wondered if Cuff-link Guy was the only attendee missing jewelry. Between the undercover security guards who stood out like NFL linebackers in a ballet company, the rude valet, and the sticky-fingered server, her mother really needed to find a new event-staffing company.

"I think you two have a lot in common," Drea said. "But you need to stay as far away from that girl as possible. Talk about a codependent relationship."

"Is she as hot coming as she is going?"

"Nope," Drea lied. "Face like a pug, luckily for you."

It worked. He was only twenty, but her brother was already a player of great renown around Magnolia, and he wasn't especially choosy about his targets. He liked them willowy thin, curvy thick, and everything in between, but he did require a pretty face. He called it his one weakness, though the cuff-link was proof he had at least one more. Damon turned away from the party and leaned back against the railing.

"Are your hostess duties done yet? We should celebrate my acceptance letter."

"I don't know . . . I promised Headmistress Fitch that I'd find her later to discuss the welcome-back gala. The committee chair bailed at the last minute so she could backpack in Europe, and now Fitch wants me to pitch in."

"By pitch in, she means do everything," Damon said, his assessment spot-on.

"She kept going on about how no one can plan a party like me and—"

Damon shook his head knowingly. "What a con. Fitch knew the magic words, and you let yourself be the mark. How are we from the same DNA?"

Drea had often wondered the same thing, but for the opposite reason. Damon only played at being truly bad. She only played at being truly good. Their DNA had made them both skilled at deception, if nothing else.

"But—"

Damon wasn't having it, and cut her off. "I remember you being the committee chair last year and hating every minute of it, complaining how it took up your whole summer. And now you're agreeing to do all that work again, except you have only two weeks to get it done."

"What was I supposed to do, tell her no?"

"Exactly. Come on, ditch Fitch. You know you want to. Let's go bowling, like we used to."

Damon was right. The last thing she wanted to do was plan a party at the last minute. She had two weeks of summer left, and she'd planned to spend them doing absolutely nothing related to school until the headmistress had hunted her down earlier today and talked her into it. Drea imagined Fitch waiting outside under the pergola, feeling smug because she'd dumped the pain-in-the-ass project on her favorite student. More like her favorite sucker.

"Let's do it. I'm going to stand up Fitch, just leave her in the garden wondering where I am," Drea said, feeling the rush she imagined Damon had felt when he got away with the cuff-link, a thought that immediately dampened her moment. "I don't think we've bowled since you...went away."

"You mean since my unfortunate incarceration. It's been four years and you *still* can't say it? I was a—come on, say it with me, Drea—ju-ve-nile of-fen-der." Damon dragged out the last two words as though she were a child learning a new term.

"Well, whatever. You're on a whole new path today, and you're right—we need to celebrate. Give me five minutes to change and we're out. But return that cuff-link first."

"Yes, ma'am. He'll think it fell off into his jacket pocket."

"Left or right pocket?"

Damon rolled his eyes at her before turning back toward the crowd, looking for Cuff-link Guy.

"I know you're good, but mistakes happen." She almost reminded him of his "unfortunate incarceration," but that would have been overkill. He got her point.

Drea would rather have stuck to her original plan of hiding out in her room and clearing space on her trophy shelf for the latest addition, from her summer at Hathaway, for Highest Academic Achievement. At least until her dad could gush about it, after which it would be forgotten until the minute she brought home the next award. But she was worried about Damon and all those fish in a barrel downstairs. As far as she knew, he hadn't done anything like that since he'd finished his juvenile-detention sentence. Drea was certain once her brother was in school and had something to distract him, there would be no more cuff-link incidents. She just had to make sure he didn't get expelled—or worse—before he even started.

When she found Damon waiting in front of the house exactly five minutes later—which included one minute to write a quick note of apology to Headmistress Fitch and find a waiter to deliver it, because as much as she liked the idea of standing her up, Drea couldn't actually go through with it— she asked, "Did you do the thing?"

"Yes, Mother."

"No more instances of 'muscle memory'?"

"No, Mother," Damon said, sounding exasperated. She had been laying on the sisterly concern a bit thick, only because she really was worried about him, but Drea knew Damon was really angry at himself for taking the cuff-link in the first place. Apparently he was going to take it out on Xavier. "Where's that damn valet? It couldn't take this long to return from parking a car around back."

They walked down the path to the driveway in silence, looking for the valet, who was just pulling up the drive in a black Maserati. Seeing as how Drea and Damon were the only people waiting at the valet stand, and Rude Boy was coming from the street end of the drive, not from behind the house where the basketball court served as a parking lot, it was a little suspect.

Xavier was an excellent face reader, because he pulled alongside them and said, "It's okay. The driver said I could take it out for a few minutes."

"Sure he did," Damon said.

"Can you keep this to yourselves? It's just that I've never driven a Maserati before," Xavier explained.

Damon clearly wasn't buying Xavier's story. "Yeah, most

high school kids haven't, even ones who work part-time as valets."

"Please? This job is important."

He sounded just like the thief in Drea's room, claiming they need a job so badly but not acting like they did. Seriously, where did her mother find these people?

"He needs his car," Drea said, handing over Damon's valet ticket, "and I need my key back. You'll likely be gone by the time we return, and I wouldn't want to find you've taken my car out for a spin too."

As Xavier unlocked the cabinet of the portable valet stand and removed two keys, he asked, "You mean the pink hamster car?"

When he handed Drea her key, he had the nerve to smile at her like they shared some kind of inside joke, at least until Damon got in his face.

"Go. Get. My. Car," Damon demanded, and not in the imperious but polite tone he sometimes used to keep up appearances, the one that made him sound just like their father. No, the way Damon stepped up to Xavier made Drea think her brother had learned to play this particular role in a place where it meant the difference between surviving and not. She'd never seen this side of Damon before, and it surprised her, but not as much as it did when Xavier didn't back down. Drea was trying to decide whether she'd have to get between them when a man's voice called out, breaking the two apart.

"Good, you have my car ready. And Damon, we keep

meeting like this, don't we?" the man asked, grabbing Damon's hand and pumping it hard, the sun bouncing off his gold-and-diamond cuff-link. It was the stranger Drea had seen cornering her father, presumably hitting him up for a donation of some kind, but given the Maserati and all the bling, Drea now wasn't so sure. He didn't look that much older than her brother, and yet he was parading around like a high roller.

"Do I know you?" Damon asked, sounding like he still wanted to kick someone's ass.

"No, I don't think you do," he said, handing a twenty-dollar bill to Xavier. "Did you get a chance to take her out?"

"*Oui, monsieur.* T'ank you for the opportunity," Xavier answered, laying the French accent on extra thick while cutting his eyes at Drea as if to say, *See, you read me all wrong, beginning to end.*

After Cuff-link Guy had driven away, Damon told the valet he'd get his own damn car and had to practically drag Drea along after him to the basketball court/parking lot. Otherwise she'd have just stood there, trying to figure out what it was about the boy that perplexed her. When they'd driven around from behind the house, Xavier was still standing at the edge of the drive where they had left him. He smiled at Drea as Damon sped by. She watched him grow smaller in her side-view mirror, almost regretting that she'd never see him again.

3

In the two weeks between the fund-raiser and the Woodruff Welcome Back Gala, three things happened that Drea had never seen coming. First, she told Headmistress Fitch that, regretfully, she would be unable to fill in as the gala planner, though her rebellion was momentary. A few days later, she called to apologize, and she offered to take on the project but was told her help would not be needed because someone else had volunteered. Not only were there no frantic phone calls by the end of the first week begging her to save the event because the last-minute volunteer was no Andrea Faraday, but the gala proved to be a smashing success, far better than anything Drea could have thrown together given only two weeks' notice.

She had to admit it was a good call to move the gala indoors this year, instead of having it on the school's back lawn as it usually was, given the record-setting heat they'd been having. The mystery event planner had gone with a beach theme, bringing in palm trees in gigantic pots and a couple of truckloads of real sand to spread along one wall of the gymnasium. It would be hell to clean up, but that's why they hired other people to deal with it. Nice touch to pipe the sound of ocean waves crashing against the shore, occasionally pierced by screaming seagulls, through the PA system, providing background noise that could still be talked over without having to yell.

This year, the door prizes weren't the usual assortment of all-expense-paid weekends to Hilton Head or a month's worth of housekeeping services. Whoever was running the event had either been given a monster budget or was brilliant at talking donors out of their money, because the grand prize was the one thing rich people really wanted—more money. The possibility of their child winning a year's college tuition to the university of their choice ensured no one would leave the gala early this year. Drea was disappointed her first act of defiance had gone unnoticed, but was willing to admit whoever had taken on the job had done much better than she would have.

"Isn't it an awesome gala?" asked Madeline, Drea's closest... well, acquaintance, which was saying something because she had a ton of acquaintances. It seemed weird to describe Maddy that way, but Drea never really had friends. Friendship required trust, and the only people she trusted shared her DNA. But if she ever decided to have a BFF, Madeline was at the top of Drea's very short list of candidates.

"Do you have any idea who did it?" Drea asked.

"Not a clue. Fitch called me after you turned down the job—shocking, by the way—but I was still in Bermuda. Even if I'd been in town, I'd have told her no, so it was just as well."

"Maybe it was your mom."

"You're kidding, right? If my mother did a beach theme, she wouldn't stop at palm trees, sand, and ocean music. She'd have added hula dancers, fire twirlers, and a tank of live sharks, safety violations be damned."

"I could see that," Drea said. Like every other Peach-lander, Madeline's family money had come in a tidal wave, fast and furious. There hadn't been enough time to learn the art of being effortlessly wealthy the way rich people were in the Hamptons or on the Main Line, both places Drea had briefly lived. Madeline's mom did not believe in "less is more."

"It would have been positively dreadful. So how was your summer at Hathaway? Meet any cute boys?"

"No, not at Hathaway," Drea said, thinking of the one she'd met on her return from school, the one who had kept her from thinking of much else in the last couple of weeks.

"Just as well. They say geek is the new sexy, but no amount of hipster chic can make a nerd hot enough for me to date him," Maddy said in between sips of her virgin piña colada. "Can you imagine? Clothes from the thrift store and furniture from IKEA. It would be *positively* awful."

After two months spent away from Madeline, Drea had forgotten her annoying habit of describing negative things as "positively" this or that. When she thought of it like the physicist she planned to be, sometimes Drea concluded the sum of

Maddy's observations totaled nothing. It also made her question how the girl had moved to the top of her almost-friend list, until she remembered just how short the list was. So when Madeline announced she'd spotted a cute boy in the crowd earlier and abandoned Drea in search of him, she took a cue from Maddy and thought it just as well.

She was still trying to figure out the mastermind behind the gala's success when Headmistress Fitch called her mom to the dais to shower her with praise and to answer Drea's question. Now she knew why everything had gone so well, and how the door prizes had gone from meh to wow.

"I can't believe you were the mysterious volunteer," Drea said after her mother made her way through the adoring crowd to join her. "Why the big secret?"

"Because I was trying to avoid something like this." She held up a shiny plaque.

"The Guardian Angel Award? I bet no one's ever called you an angel before." Drea meant it jokingly, but it was clear from her mother's expression that the joke had fallen flat. "I mean, I'm just surprised Fitch talked you into it. Didn't she tell you that I'd agreed to plan the party but reneged?"

"Yes." Her mother's response was unusually succinct, and she seemed distracted, looking around the gym, at her watch—everywhere except at Drea.

"So wouldn't my bailing on Fitch have been one of those 'teachable moments' you and Dad love so much?"

Her parents were not of the helicopter variety. They were always preaching independence and personal responsibility,

31

and would have made her honor her commitment to Fitch, not honor it for her. Drea expected a delayed sermon and wondered why she'd opened herself up for it, but all her mother did was briefly put her hand on Drea's cheek before smiling and walking away.

As Drea watched her mother disappear into the crowd, she saw the second thing she'd never seen coming: the rude valet from her parents' party talking to Headmistress Fitch. He wasn't wearing the white-shirt/bow-tie/black-pants uniform of male event staff everywhere, which meant he wasn't working the gala. In fact, he was wearing a different uniform altogether, as if he'd stepped out of a Tommy Hilfiger ad— khaki pants and a polo shirt tucked in only partially at the front—just like every other boy at the party. Was it really possible he was there as a guest?

"I guess we'll be classmates."

Drea shifted her gaze to find the thieving waiter from her mom's party standing next to her. "What the hell?"

"Not the most *gracious* welcome, but thanks. I guess your mom didn't tell you."

"My mom? Why would she—"

"I'm Gigi, by the way," the girl said, handing a speechless Drea one of the cups she was holding. "Who'd have thought you could make a rum punch without the rum? My abuelo is turning in his Puerto Rican grave right now."

Drea took the drink, wishing it wasn't virgin. "What are you—"

"Good thing you didn't bust me to the police, right? You

know what that would have been—*awwwkward*. Especially since we're going to be locker buddies."

"But…" was all Drea could manage, though the girl had plenty to say.

"I told Headmistress Fitch we knew each other, so she said she'd be sure to give me the locker next to yours since the old occupant graduated. She's *really* a sweetheart. The headmistress, I mean."

Drea took a few unladylike gulps of punch as she ordered her thoughts enough to make sense of the possibility this girl and the valet might be Woodruff's newest students.

"Of course, we don't really *know* each other, but now we'll have plenty of opportunities to remedy that, right? We'll be best friends in no time, and you know what that means— sharing clothes! I cannot *wait* to get a better look at that closet of yours—"

"Shut up," Drea said when she could finally form words. She raised her hand, palm in Gigi's face. "I mean… hold up a minute.".

Sticky Fingers looked stunned, but only for a millisecond. "They really aren't into teaching manners at the Woodruff School, are they? I'd have thought—"

"Why would you possibly think we'll be best friends? You stole from me."

"Oh, that was just a little misunderstanding. I figured since your—"

"How are you here?" It was Drea's turn to interrupt. "How are either of you even here?"

"Either of who?" Gigi said, looking around them and then at Drea as though she might be hallucinating a third person in their conversation.

"The valet. What's-his-name." Drea knew full well his name, since she'd been cyberstalking him for the last two weeks and finding absolutely nothing. "The one from my parents' fund-raiser—Xavier."

"I don't know anyone named Xavier." Drea got the feeling she was telling the truth. "But seriously, a *valet*?" Gigi continued. "I'm beginning to think Woodruff standards are not all they're made out to be. They'll let just anyone in here, right?"

Drea was about to point out the irony of the girl's assessment, but like her mom moments earlier, she just walked off into the crowd before Drea got the chance. By the time she turned back to where she'd spotted Xavier and Ms. Fitch, neither of them was there. That was because the headmistress had been called away to deal with the third thing that Drea, or anyone else at the party for that matter, had never seen coming.

While all the guests were attending the party inside the air-conditioned gym, many of their cars were being stolen right off the Woodruff parking lot. And once they made it home, thanks to rides from guests whose cars hadn't been stolen, they discovered they'd also been robbed while they sipped rum-free beach drinks and listened to Fitch wax on about their generous support and brilliant children. The police would later say they were baffled because there was not a single case of forced entry. Home-security systems did not notify the security company. Car-alarm systems did not alarm any-one. There had been no guards posted in the parking lot—Why would there be? It was Peachland!—but surely neighbors across the street should have noticed a bunch of thieves hotwiring twenty cars.

The Faraday house had not been spared, despite having one of the most secure homes in the state of Georgia, but they'd only lost the Childe Hassam painting, her father's Austrian nineteenth-century hunting sword set, and Drea's jewelry box. She had driven them to the gala, and apparently no one was interested in stealing an economical, gas-friendly compact. So they didn't discover the breach until they arrived home, but the Faradays were as much victims as some of the other unfortunate Peachlanders. At least, that's what the thieves wanted everyone to believe.

It wasn't lost on Drea that the guests who hadn't been ripped off were the same people who'd declined her parents' last-minute fund-raiser two weeks earlier. Luckily for them, they'd been doing August in Europe, or ending summer break in some Northern state where the dog days didn't have quite as much bite. She recalled the stranger who'd cornered her father at the party, the man whose bling stood out in a room full of people working hard at understated elegance, making him an easy mark for Damon. She wondered if the stranger hadn't been the only mark in the room—whether he had his own list of marks.

Then, during the week that followed the party, there were the whispered conversations between her parents that stopped the minute Drea walked into the room. Of course, parents kept things from their kids, but these were not the usual secrets. Since they'd arrived in Peachland, her parents had played it straight as far as Drea knew, which was why it was the longest she'd ever stayed in one place. Before Peachland, in every town her parents had run a successful antiques-auction scam, they'd have to move before they overstayed their welcome and raised the attention of the local honest dealers, or worse, the police. They really were private antiques dealers now—it wasn't just a cover story. So it had been more than three years since she'd seen them like this, conspiratorial and evasive, but Drea recognized the signs just the same.

And she should have known something was up after her mother's revelation that she had secretly managed the gala without so much as giving her the side-eye for breaking a commitment. Drea didn't know exactly what had transpired, but in hindsight, she realized the third surprising thing shouldn't have been. Had she been paying closer attention, she'd have seen it coming, after all.

now

4

The Last Week of Eleventh Grade

Another thing Drea hadn't seen coming was the way her seemingly perfect life would begin to implode after that day. It began with her suspicion-turned-obsession about her parents' roles in the thefts. She never found any proof—her parents were way too experienced to leave any—but Drea was certain they were behind it, even if car theft wasn't their standard modus operandi. And if they weren't the masterminds of the heist, they at least knew something about it. There were just too many coincidences: the last-minute fund-raising party and the sketchy event staff; her mother's willingness to take on the gala planning instead of making Drea do it; her decision to move the gala inside where no one could see their cars being stolen, and to blast the sound of crashing waves through the PA system to cover the sound of twenty high-performance car engines starting all at once.

Drea learned the police had questioned Woodruff School neighbors who hadn't attended the gala as well as car security-system companies but found not a single alarm had gone off, almost as though the thieves had used keys. Not that they had needed keys, since they'd also made off with cars that had keyless entry. That was what threw Drea off—the whole thing was too high-tech for her parents. There was a reason they were in the antiques business.

Trying to figure it all out drove Drea perilously close to crazy, and it didn't help that the only person she could talk to about it didn't want to hear it. Every time she brought it up, Damon would stop her, saying it was best for all of them if he stayed out of it.

That's why she'd tried to blame him when, just two months into her junior year, he was called to pick her up from the security office at the Promenade, Magnolia's swanky mall.

"What the hell, Drea?" he had asked once he'd convinced the security guard that it would all be taken care of and would never happen again.

"You know what the hell," was all Drea had said in response, and Damon never mentioned the incident again.

Drea had gotten the idea to take the hand-beaded clutch when the store owner told her to take her time looking at the evening bags she'd pulled from the display, and left Drea to follow another customer around the store. The owner had profiled the girl the moment she had walked in: fifteen or sixteen years old, huge backpack, brown skin. The girl could have been Drea, save for her Woodruff School uniform and that her mother dropped thousands of dollars a year in that place.

The other difference was that the girl was probably not a thief. Drea, on the other hand, had convinced herself she was just like her parents.

Except her parents wouldn't have gotten caught. Neither would Drea, if the mall security guard hadn't been walking by the store and seen her put the clutch into her bag. He hadn't known anything about how much her mother spent in Natalia's Fine Accessories or their money and position in Peachland, and even when Natalia tried to persuade him it was a misunderstanding and that she'd never press charges, he still hauled Drea down to his office.

When she replayed the whole thing later, it had made her angry. She'd done it to give the finger to her parents and their money and status, but those were the very reasons she would have gotten away with it if the guard hadn't seen her. All those things made it possible for her to ruminate about it from the comfort of her authentic Victorian four-poster bed. Had that other girl in the store stolen the bag, she'd be thinking about it from juvenile detention.

There was another thing that had put Drea on the crazy train and that she had absolutely not seen coming: She got stupid over a boy. She'd been on plenty of dates and she was a skillful flirt when she wanted to be, playing the part of the charming ingenue even if she didn't come by it naturally. None of that prepared her for how hard she crushed on a boy she didn't even know, or how devastated she was when he was gone before she ever got the chance to try out her skills on him.

But all of that had happened months ago. It was now the end of her junior year and, for the most part, she'd gotten her act together. She'd forgotten about the boy (mostly), had recommitted to her studies, and just recently, her parents had given her a whole new thing to worry about and focus on. On top of everything else this year, they'd suddenly left two weeks ago, claiming they had a lead on a very expensive Napoleon III–era chandelier and hadn't called in since. Of course, everyone knew they often traveled around Europe looking for priceless antiques, so that was the story Damon and Drea went with this time. But the fact they'd heard nothing since their parents had left, except the occasional *we're fine, be home soon* text, meant this time was different.

So she was shocked when an aide from the counselor's office interrupted AP Chem and asked her to step outside. In her four years at Woodruff, Drea had never been summoned to the counselor's office, at least not by a hand-delivered note in the middle of class with the word URGENT scrawled in all caps across the sealed envelope, and certainly not during the last week of school. She walked down the hall as though she were headed for the gallows instead of the counselor's office, with that familiar sinking feeling that made her wonder if she'd finally been found out.

"Ah, Andrea, come in," Ms. Vance said. When Drea continued standing in her doorway, she added, "Please, have a seat. Would you like something to drink? I have tea and coffee."

Ms. Vance had never offered beverages before. This meeting was either going to be very long or very difficult. Or both. Drea declined the offer.

"Let's get right to it, then, shall we? I've received the grades from your final exams, and—well, I don't think I'm divulging any big secret here since you won the last three years—you're the top contender to be the junior-class recipient of the Top of the Class Award."

Drea smiled demurely, as though Ms. Vance had indeed told her something she hadn't already suspected.

"But I was doing a last-minute check of your records and I found a slight problem." She placed a hand on top of the open file folder on her desk. "You don't quite have the highest GPA."

This was it.

"Last semester, you failed to turn in a project in art class. That's so unlike you. What happened there?"

What Drea wanted to say: *Uh, my whole world went to hell after I figured out my parents were behind a massive car and home heist that ripped off a bunch of Peachlanders. You and everyone else think they're these fine, philanthropic citizens and successful fine-antiques dealers. What you don't know is how they started that business, and none of it was fine. They sold masterful reproductions as the real thing, ran bidding rings that fixed prices at auctions, and told little old ladies their family heirlooms were kitsch at best—before buying them for a fraction of their true value. Oh, and in the very beginning, they weren't even white-collar about it, and just flat-out stole the merchandise they sold online.* Like everyone else in Peachland, the Internet had made the Faradays rich too. Thanks to the web, just about anyone can fence a matching pair of stolen Tiffany lamp shades. It's even easier when the thieves are the best con artists in the antiques business, spinning stories of how they acquired their loot that convinced even people who ought to have known better.

What Drea actually said: "Oh, that's a mistake. I mean, it's true I didn't turn in the assignment initially, but I made it up before the end of the semester. I guess Ms. Arpel forgot to credit me for it."

Or maybe when your parents go back to a life of crime after years of playing it straight, and you're worried about the police showing up at your door to haul them away almost as much as you worry that you're really just like them, you forget to turn in the make-up assignment too. In fact, you say "Screw the make-up assignment," which is definitely not like you. And then you proceed to go off the rails, and even though school is the least of your problems, shouldn't you get credit for somehow managing to keep your shit together enough to maintain an almost-perfect GPA? Apparently not, so you smile and pretend everything is all under control.

"I'll talk to her today and get it sorted out."

"I knew there had to be an explanation," Ms. Vance said. "How are your parents? Are they still out of town? I was hoping to speak to them about next year's scholarship fund-raising drive."

"Woodruff gives scholarships?"

"We did as of last year. We gave two students full rides,

43

and while it didn't quite work out as well as we'd anticipated, we'd like to try it again next fall but time is running out to recruit candidates. I'm committee chair again this year, and your parents were so generous—"

"Really? Who were they? The students, I mean."

"That's confidential. Can't divulge that kind of thing, you know."

That's where Drea was so unlike her parents and Damon—no subtlety. Ms. Vance would be divulging every detail right now had one of them asked. But it had only taken a second for the pieces she'd been missing for months to fall into place, and Drea just blurted out the question the moment it occurred to her. At least she hadn't named the suspected recipients, but knowing there had been two of them, and that the scholarship money had been donated by her parents, explained a lot.

"Right, of course. Well, yes, they're still out of town."

"I imagine they live a very glamorous life, traveling Europe looking for beautiful treasure."

"Yes, it's all very glamorous. The bell should be going any second, so . . ."

"Of course, don't let me keep you," Ms. Vance said, closing Drea's folder. "Once you get that issue resolved with Ms. Arpel, everything will be perfect."

And really, wasn't that the whole point?

5

Thursday, 11:47 p.m.

Drea had a thousand reasons why she wished they lived in the
city instead of boring Peachland, but tonight, she was thank-
ful only the crickets were still awake. The night was full of
their song and the heavy scent of honeysuckle, but nothing
else, and she reached the target without seeing another living
soul. That small bit of luck boosted her confidence. It was one
thing to hear about a crew that planned their heist down to the
letter only to be surprised to find an easy-to-pick tumbler lock
during the Chippendale job, or for Dad to recount how difficult it was during the Tiffany job to detect the false gates from
the true ones on a BiLock. Actually pulling off her own break-
in, which Drea had never done in a live situation, was another
matter. But arriving undetected was just the first step.

First she had to get past the alarm, though she didn't
expect that to be a problem. She had staked out the front

entrance for the last three mornings, arriving before the early custodian. Unlike tonight, during her custodian surveillance she'd had a perfect cover—early-morning jogger who had stopped to retie her laces behind the big sign out front that read "The Woodruff School, Home of the Falcons." And if anyone had caught her on those mornings, watching through a tiny pair of binoculars as the custodian punched in the alarm's access code, she would have become an early-morning jogger who also enjoyed bird-watching, but she saw it as a good sign that no one ever had.

The custodian, a woman named Gladys, had small hands, making it easier to see the numbers she pressed on the keypad. Drea had taken that as another good sign, since she'd expected her view would be partially obstructed, or that she'd have to guess some of the numbers based on the woman's hand movements.

But Gladys had made it easy, punching in the same number three days in a row. 8124.

So why hadn't 8124 worked tonight? Drea had already tried it five times, and the little light on the keypad continued to glow red. What if the alarm company monitored the number of failed attempts? They'd probably send a patrol car and it would be there any minute.

After the sixth failed attempt, Drea noticed how bright the light high above her was, illuminating her presence at the front door for any passerby to see. If she'd had a decent arm, and if the bulb wasn't protected by a metal cage, she'd have tried throwing a rock at it. Her watch told her she'd been working on the keypad for a minute now, but no cars had gone by. She'd have heard it. On such a quiet night, she was certain she'd have heard footsteps from fifty paces. Drea stepped away from the light and scanned the street anyway, just in case. Everything looked the same as it had almost two minutes earlier.

Drea returned to working the keypad, suddenly feeling exposed. She wished she had an accomplice, someone to watch her back. *Or someone to snitch you out when they get caught.* She'd heard that warning a million times. But going solo still didn't save her getting caught.

"What the hell are you doing?"

Drea froze, deciding whether she should talk or fight her way out of this, but her heart felt like it was beating double-time. She turned, expecting the voice behind her to belong to someone from the neighborhood out walking their dog, or maybe even a cop, but she startled at the sight of Xavier Kwon.

Drea had guessed right when she'd spotted Xavier talking to Headmistress Fitch at the gala last summer. When he'd shown up at Woodruff last fall, Drea had learned his last name and anything else she could through gossip, which she'd hoped wasn't accurate (he had a criminal record), and a mild web-searching obsession, which she'd found wasn't much (he apparently wasn't a fan of social media). In spite of how well she'd played the rich snob when they first met, Drea had imagined fifty different scenarios in which they were accidentally thrown together and she'd be given the chance to prove she wasn't really that girl. But she could never translate what was in her head to real life, and the longest conversation they'd ever had was that first one in her driveway, when he'd pretended to be French to get bigger tips. He'd left school before first-semester midterms, and during his very short stint at Woodruff, they had run in completely opposite circles.

Okay, even that wasn't true. Drea had a circle to run in. Xavier Kwon did not. Woodruff was small, private, and expensive, which meant it had a long waiting list that all but assured everyone entered the lower school and didn't leave until graduation. It was strange enough that Xavier had arrived at the start of eleventh grade when every other junior had already been in the same clique for two years. The bigger mystery—at least until Ms. Vance had told her about the scholarships—was how he'd managed to be there at all, given his background, which was decidedly not the Woodruff standard. For one thing, rumor had it he was poor, to which Drea could attest since he was working as a valet when she first met him. It also didn't help that everyone was afraid of him. But those weren't the reasons Xavier didn't run in a group. It was mostly because he was too cool to be a joiner, as one would expect of a guy people only called X, never his full name. X was a circle of one.

Or not.

"Is this who's been screwing around with the alarm system?" A boy appeared out of the darkness beside Xavier, who was standing clear of the light overhead.

Drea waited for her fight-or-flight impulse to kick in, but it didn't. Maybe it was the way Xavier was smiling at her—

part amused, part intrigued—that made her stay.

"Who is she and why are we just standing here? We got work to do, man."

Xavier stood close beside her, putting his arm around her shoulders. There was a time she would have been thrilled that he noticed her, but when she felt him run his hand down her back ever so lightly, she broke herself free of him. It was too intimate now, all these months later. They hardly knew each other, after all.

"This is Andrea. She goes here," Xavier explained to his friend.

More likely, his accomplice. Like her, they couldn't be up to any good this late at night, talking about the very alarm system she'd unsuccessfully tried to get past.

"Drea," she said.

"What?"

"My friends call me Drea."

"Oh, so we're friends now?"

"No, I just meant—"

"Can you run game some other time?" the accomplice asked, pointing to his wrist and an imaginary watch. "Get her number and get rid of her."

"Um, I'm standing right here," Drea said, hoping she sounded exasperated and not excited that Xavier may have wanted her number. His friend was rude and pushy, but he was right—this wasn't the time. If Xavier was even interested. But he must be, considering how he had just greeted her.

"So you are. And doing what exactly?" Xavier asked.

49

"Same thing you guys are doing: breaking into the school. Though I suspect for different reasons."

This made Xavier smile, and made his friend look like he might explode.

"That ain't the only difference," the friend said. "We actually know what the hell we're doing."

When the accomplice headed toward the back of the school, Xavier followed. Drea continued to stand in the glaring light until he turned back to ask, "You coming, or what?"

Across the street, a man idled in the small hybrid car he had rented just for tonight, marveling at how quiet the engine was. Too bad they didn't make these back in the day. What you sacrificed in style and comfort you made up for in stealth. He knocked wood three times even though there was no wood in the car, grateful for the half-moon, which made driving the neighborhood without headlights a bit easier. He was also glad he'd stocked up on his favorite gum, a treat to help the time pass. He could go through several packs in one night, an old habit formed during years of surveillance. But he'd been off the job a long time now and wasn't as young as he'd been back then. Let someone else handle it. He unwrapped a stick, savoring the first biting taste of cinnamon, and waited.

Thursday, 11:51 p.m.

Even though instinct told her to run, that there was still time to undo a monumentally bad decision, Drea followed Xavier. As he walked ahead of her, she took in the broadness of his shoulders, the leanness of his back under his shirt. It reminded Drea of the days she had watched him in the hallways of Woodruff. Stalked him, really—learning his schedule, changing one of her electives on the last day of drop/add so she could be in his art class, and finding reasons to be near his locker between classes.

"I take it this is your first break-in," he said.

The question jolted her back to the present. The memory of him had been so intense, she'd nearly forgotten she was right there with him, in real life.

"Yeah, I thought so. I still remember my first time. It was at the Seven-Eleven down the corner from my house. I was seven years old and it was eleven in the morning. Seriously, I'm not making that up."

"Seven? Did you lift some Skittles and comic books to show off for your friends?"

"No, I took a loaf of bread and some lunch meat because I was hungry."

Drea didn't know what to say to that, so she said nothing.

"I was a lot older when I figured out you could steal because you wanted something, not just because you needed it. I'm guessing you're here for the second reason."

Drea was still quiet, not because she didn't want to answer, but because she was still thinking about a seven-year-old who had to steal his dinner.

"I get it. It's tough to admit you're about to commit your first crime."

"This is hardly my first crime." It was a strange thing to sound so proud of.

"Really? I didn't expect that. Well, whatever other crimes you've committed, they couldn't have been breaking and entering, or you'd be in jail on a B&E charge right now."

"What makes you so sure?" she asked, hoping he didn't realize how nervous she was, and that it had nothing to do with being caught attempting a B&E.

"You picked the front entrance—the one anyone going down Magnolia Street can see, especially since it's lit up like Christmas."

They reached the back entrance, and Drea saw his point. This door was the better choice. Visibility from the street or nearby houses was practically nil, and the lighting in the teachers' parking lot was dim this time of night. But it wasn't like she didn't know that, which she was about to explain when Xavier continued.

"But the locks back here and at the side entrance are swipe card. If you'd stolen a teacher's card, you risked them discovering it and having the card deactivated before you could break in." He stepped back to appraise her, looking her up and down, making her feel both vulnerable and a little warm. "You're what, five foot two?"

"And a half," Drea said, knowing her correction was weak. "Closer to five three."

"I'll give you another inch if you want, but unless you've got an NBA-like vertical leap, you still couldn't reach the windows. So you were forced to use the front entrance, which has a number pad. It was easy to watch the staff and learn the code, right?"

Xavier stopped long enough for her to acknowledge his brilliant deduction, but Drea didn't oblige, so he continued. "Whoever designed the system probably didn't bother switching the front door to a swipe-card entry because they never expected anyone to use the front door. The bright light and visibility from the street would deter break-ins. And they'd be right if they were dealing with professionals."

"I suppose we should give her some credit for figuring out the alarm code," said the surly accomplice, who was too busy with his phone to look up when they joined him. "Where'd you learn how to do that—online? Thought you'd become a thief so you spent a few days on CrowdTutorial, right?"

"I may not be as good at larceny as you guys, but shouldn't

you be trying to break into the school instead of playing on your phone?" Drea said. "Seems like a stupid time to send a text."

Surly Boy looked up at her only briefly, as though giving her any more consideration would have been a waste of time.

"That's Jason, and he isn't texting," Xavier said. "Sad social skills, mad hacking skills. He's disabling the entire system. We're hacking the alarms, the locks, inside motion sensors, everything."

"*We're* hacking? You mean *I'm* hacking."

Drea was captain of the Woodruff debate club but she was at a loss for words, which never happened. Unless Xavier was around. The way this boy had read her, like he'd known her forever, was unnerving. And she hadn't even considered motion sensors. Drea had done her research on the system and thought she knew every detail. She'd have preferred to look at the alarm-system schematics, but they apparently weren't on paper, only in the designer's head, because she could find no trace of the specs in her father's office. When he'd mentioned having the system installed a couple of years ago, Drea didn't recall him saying anything about motion detectors.

"If he's the hacker, what do you do?" Drea asked Xavier.

"I'm very good at asset transfer, breaching offline defense systems, and target protection."

"Okay, I see. You're the bullshitter," Drea said, recalling the French accent that made her fall for him almost immediately, even if it turned out to be fake.

"He's a thief who can break into anything that isn't

electronic," Jason clarified. "And he can also deliver a major ass-kicking when necessary."

It was Drea's turn to size up the boys, and she quickly concluded they were in the wrong jobs. Jason was slightly built, only a few inches taller than she was, and quite stealthy, considering the way he had just magically appeared out of nowhere a few minutes earlier. He should have been the thief, because there was nothing covert about Xavier. He was six feet, maybe an inch more, lean but mostly muscle, which Drea could see being a plus when it came to delivering a "major ass-kicking." But he also had that thing some people have that announced when they've entered the room. She searched for the right word for it but only came up with *presence*. He had plenty of that. Not a great attribute for a thief, but it worked wonders on making a girl forget she had a mission of her own to execute.

"Now I get to ask a question," Xavier said. "Why is Little Miss Perfect breaking into her own school?"

"Don't call me that."

"But it's true, isn't it? Junior class president. A lock for valedictorian next year. Voted most likely to do everything right. I bet none of your fans saw this coming," Xavier said, his smile nearly throwing Drea off again.

"Are you one of them?" she asked.

"One of who?"

"My fans. You clearly know a lot about me and my current status, considering you vanished from Woodruff months ago," she said, not adding that he'd left with no explanation. Not

55

that he owed her one, since she'd barely said hello to him. Remembering how hurt she was by his disappearance helped her play it cool now. "I know nothing about you."

"Oh, I think you know more than you let on," Xavier said.

"Okay, we're in," Jason said. "Let's go. We've got about five minutes before things start looking wrong to the alarm-monitoring company."

"I guess this is where we go our separate ways," Xavier said, following Jason through the door but blocking Drea from entering.

"I'm going in, too."

"No you aren't. We've got business. You don't even have gloves."

Drea produced a pair of leather gloves from her back jeans pocket, though she'd completely forgotten about them until he mentioned it.

"Tell me why you're here," Xavier said. No, *commanded*.

Maybe it was because she'd watched him walk through the halls of Woodruff like he owned the place from the day he'd arrived, or because she had moved to the back of English Lit just to sit behind him, when normally she always sat up front, or maybe because she wasn't over him like she'd believed, but Drea told him the truth without a second thought.

"I need to change one of my grades or I won't be top of my class, and I'm always top of my class."

Xavier looked at Drea like he suddenly didn't know who she was, and smiled. "Let me do it for you. It's kind of the reason we're here, to hack the school records system. Well, that and I also have to—"

"Dude, move your ass," Jason yelled from halfway down the hall.

"I'm coming," Xavier yelled back.

"You're committing a felony just to change your grades?" Drea asked. "I thought I was the only person neurotic enough about my GPA to do something that stupid. You don't even go here anymore."

"Hey Poser Girl, it's past your bedtime. X, we gotta move," Jason practically screamed, aware they had already lost thirty seconds of the precious little time they had before the alarm company figured out their system had been overridden.

"Jason is right. Go home, Drea. Let me do this. If your hacking skills are anything like your B&E skills, you need to let me handle it. You don't want to screw up your life before it even starts. Believe me, it sucks. And besides . . . I owe you."

Before Drea could mount a protest, Xavier pulled the door closed until the lock clicked. He ran down the hall to catch up with Jason, turned right toward the school office, and disappeared.

The man waiting in the quiet car across the street received a phone call that only lasted a few seconds. He disconnected the call and made one himself, noting the time on the dashboard's clock. Four minutes before they should arrive, give or take a minute.

7

Thursday, 11:55 p.m.

Drea wondered what Xavier had meant about owing her, but only for a second. He probably felt guilty about what he'd done last summer, even if he'd done it at her parents' request. She had suspected for months that he'd been part of the heist. But Drea wanted confirmation just the same. She didn't go home; instead, she took a seat on the stone bench in the small rose garden near the back door.

Back when Peachland was on the verge of financial collapse, Woodruff had been facing closure, but her parents had arrived in town just in time to save the day, and it was the kind of school that required a rose garden, at least according to her mother, who had suggested planting it. That was why the bench had their family name etched into it. It was her mother's attempt to prove they were not only wealthy enough to save the school from financial ruin, but that they were respectable, too. For their efforts, they'd lobbied to have the school named after them, but Peachland parents, while appreciative, had thought that was a bit much. Instead, her parents got a rose garden and a stone bench where the family name became a place for people to rest their asses.

She laughed at the thought. It was the kind of moment she'd love to share with her mother, but Drea had no idea where she or her father were, despite what she'd told Ms. Vance. She was certain their sudden disappearance had something to do with what had gone down during the Woodruff gala last summer, like everything in Drea's life had since that day.

After the initial shock that money, class, and security systems could not protect them from the very reason they'd escaped the city, Peachlanders got back to their lives after the heist, upgrading security systems, buying new luxury cars, and replacing the antiques her parents had sold them with even more items from the Faraday collection. No one had questioned why, given the treasure held there, the Faradays had only lost a couple of things. No one suspected, as Drea had, that their stolen items were only a cover. Well, Damon probably had, but he never said as much to Drea. Her father never mused how Cufflink Guy had cornered him against the stolen Childe Hassam painting. Because only one other person knew about the black-pearl ring thief, no one considered the missing chinoiserie jewelry box—only that particular ring left in its place on the dresser like a taunt—a major coincidence. When the ring thief turned up, as promised, with the locker next to hers, Drea didn't mention it. It was easier, smarter, to act clueless and pretend she barely remembered catching Gigi in her room that day and to ignore her attempts at friendship until the girl finally gave up. They both knew it wasn't Drea's friendship Gigi was after, anyway.

"Really respectable, Mom. If only you could see me now. I've become a burglar."

Well, maybe only a burglar by association. The second she had lost sight of Xavier, she knew she had to wait for them. It wouldn't be long; they had less than four minutes left. Not only did Drea have a few questions for him about the heist, she needed to make sure they changed her grade or she wouldn't be able to sleep tonight. She also needed to set Xavier straight on this whole idea of her being Miss Perfect. He ought to talk to Damon, if he really wanted to know who she was. If not for him, she'd be in juvie right now, or at least on probation.

Damon hadn't thought she was so perfect when he picked her up from the security office at the Promenade. He didn't even know about the wall she'd spray-painted during her temporary downward spiral, a really sad attempt at tagging that she wouldn't admit to now, even to convince Xavier Kwon she wasn't such a straight arrow. *Little Miss Perfect.* Perfect people don't tag a wall with letters that aren't uniform in size or that go uphill. They also don't ruin a chance to win Top of the Class by getting a 3.8 in art, an elective she'd taken only because Xavier was in it. There was no such thing as an AP art class. Given her line of work, you'd think her mother would have lobbied for that at Woodruff instead of a rose garden.

"Xavier Kwon doesn't know me at all," Drea said, making her case to no one. She smiled. Maybe she'd get a chance to change that.

One thing Xavier did get right was pointing out how she'd forgotten to use her gloves when pounding numbers on the alarm keypad, a rookie mistake. She was smarter than that. Drea checked her watch. Three and a half minutes. Plenty of time to run around to the front door, clean off her prints, and be back here before the boys finished the job. If breaking into a high school to change your grades could qualify as a job.

As Drea rounded the corner of the building, she noticed a car driving slowly down Magnolia toward the school. Probably about two blocks away. It was the first set of headlights she'd seen all night. Brushing it off, she kept heading for the front entrance as she twisted her long hair into a tight bun, something else she hadn't remembered to do until she found the ponytail holder in the same pocket as the gloves. Perfect. Another clue for the cops, since she was the only girl at Woodruff with hair that curled like half-cooked ramen noodles in a weird shade of blonde-auburn-brunette the exact color of the rosin she rubbed on her violin bow. Like the school's alarm system, her worry was probably overkill. Not only couldn't she imagine Magnolia PD calling their CSI unit—if they even had one—to the scene of a high school break-in, but she'd been at Woodruff for three years. Her hair was probably all over the place. But old lessons died hard.

At the front of the school, Drea put on her gloves before using the hem of her T-shirt to wipe the keypad, careful to use a light touch, in case pressing any of the buttons too hard screwed up Jason's hack into the system. By the time she'd finished destroying any evidence she'd ever been there, the car had stopped half a block away. Drea moved away from the door and the bright light to get a better look. It was a patrol car.

Just stay calm, she told herself as she ducked between the building and the hedge that ringed it. If this had been about the school break-in, if someone had seen them and reported it, the cop would be pulling into the parking lot, not pulling behind a car parked across the street. She hadn't noticed the car before, but if it had been there when she was working the keypad, she wouldn't have. The little car would have been blocked from her view by the school sign. Now that she was about ten feet down from the door, she could see it plain as day: a Toyota Prius, a car with practically the quietest engine on the planet, so she wouldn't have heard it approach.

Now another patrol car was coming toward the school from the opposite direction, but it didn't pull into the school lot either. It joined the first car, which must have called for backup. Except that second car arrived way too quickly—it had to have been en route to the school already. Now the first cop got out, walked up to the Prius, and shined his flashlight into it. He started talking to someone inside while the second cop, who looked like he had his hand near his gun, stood back. That was probably how they handled a routine traffic stop in Atlanta, but it seemed a bit much in Peachland.

The Prius must have arrived after she did. It must have been someone who lived on the street, coming home late, parking in front of his house, when he noticed a silhouette under the bright light at the school's front entrance. She could understand not hearing the car's approach, but how did she not see his headlights? But none of that mattered now. The driver never went inside his house, staying in his car for a reason. He must have watched her messing around with the keypad, then saw the arrival of Jason and Xavier. He must have called the police.

Drea checked her watch again. Only a minute had passed, though it seemed like it had been forever. The boys had two and a half more minutes. *Please stay over there, cops, across the street.* Even as she thought it, Drea knew it wasn't going to happen. Now both officers were looking at the school. The first cop leaned down to say something to the driver of the Prius, who drove away a few seconds later, before both officers got back into their cars. She didn't wait to see where they were headed. She already knew.

There were no windows in the registrar's office, so Jason wouldn't know the police had arrived. Even if Xavier was acting as a lookout, he couldn't watch both sides of the building. And hadn't he mentioned a second part of their mission, at least before Jason cut him off? Xavier was probably busy doing that second thing and nowhere near a window, either. After all, they weren't expecting the alarm-monitoring company to have a clue for another two minutes now.

She figured the cops would split up, driving the perimeter from opposite directions before stopping to check the front entrance, since that was where the tipster probably directed them. Running between the hedges and the building, careful to stay low, Drea went around back, hoping the boys had finished in less time than they'd anticipated and she'd find them already outside. No such luck.

Drea couldn't stay behind the hedge forever; the cops would know as well as she did that it was a great way to move around the building without being seen. If only she'd gotten Jason's number. Then she could warn them while hauling her ass out of there. She left the cover of the hedges and made a break for the Dumpster enclosure behind the school, praying the whole way, even though she wasn't the tiniest bit religious. There, she had a view of both the back door and part of the front parking lot.

Drea watched through the wooden slats of the enclosure for the cars to slowly circle the school grounds, waiting for her moment to get to the back door undetected. What she'd do when she got there, she didn't know. Maybe break the little window on the door and try to reach the lock so she could get inside to warn the boys. But if it were that easy, Jason wouldn't have had to hack the electronic lock. At the very least, she could try to get their attention through the window when they rounded the corner at the end of the hall and wave them on to run faster.

The boys should be coming through the back doors in about two minutes. By then, the officers should have completed the perimeter check and be back at the front entrance looking for signs of a break-in. Except nothing went as Drea had expected. The patrol cars didn't split up and they didn't check the front entrance before investigating the back door, because two sets of headlights were now headed toward her.

8

Thursday, 11:57 p.m.

Drea's instinct to run finally kicked in. Once the second patrol car's headlights cleared the Dumpster enclosure and turned toward the back door, Drea took off up the hill that rose behind the school. There was nothing she could do for the boys now. Her getting arrested wouldn't help them. Good thing she hadn't tried to break the little window, leaving an obvious sign someone had tried a forced entry. Hopefully the cops would have a look, determine nothing was wrong and that the tipster hadn't really seen anything at all, and just drive away. But nothing tonight had happened as she'd predicted. Or hoped.

At the top of the hill, she lay on her stomach and watched as the officers got out of their cruisers and went straight to the back door, which was apparently unlocked. Had it been unlocked all this time? Could she have gone in to warn the

65

boys after all? If she'd done that the minute she saw the first patrol car pull in front of the school, maybe they'd all be up the hill right now, disappearing into the night. But Drea was certain Xavier had locked the door from the inside, keeping her out. She remembered hearing the bolt click. The cops must have gotten the alarm company to open it remotely.

Through the windows Xavier had pointed out, the ones that were too high for her to reach, Drea could see the officers' flashlights moving around the building. She noticed how they moved with purpose instead of clearing the school room-by-room, or at least moving tentatively through the building in case there really was an armed intruder. Thanks to their flashlights and open classroom doors, Drea could see them proceed directly from the back door to the main hall, where they took a right turn. It was as though the boys had left a trail—the cops were heading toward the registrar's office, where the boys were probably changing her grade right now. They were heading straight for Xavier.

After the way the night had gone so far, she shouldn't have had any hope left. But she tried to convince herself the boys had finished their job two minutes early and had already exited the rear door before she'd returned to the back of the building. Maybe they'd spotted the patrol cars' arrival after all, and had already taken off through a side entrance, or even the front door. Yeah, that was probably what had happened, but she still waited for the officers to finish their search and exit the building.

When they did come out just a minute later, her hope was

crushed again. They weren't alone. Each officer was holding the arm of one handcuffed boy, whom they led to their patrol cars. She watched Xavier hesitate before he got into the backseat of one of the cruisers. Jason was placed in the other car and both cruisers drove away. She looked at her watch. The whole thing had taken five minutes, just as the boys had planned—except for the ending.

There was nothing for Drea to do now but go home. She decided to take the long way around to her street just in case. Strange that the officers didn't search for her. Surely the tipster reported seeing three people. *Just be grateful,* she told herself as she pulled off her gloves and stuck them in her back pocket. That was when she noticed her phone wasn't there. It wasn't in the other back pocket either. She checked her front pockets . . . and nothing. It was gone.

The last time she knew for sure she had it was when she'd left the house, which meant it could be anywhere. What if the cops came back to do some actual investigating and found it? Or what if they already had? She could always say she'd lost it at school earlier in the day. That would make sense. But Drea didn't want to take a chance. *If you're going to do a job, do it right.* She'd have to retrace her steps down the hill, into the Dumpster enclosure, to the back door, in the rose garden, around to the front of the school, and back again through the hedges. It could be somewhere on the street between home and school. It would be a long night, but at least she had plenty of darkness left to search. Except that there was only a half-moon, and she couldn't risk wandering around with a flashlight.

As she began her search around the grass where she'd lain flat watching the boys be taken away just a couple of minutes ago, she kept replaying two thoughts. One was Xavier's last words to her before he'd gone inside the school: *You don't want to screw up your life before it even starts. Believe me, it sucks.* The second thing was something her father had told her more than once: *You're great with a plan, but execution was never your sweet spot.*

As though to prove them right, as though her execution tonight hadn't already been enough of a disaster, as Drea started her descent down the hill toward the school, her foot landed on a large rock. She felt her ankle turn and the ground fall away. Then she was tumbling down.

The tipster hadn't left as the officers had directed him. Who were they to tell him what to do? It was a free country, and he'd been parked on a public right-of-way. He remembered when both of them were rookies. Hell, he'd trained one of them. Instead of leaving, he'd driven around the block once before parking on the street that ran alongside the school. That gave him a decent view of both the back and the front entrances. From that position, he could watch it all play out, including the girl lying in the grass at the top of the hill, whom he had neglected to include in his report to the officers.

Friday, 12:02 a.m.

Even though the Woodruff School was not in the rookie's patrol area, it was in his neighborhood. He figured it was his duty to help out—at least that was the story he'd tell his commanding officer if asked why he was out of zone—but it must have been the fastest apprehension and arrest on record. By the time he had arrived at the school, the suspects had already been taken away. The two officers who first responded to the call were more than enough to arrest two unarmed juveniles pulling a classic end-of-school prank, but in the week since he'd been out of field training and patrolling on his own, the most action he'd seen was routine traffic stops and an old lady who had mistaken her neighbor for a prowler. Back when he'd enrolled in the police academy, he'd expected a lot more excitement than he'd seen so far.

He was about to return to his own patrol zone when he thought he saw something creeping along the front of the

69

school. It was not fully upright, walking with a slow, dragging gait. Perhaps an animal. The moon wasn't bright enough for a good look, and by the time he switched on the side-mounted spotlight, whatever it was had disappeared.

May have been a bear, but he doubted it. You might see a bear up in the mountains, but not down here. Then he spotted it again, this time at the side of the building. The figure was more upright now and moving faster. Bears could stand upright, but with the lights shining on it, the rookie could see the figure was too thin to be a bear, even a cub. He radioed dispatch, realizing he'd probably be asked why he was out of zone, but if he could catch whoever the shadowy figure was, no doubt he'd get a pass.

"Unit Two Twenty-Seven checking in on the call from the Woodruff School. How many prowlers did the nine-one-one caller think he saw?"

"Two were reported. Responding officers report arresting two suspects: one sixteen-year-old Caucasian male and one seventeen-year-old Asian male."

"You sure there was no mention of a third prowler?" the rookie asked as he got out of his cruiser and started his approach on the building.

"Affirmative. Unit Two Twenty-Seven—confirm your position. GPS indicates you are out of zone."

"Right. I'm at the school. I thought maybe the responding officers might need assistance."

"Responding officers are already en route to juvenile detention with suspects. Please return to zone."

"I will, but I want to check out something first. Thought I saw someone moving around the rear of the school. I'm on foot now."

"Do you request backup?"

"No," he answered, not wanting to get into any more trouble than he already was. "It's probably nothing. I'll radio if I need help."

He closed communication with dispatch and moved slowly along the side of the school, his heart pounding so loudly he was convinced his target could probably hear it. The tipster clearly hadn't seen the third kid. Maybe he'd been the lookout—albeit a very bad one, since his friends were about to be booked into juvie right now. The lookout got at least one thing right—he picked a loyal crew to run with, since the other two suspects never gave him up.

But why would a lookout still be hanging around the scene of the crime? The rookie may have been a fresh recruit, but his experience dealing with criminals went back long before someone had paid him to do it. Either the lookout was hanging around to finish whatever his accomplices couldn't, or he'd stayed behind to eliminate evidence. The officer leaned toward the last option, which would mean this break-in was probably more than just a high school prank. Maybe the lookout would be the better arrest—the one with information that might save him from a lecture about staying in zone, perhaps even get him a commendation for his probation period.

As he turned the corner to the rear of the school, he heard a faint moan, the sound of someone in pain. The perp was obviously close, but the rookie couldn't see him. There were plenty of places a suspect could hide and still watch him with a clear view: the hedges lining the building, the rose garden at the back entrance, the enclosure used to conceal the trash cans.

Now the pounding in his chest was so loud he could visualize the valves in his heart opening and closing, sending all the blood to his ears. It was just another kid, or at least he hoped it was, but now he regretted declining backup. It would have been so easy to call it in using the radio on his shoulder, but the suspect might hear him; he'd be giving away his location if he hadn't yet been spotted. Instead of clicking on the radio, he drew his gun. Even though the perp was hurt, and probably only a high school kid, if he was armed, none of that mattered.

When Drea finally stopped tumbling, she knew something was very wrong. She'd felt something in her foot pop right before her leg went out from under her. It hurt to stand, much less walk, but she had to find that phone. If she had dropped it someplace obvious, the police would never buy her story that she'd lost it during the school day, because someone would have noticed the phone and either turned it in or kept it. The only way a phone could be lying in plain sight was if it had been lost after the last student, teacher, and custodian had gone for the day.

She retraced her footsteps, checking the front of the school, the rear entrance where the boys had gone in, around the bench with her family's name. If she'd dropped it at the back door, the police would have found it. Drea kept her phone locked, but the hot-pink case with tiny red hearts printed on it still would have given her away. The police would know the boys weren't the only suspects, and they'd still be here, looking for her now, assuming it was no coincidence.

So if she lost it on school grounds, it had to be inside the Dumpster enclosure. She had half limped, half dragged herself there, only to collapse, too tired to search even on hands and knees. The pain was now close to unbearable. There was no way she could walk home; she could'n't even walk to one of the houses across the street. Finding her phone had become less a legal necessity and more a medical emergency. If she didn't find it soon, she'd have to crawl to the nearest house for help.

If the pain hadn't been about to kill her, she'd have laughed at the whole night, though there was nothing funny about a single part of it. First, getting caught by Jason and Xavier. Actually talking to the guy she'd only stared at for two months, too afraid to even say hello. Then letting him get caught, though she wasn't sure what she could have done to save him. As she'd watched the boys being led out of the school by the police, she had noticed Xavier looking around for something before he got into the cruiser. Not looking down at his feet like he might have dropped something, but looking around the school grounds and beyond. Drea imagined he was looking for her, wondering if she'd gone home before the police had arrived.

Now she heard footsteps moving outside the enclosure. It couldn't be the police—she'd watched them drive off. While she'd been busy falling down the hill and busting up her leg, could they have returned for some reason? No, probably a neighbor who had seen the commotion and came to see what the fuss was about. For a brief second, fear-fueled adrenaline surged through her as she realized it might be the neighbor who had sat in the car and watched them, who'd probably called the cops in the first place. But as the door of the enclosure swung open, Drea was more grateful than afraid. At this point, she would take being caught at the scene of a crime over the pain shooting from her foot to her knee—until she saw the Glock 22 pointed at her, and the cop behind it.

Friday, 12:05 a.m.

"Jesus, Drea. What are you doing in here? I damn near shot you."

"You would have put me out of my misery."

"What?"

"I'm hurt."

"Hurt how? Why are you even out here? You're supposed to be—"

"Damon, stop being a cop. Can you just be my brother long enough to get me to a hospital?" Drea asked between moans. "I may have broken my ankle. I can barely walk on it. Can you bring your car closer?"

"I'll carry you," Damon said, helping her up.

"You don't have to carry me. Just be a human crutch. I'll hop on the good leg." She put one arm around his shoulder.

Once she had Damon to lean on, Drea mentally downgraded her injury from *I might die* to *I wish I had some strong drugs.* "I don't think it's broken. If it is, maybe just a hairline fracture," she said, hoping to get Damon to talk instead of repeatedly clenching his jaw, clearly trying not to explode from whatever emotions he was working to suppress—worry about her injury, anger that she was somehow related to the suspicious-activity call he had just responded to.

But Damon didn't talk about things. He fixed whatever he could exert control over, and the stuff he couldn't control, he gave up on.

When he finally spoke, it was clear he thought this situation—the whole "Drea situation," as he liked to call it—was still one he could fix.

"We need to approach the car from the rear," Damon ordered, "out of view of the dashboard camera. That's why I didn't want to move the car closer to you. It would have been recorded. Before we get inside, use your cell to call mine—"

"My phone," Drea said, remembering why she was in the enclosure when Damon found her. "I lost it somewhere, maybe around the Dumpster. I was looking for it when you found me. Call my number. It has to be around here somewhere."

Damon did as his sister instructed, but not before giving her a look of exasperation.

"It's ringing," Damon said, but apparently only in his ear. The only thing Drea heard were crickets.

"Oh, that's right. I put it on vibrate because I didn't want anyone... I mean, we'll have to listen harder. Call it again. But get closer to the Dumpster first."

"Damn it, Drea..."

He didn't finish the sentence, though Drea was pretty sure the end went something like, *why are you turning into such a screwup?* Instead, he helped her to the stone bench with Faraday etched into it, then went back to look for the phone after reminding her to stay put, out of sight of the front dash. Like she was going anywhere. While she waited for him, Drea replayed the night again, and concluded Damon was right, even if he wouldn't say the words. She had become a grade-A screwup.

"I couldn't find it," Damon said when he returned a minute later.

"Did you check inside the enclosure?"

"Of course I checked—didn't you just see me go in there?"

"Even on vibrate, you should have been able to hear it."

"Obviously I didn't because the phone isn't out here. Did you use it while you were…doing whatever it was you were doing on campus?"

"No."

"Then you probably left it at home."

"I'm pretty sure I didn't," Drea said weakly, beginning to wonder if that was true. She'd made so many mistakes tonight that she was beginning to doubt it herself.

"I'm taking you home, where I'm sure we'll find your phone."

"I need to go to the hospital."

"You'll go to the hospital, but first we need to go home so you can call me from the landline. We have to set this thing up right."

"What *'thing'*?"

"I'll be taking you to the hospital in my squad car, in uniform, at one in the morning, after having gone out of zone on a prowler call at the school my sister attends, during which I suggested to dispatch there might have been a third suspect."

"Okay, okay, I get it." Drea gently touched her ankle to check for swelling. It already felt like a baseball was growing inside it.

"We'll park on the corner and walk the block home. If anyone asks, I stopped there to finish a report before going back to my zone."

"Walk? And what about our hella-long driveway? I can't—"

"Can't what? Go to jail? Get me fired? Damn right you can't. So do what I tell you."

Drea had pissed off Damon a lot in the last year, but he'd never been this angry with her. Even her pain didn't soften him. So she shut up and listened.

"We'll walk—hobble—to the house. You go inside, call my cell from the landline. Stay on the line for a full minute. In the meantime, I'll be running down the drive to my patrol car, then I'll come back to the house to get you. Got it?"

"Got it."

"And don't say a word inside the car until I pick you back up from the house."

"They record inside the car?"

"I'm serious, Drea." Damon pointed his finger in her face to make sure she understood just how serious. "In fact, let's make it easy. Silence until we get to the hospital, okay?"

A faraway voice joined them in the quiet night, startling Drea.

"Two Twenty-Seven, confirm whether assistance is needed at four twenty Magnolia Street."

"This is Unit Two Twenty-Seven," Damon said into the radio on his shoulder before shaking his head at Drea, as though she'd actually talk right now. She wasn't *that* much of a screwup. "False alarm, didn't find anything. No assistance needed."

"Check. Return to zone three."

"Ten minutes for a thirty-one, then back to zone three."

"Check, Two Twenty-Seven."

When the voice left them alone again, Drea mouthed a question to Damon, asking if she could talk.

"What?" Damon asked. More like growled.

"What's a thirty-one?"

"It means I need to take a piss. I bought an excuse to be at the house right now," Damon said as he helped her to her feet to finish the walk to his squad car. "So we'll just go by the house to make it look good, wait a few minutes, then go to the hospital. I can say I took my thirty-one at home since the school is just a few blocks away, and while I was there, you tripped down the stairs. Luckily, I was home to take you to the hospital."

"Aren't you worried someone might see us—me sitting in your patrol car instead of hobbling down the steps to the car on my broken leg?"

"Yeah, but we'll have to just hope everyone's asleep, which they should be this time of night. Like you should have been."

"Why did you think there were three suspects?" Drea asked before she realized her question only confirmed for Damon that she knew what had gone on at the school. What she really wanted to ask was whether Jason and Xavier had given her up, but she knew better than to implicate herself further.

"I didn't until I saw you creeping around the building."

"So there wasn't a report of three people?"

"The tipster only reported two, and that's what Magnolia PD found when they got here."

"Two what?"

"Two boys, both with juvie records. But I guess you already know that."

When they reached the car, Drea half expected Damon to handcuff her and make her ride in back, his anger at that moment was so strong. As he directed, she scooted down low on the passenger seat and rode in silence, looking for the silver lining.

That was one of the things that made her popular and won her the votes that made her junior class president. Her classmates thought Drea was an eternal optimist, always hopeful. It was a sham, but after attending eight different schools before Woodruff, back when they'd had to run before her parents' scams were discovered, she'd learned what to do to make people like her, even if she never learned to make true friends. How could she when she never stayed around long enough to get past the pleasantries? So as Damon drove in silence, Drea pretended to be the girl everyone thought she was, and despite how badly the night had gone, she was able to find tonight's silver lining. No doubt the cops had asked the boys if there were any other kids involved, no matter what the tipster had told them. Xavier owed her nothing, but given what Damon had learned from the arresting officers, he must have told the cops that there had only been him and Jason.

The man in the quiet car was still there when the third patrol car arrived. He backed up the street half a block, taking a less visible position, and with the small binoculars he always kept on him, watched the police officer help the injured girl to his vehicle. He made note of the fact that the officer hadn't hand-cuffed the girl and had let her ride in the front seat. He wasn't sure who the girl was or why she'd been there tonight, but it was clear she hadn't been arrested. Might not have been any-thing, but it might have been something. His experience told him it was usually something, so he was glad he had stuck around.

While he'd appreciated the night's half-moon earlier, he was glad he could use his headlights again. He waited, watch-ing the third police car pull away before he switched them on. Satisfied that his mission was complete, even if it hadn't gone exactly as planned, he drove away.

11

Friday, 1:05 a.m.

At the hospital, Drea learned she was right about her ankle. It wasn't broken, but she had a severe ankle sprain with a possibly torn ligament, which the doctor had told her could be even worse since they didn't always heal right. Best case, she'd have to keep her leg immobilized for a few weeks. The doctor had left her alone in the examination room before he'd told her what the worst case might be, and now she had begun to wonder if he'd forgotten about her.

When the curtain moved, it wasn't the doctor or nurse Drea expected to see, but Damon. "They said I could come back here. Is it okay?"

"Yeah. I'm waiting for them to fit me in a walking cast, but I'm not supposed to actually walk on it for a while. They're giving me crutches."

"It could be a minute before they get to you. I just heard

over the radio there's a traffic accident with multiple injuries. EMS should be here in a second. That's probably why they said I could come back. To keep you company. Is it still hurting?"

"No. They gave me the good drugs."

Drea was suddenly uncomfortable with Damon acting more like a brother than a cop. Maybe uncomfortable wasn't the right word. More like...guilty. She was sitting in a hospital getting the good drugs, and soon would be going home. Xavier and Jason were probably sitting in juvie lockup right now, waiting to make bail. Drea knew about Xavier's criminal history, or at least what she'd heard about him around Woodruff. That was all she had to go on since juvenile arrests don't turn up during Internet searches. But she had been more inclined to believe the rumors when she put them together with her suspicions about a car heist in which the thieves apparently had keys—the very keys Xavier had access to during his valet job just two weeks before the heist, coincidentally enough. She knew nothing about Jason except what Damon had said about the two male suspects with juvie records.

"All that stuff you did—making sure the onboard camera didn't record us, going home before you brought me here—"

"Shhh," Damon admonished, looking around the curtain for potential eavesdroppers.

"There's no one in the next bed. I may be on drugs, but I'm not stupid."

"Keep your voice down just the same."

"You went through all that, but if someone really cared,

they could figure it out. A neighbor could have seen us at the house. It was a nosy neighbor who busted us in the first place." Drea said *us* before she could stop herself. She was certain Damon noticed, but he didn't ask the question she thought he was dying to ask, probably because he didn't want to know the answer.

"Stop playing cop. That's my job."

"It wasn't your job tonight, apparently. Maybe you're just like the rest of us after all."

"What are you talking about?"

"You didn't arrest me even though it was obvious I was involved in...that thing. Maybe you have a little larceny in your blood, just like Mom and Dad. And me."

"First off, no matter how much you try to convince yourself you're like them, you aren't." Damon whispered, sounding as though she'd worked his last nerve. "I'm the one with the expunged record, remember? My first job now is looking out for you. Being a cop comes second, but it *is* the second-most important thing to me, and I wish you wouldn't try to ruin it." He paused before adding, "Look, we're both in a situation we didn't sign up for. I don't know why they left—"

Drea lowered her voice until it was nearly inaudible. "I think we both have some idea, Damon."

"Do you have any real evidence?"

Drea considered lying, telling him she was working on more than a hunch, but he'd see right through her. Not only did he know her better than anyone else, he could read people better than anyone she knew, which is why he was going to be a good cop. He'd been raised by professional grifters, so he'd been learning how to lie, and how to read liars, for pretty much his whole life. Damon could spot the way a person's pupils dilated when they lied or which direction their eyes darted, unknowingly revealing the truth.

"No, not real evidence, but I think—" Drea began, but went quiet when she heard soft footsteps approaching. A nurse pulled back the curtain at the same time Damon's phone rang.

"It's work," he said, looking grateful for an excuse to make his getaway.

The dispatcher on the other end told Damon there was an urgent call for him and then put him on hold with no further explanation. After a minute of holding, he finally heard a woman's voice on the other end. It didn't sound nearly as urgent as dispatch had described, but they wouldn't have put the call through if it wasn't important.

"Officer Faraday?"

"Yes, this is Faraday."

"My name is—well, I don't really want to give my name. I'd like to remain anonymous, like I told the nine-one-one people."

"What's this about?"

"The case you'll be going to court on tomorrow."

"Who are you?"

Damon looked around the emergency-room lobby as

though whoever was on the other end—this anonymous caller who happened to know his court schedule—was one of the people waiting their turn to see a doctor.

"No names, I told you. But I know the girl, she told me all about it."

"What did she tell you?"

"Oh, *everything*. We friends, real close."

Damon was surprised to hear the caller was just a kid. She sounded older. And what was she doing calling him in the middle of the night? But he didn't interrupt her to ask. The girl gave details about the perp and the case that Damon figured only a close friend would know, so when she also told him where he could find the evidence that would surely lead to the suspect's conviction, Damon believed her.

"You might wanna check her alibi while you at it. When the lawyers ask, she plan on saying she was at school the day she stole it, but I know for a fact she wasn't."

"Look, Miss . . . ?"

"You keep trying to find out my na`me when we both know you don't need it. You don't need no witness for that kind of evidence."

"You seem to know a lot about the law for someone in high school."

"My daddy is a lawyer."

Damon doubted it. In fact, he didn't know whether to believe anything the woman—the *girl*—was telling him.

"If she's your friend," Damon asked, "why are you telling me all of this?"

The woman paused for a few seconds before saying, "Bitch stole my boyfriend."

When the line went dead, Damon considered calling dispatch. Whatever story she had told was convincing enough to put her call through, and it must have included some contact information. But Damon didn't bother because he knew none of it would be true, though he hoped that the caller's tip would be.

Two hours later, and after a few practice runs down the hall on crutches, the hospital released Drea without even a wheelchair ride to the front door.

At the sliding doors of the emergency entrance, Damon said, "Wait here and I'll get the car."

"No, I might as well practice, though it might take me an hour to get there." After she negotiated the curb, Drea resumed the conversation where they'd left off, as though Damon had never stepped away to take that call. "I think they left because they're on a job. Or running from the consequences of one."

"If you're right, they aren't coming back, at least not until *they're* ready. Not until it's beneficial to *them*. That's what con artists do."

"But it hasn't been like that since we moved here. They said the cons were over, that I'd get to graduate from Woodruff. They even put our name on that stupid bench, like it would be the last surname we'll ever use. We've been Faradays longer than we've been anyone else. Sometimes I even forget what our real name is. I mean, they were straight for three whole years...weren't they?"

"As far as I know, at least until last August."

"So you think they were in on that too."

Damon didn't say anything, which said everything.

"Maybe you can find them, use your police contacts."

"I've been a cop for about a minute. I have no contacts."

Once they'd finally made it through the pedestrian crossing, Damon stopped her. "You sure you don't want me to get the car? I'm parked way out there. Couldn't find anything closer."

In answer, Drea pushed on. She was going to master those crutches if it killed her. "Stop trying to change the subject."

"At least use the walk. We don't need you getting hit by a car, too."

Damon guided her toward the walkway that cut through the center of the lot, bordered with yellow rose bushes and illuminated by soft lights spiked into the soil. Tall crape myrtles planted on either side leaned toward one another, forming a pink-and-white archway. Drea wondered if the hospital hoped to fool people into thinking they were spending a day in the park rather than visiting sick people, or maybe being cured themselves. It worked. It made Drea hopeful.

"Maybe if you found them and told them about tonight."

"Drea, I swear, I don't want to know what happened tonight."

"Not that. I mean that my leg is broken."

"Your ankle is sprained."

"The doctor said that can actually be worse. We'll tell them I need surgery. We'll tell them I need a kidney transplant, or that I actually was hit by a car, or whatever lie we need to tell to make them come back."

Drea stopped to sit on a bench on the walkway. "I'm already tired."

Damon sat beside her. Maybe he knew she wasn't only referring to the crutches. "They're on the run, and we don't even know how to reach them. Something must have happened on the last job that scared them. They won't come back until they're sure the threat is gone."

"Maybe you're what happened, Damon."

"What?"

"*You're* the threat."

"How am *I* a threat?" Damon asked.

"If it was the car heist and home thefts that made them run, why are they just now running? That job was a whole school year ago. Your parents are life-long criminals, and you go off and become a cop? In their own town, no less."

"Hey, you were my biggest cheerleader when I decided to enter the police academy."

It was true, but that was before she knew her parents had fallen off the wagon. But she needed an explanation, or at the very least, someone to blame, and her parents weren't here.

"They may not be the greatest parents in the world, but they don't want to ever make their son have to take them down one day."

"The police department would never let me arrest my own parents. It's a conflict of interest. Besides, I'd been on the street a whole month before they left—I was still a full-fledged officer while I was in field training. It's just a coincidence they left when they did." Damon started out angry, but by the last sentence, sounded as though he was trying to convince himself as much as Drea. "Blame me if it makes you feel better. But you know the same truth I do, Drea. They were cons long before they were parents. The next big job, and their self-preservation, has always come first. It always will."

12

Friday, 7:00 a.m.

Since it was the last day of classes before summer vacation and Drea had already taken her finals, Damon said there was no real point in her going to school, insisting she stay home to recuperate. He had dropped her at home just before four in the morning, made up the sofa in the salon for her since she couldn't manage the stairs, and left to finish the rest of his graveyard shift. Three hours later, despite being on the good drugs, Drea hadn't managed five minutes of sleep. The guilt of being a coward, the fear that Xavier and Jason would eventually narc on her, the phone she still hadn't found, and worry that, after all of this, she still wouldn't have a perfect GPA because they hadn't had time to hack her grade—they were all stronger than the painkillers. She needed answers or she was going to lose it.

It was now seven o'clock, which meant Damon had another hour before he finished his shift, plus another half hour before he got home. Grateful that she had never bothered to change into the pajamas Damon had brought downstairs to her, Drea checked her hair and face in the foyer mirror and decided she would do. She wasn't sure what she hoped to learn by going to school, but she called a taxi, told the dispatcher she might need help from the driver to get down the front steps, and managed to get herself outside. It turned out she was a quick study on using crutches, even if she was a little tipsy from the painkillers, and she was waiting at the driveway when the cab arrived ten minutes later.

Once they pulled into the school parking lot, Drea realized she had no plan. There would be questions about the crutches—she had been just fine when everyone saw her leave school yesterday. Then there was the grade change, assuming the boys had been successful before they were caught. The art teacher was about a hundred years old and would be retiring after today, which was the only reason Drea had decided to change the grade. She figured the woman wouldn't be checking on who made top of the class, and even if she did, she would think the grade in the system was the grade she'd given. But what if Drea had underestimated the old lady? She might want to question her about the change, and even though Drea had learned to lie from the best, in her current condition, she wasn't exactly confident in her con-artist skills.

"You need help inside?" the driver asked.

Drea scanned the front entrance: the keypad, the bright overhead light that was now turned off, the hedges that circled the building. Everything looked the same as it had last night, before all this started. What had she expected to see?

"No. I think this was probably a bad idea," Drea said, as if the driver cared. He just wanted her to pay her fare and get out so he could get to the next one.

"Okay. So what now?"

She was about to tell him to take her back home when she got an idea. "I'm not going in. Can you pull in front of that house over there? Across the street—the blue one with white trim." She pointed to the house where the person she assumed was the tipster had parked.

"All right, but the meter's running."

"That's fine. There'll be a good tip in it for you."

"Them's the magic words."

This was Drea's neighborhood, and she'd been going to Woodruff for four years, so she'd walked past this house a thousand times. But she'd never sat in front of it in a car, and she wanted to see what the tipster must have seen. Of course, the lighting wasn't the same, since the sun had been up for two hours now, but at least she'd know his line of sight.

When the cabbie parked, the view wasn't what she'd expected. The responding officers could see the school's front entrance from where they'd parked their patrol cars in front of and behind the tipster, but from her seat in the back of the taxi, there was no view at all. It was blocked by the big brick sign with the school's name—the very one she'd hidden behind while spying on Gladys, the custodian, entering the alarm code, through binoculars.

"Can you do me a favor?" she asked the driver.

"Give nice tips, you get favors."

"Tell me if you can see the front door of the school from here."

"No, that sign is blocking the way."

"Now can you pull forward a few feet, and tell me if you can see it?"

The driver did as Drea requested. "The bushes around the sign are hiding it."

"Okay, now back a few feet from our original position."

"What's going on here, kid?" the driver asked. He probably suspected she was pulling some prank, and more importantly, that the tip she'd promised was a lie. Drea pulled out a twenty and passed it through the partition between the front seat and back.

"I'm good for it."

"My view is still blocked," the driver said after shifting into reverse.

"Okay, let's just sit here a minute."

"Your dime," the driver said.

She'd been wrong in her earlier assessment. The busybody must have been in that spot before she arrived and seen Drea as she approached the school. So why not report three prowlers?

It was 7:40. She needed to get home so Damon could find her pretending to be asleep on the couch. She wondered where Xavier was right now, whether he would soon arrive at whatever school he attended now, or if missing the last day of school was the least of his worries. Unless he was still sitting in a juvie detention holding cell. Drea had spent two months watching Xavier and had learned very little; she still didn't know much more about him than she did before last night went terribly wrong, except that he actually did know she existed. In fact, he seemed to know more about her than she did him.

But despite his being a criminal, she assumed he had family, someone who cared enough about him to do whatever it took to bond him out last night. Five years ago when Damon was caught attempting, on his own, a job their parents had planned, they stopped running long enough to see him through his trial. And when a condition of his probation was living with his family, they moved to Peachland and started an honest antiques brokerage firm—even if they weren't exactly honest about their background or in telling people they had a son away at boarding school. They promised Drea she'd do all four years of high school in the same place.

She figured if Damon had family to see him through his felony screwups, Xavier probably did too. Her parents were criminals, but they'd always been good, if unconventional, parents. At least until they bailed on her to save their own asses.

A few minutes later, a van pulled into the school lot. The side of the van said Southern Security Cameras.

"Does that van have anything to do with what's going on here?" the driver asked.

"A nice tip should also buy me a driver who doesn't ask questions."

"I like money as much as the next guy, but I won't do anything shady."

Drea didn't believe that for a second. Damon was good at reading liars, but Drea's skill in detecting a lie went beyond science or observation. It was a quirk she'd discovered about herself when she was just a little kid. Her mom called it "the gift," something her grandmother had passed down to them both. In fact, they came from a long line of women who were human lie detectors. If she was physically present when someone lied to her, Drea would know. It may have been a long time ago, but the cabbie had done all sorts of shady things.

"We're just sitting in a car. Nothing shady about that," Drea said, not helping her argument when she pulled a pair of mini binoculars from her bag and peered through them.

The van parked at the front entrance. She guessed the school was aware of the break-in. The arresting officers had probably called Headmistress Fitch the minute they got Jason and Xavier into booking.

"What if the people who live in this house wonder what's going on?"

"I doubt it, but drive around the block and park one house behind us. I need a view of the front entrance, anyway." Drea said, slipping another twenty through the plastic door to make sure the driver did as told.

Good thing she'd had the sense to save most of the allowance her parents had given her over the years, which was way beyond generous. She'd also exchanged all their outrageous gifts for cash—at least, the ones that had been legitimately purchased and came with receipts. Considering it was their business to be observant, it was odd how her parents hadn't seemed to notice that Drea had come home with an economy car on her sixteenth birthday, even though they'd dropped her at the dealership with fifty thousand in cash. *Nothing too expensive. We don't want to be those parents who spoil their kids.* Or how they'd never seen her in the fur coat they'd given her last Christmas. *Mink in Georgia—really, Mom? Besides, no one wears real fur anymore.*

She'd been hoarding money for years, even as a little kid, but hadn't thought to open an account until they had given her ten thousand dollars when she turned fourteen, which was, according to her father, the age you became an adult where he was from. He was from Kansas, but even in the privacy of their home, held fast on that story about his princely great-great-grandfather. A grifter claiming Nigerian ancestry seemed too obvious to be made up, but Drea was never sure what to believe. Not only didn't her gift of lie detection work on her parents for some reason, but they also had trouble separating the truth from the cons, even with their own kids. She was just as skeptical about her mother's royal family history. What were the odds they both came from such distinguished lineage? Not good.

The only part of their story she had ever believed was why they went into the antiques business, and how they became thieves in the first place. Both sets of Drea's grandparents had been small-time dealers who had worked the antiques circuit, traveling in a rented truck to trade shows in neighboring states to buy, sell, and trade. As teens, her parents had worked their families' respective booths in the summer. When they weren't setting up the booths and making sales, they had always sought each other out, first sharing furtive glances, then lunch breaks, and later, their dreams of something bigger than the small, dusty towns they were from. After a couple of summers, they had fallen in love.

Her father's parents were a little more open-minded about the romance, but her mom's parents were what she called old-school, and what Drea's dad called racist, and they weren't having any of it. So in their seventeenth summer, they met at a trade show in Colorado as they had the previous two summers, except they didn't go back home. They became runaways, moving to Denver and learning to live on the street, "hustling a dime," as her father called it—but Drea called it stealing.

Eventually they decided to put all that antiques knowledge to work. They already knew what to steal, and quickly learned how to steal it. The problem came in selling it. Two seventeen-year-olds trying to pass off a Victorian copper harvest jug was a hard sell, even if it was clear they knew their English kitchenware. That's when they learned the art of disguise and the science of grifting, becoming thirty-something New Yorkers at an estate sale in Arizona, or distant cousins of an English baron on holiday, during a visit to a Napa Valley auction house.

Their marks may have bought their cons without reservation, but Drea knew better. Since they'd never spoken to any of her grandparents again, and Drea had no idea who they were, she could only have faith that the story of how her parents met was true. It was too romantic and beautiful, in a criminal sort of way, not to be.

Whatever their real story was, the one thing she knew for certain about her parents was how great they were at what they did. Thanks to their special skills and their generosity—Damon called it bribery—she now had a secret bank account with a low six-figure balance. There was probably twenty times that amount in the account they'd given Damon access to, but he refused to use it since he knew where the money had come from. Maybe Drea had known all along that one day she'd need it because they would abandon her. How was that for being an optimist?

By the time they had circled the block, the driver of the van had gotten out of the car and was taking photos of the front entrance. A patrol car had also arrived and parked behind the van. Through her binoculars, Drea saw the cop was Damon. Was he there looking for her phone? If so, it was crazy to look for it now, with teachers already in the building and kids starting to arrive. And why do it in uniform, driving his squad car, if he was already off duty? He'd only draw attention to himself.

"Hey, wait a minute. Now there's a cop here," the driver said, confirming Drea's concern. "No tip is going to buy me that kind of trouble. I got my own problems."

"Just a minute more, I promise."

Drea watched Damon talk to the security cameraman for a few minutes, and then he went inside the building. Her phone was definitely not inside the building.

13

Friday, 8:05 a.m.

When Drea got home, she found a message from Damon saying he would be late, which she already knew because he was busy doing something at her school other than looking for her lost phone. Even though she was glad for the chance to catch him doing whatever he was up to, now her foot was killing her, thanks to putting her weight on it while trying to manage the porch steps.

She took two painkillers—one more than she was supposed to—before she logged into her school account. Her grades should have been posted by now. And there it was—the GPA box on the front page showed the highest average possible at Woodruff. Xavier and Jason had come through for her. After everything that had happened since she'd gone to school last night intending to change her grade, her GPA didn't seem as important, but it also would have been a shame if all that had happened and she still didn't have a perfect grade.

Drea was about to log out when she noticed her inbox had a message. What if the art teacher had discovered she was a cheat? Only teachers and administrators could access the system, but she didn't recognize the sender's name, which was really just a single letter: *J*. She clicked open the message.

It's all your fault, Poser Girl.

Now Drea knew what the *J* stood for. Jason. But how? Could he have sent it last night while he was at the school, changing her grades? But at that point, nothing was yet her fault. She wasn't sure if anything had been her fault even now. No, Jason must have hacked the system since his arrest. That meant he was no longer in jail, so Xavier should be free too.

Or maybe they were never booked into holding. Maybe the police didn't have enough evidence or something and had to turn them loose. Was that possible? Catching the boys inside the building was enough for at least a B&E charge. Still, you never knew. Oh, wow. She was turning into the girl everyone thought she was, the one who believed in rainbows and unicorns. It must have been the drugs kicking in, but she suddenly felt relaxed. Better. Until the inbox showed the arrival of a new message.

Happy with your grade?

Of course Jason could see when she was logged into the system. He must have been watching, lying in wait. While Drea debated whether she should respond, another message appeared.

We can talk here. I've firewalled our messaging.

Talk about what? Drea didn't plan to find out, because she didn't trust him. Emails and texts left evidence trails.

I know you're there. You better talk to me. You owe us at least that.

She typed: *Nothing to talk about. Change it back if you want. I don't care.*

Drea logged out, turned off the Wi-Fi access, shut down her tablet, and pulled the plug from the wall. Jason was obviously good at what he did. For all she knew, he could hack into her computer and set her up somehow. He'd apparently forgotten he'd been at the school last night to do his own job, and whether she'd been there or not, he could have been caught. She wished she'd never let Xavier convince her to let him change her grades, that she'd run the minute they found her trying to break into the school. She wished she'd never seen Xavier smile at her that way just before she agreed to his plan. When Drea told Jason she didn't care anymore, it was true. He could change her grade to an F if it would make him leave her alone. She just wanted it all to go away. And for a little while, it did, thanks to that extra pill she took.

Drea woke to a sound she thought came from the kitchen even though it was several rooms away. It sounded as though someone had clanged into the pots and pans that hung over the kitchen island. The clock on the fireplace mantel told her she'd been out for three hours. Damon must be back. As she shook off her drug-induced sleep, something felt wrong. Drea was a light sleeper. Even on drugs, she should have heard Damon come in the front door and through the gallery. Since he'd moved out of the house after his probation ended a few years ago, he'd stopped using the door that led from the garage into the kitchen, and hadn't picked up the habit again since coming back home while her parents were gone.

She looked around the room. There were no signs her brother was home—not the messenger bag he always carried, no paper coffee cup. Like an alcoholic who wouldn't leave the house without his flask, Damon couldn't go two hours without fueling his caffeine addiction. But it had to be him. She was a little foggy headed right now, but she remembered setting the alarm system when she got home, and if that wasn't Damon in the kitchen, the alarm should have gone off.

Drea sat up on the sofa, now fully awake and aware that she was nearly immobile thanks to her bad ankle. The only landline downstairs—because only her parents ever used it—was in the kitchen. The footsteps were way too quiet to be Damon. He wouldn't walk that tentatively through his own house. She looked for the closest weapon. Her crutches. Impossible to get sufficient leverage from a sitting position to swing hard enough to hurt anyone. No, she'd have to get up, try to get out of the house.

It was too late. Before she could even lift herself from the sofa, he was standing across from her, blocking her escape through the front door or the back. She stood anyway. She'd have a better chance of fighting him off if she had to.

"Get out of my house or I'll call the police."

"And tell them what—that you're guilty of a B&E at the school last night, that they didn't catch all the bad guys?"

"I never entered the school. I'm not guilty of anything."

Surprisingly, Jason's response to her defiance wasn't to argue or attack her, but to collapse onto the love seat across from her.

"Right, because you conned X into doing it for you," he said, pulling a pack of cigarettes from his pocket.

"Don't smoke in my house," Drea said with all the authority she could muster, and it worked. Jason returned the cigarettes to his pocket. "Xavier offered to do it. I had nothing to do with whatever job you guys were pulling."

"So we just randomly decided to change the grades of a girl we don't know? We don't even go to that school. No cop would believe you weren't involved. We could say you were the lookout man, except you sucked at it and bailed."

"*You* were the one who dismissed me, remember? Said I should go home like a good girl."

Jason leaned forward, put his elbows on his knees, and dropped his head into his hands. Drea was no longer afraid of him. He didn't want to hurt her. He had come because he was angry and wanted to yell at someone, even if it was the wrong someone. Now she knew how Damon must have felt after their conversation at the hospital last night when she did the exact same thing to him.

"If I hadn't been there, if you'd never met me last night,

the police still would have come. You'd still have been caught."

When Jason looked up at her, his anger was fresh, hotter than before. Maybe she'd read him wrong. She wished she could detect anger as well as she could sense lying.

"Not if we'd gotten out as soon as we finished our own job instead of sticking around to change your grade."

Drea was quiet for a moment, not wanting to say the wrong thing. Damon had told her both of them had juvie records. For all she knew, Jason could have been arrested for assault. Just because Drea had a crush on Xavier didn't mean his partner in crime wasn't dangerous. For that matter, her crush could be dangerous too. The most she knew of Xavier was what she had imagined, and she'd only met Jason last night. It may have been a mistake to assume he wasn't there to hurt her.

He stood up and began to pace, running his hands through his hair. It didn't match the rest of Jason. It was like a baby's hair—pale blond, almost white, and wispy fine—but there was a lot of it, forming soft curls, reminding her of the women in Botticelli's paintings. But he was definitely not a girl, despite his slight build and the fact he was so light on his feet—like a dancer or a cat, which was one of the reasons Drea thought he'd make the better thief. Drea suspected that unless he was with Xavier, to whom Jason seemed to defer for some reason, this boy would be an alpha. His physical appearance was a great disguise, because nothing else about him was soft. She hadn't known him twenty-four hours, but of that much she was certain.

Drea kept her voice even, not wanting to sound falsely cheerful, and said, "But you're not in jail. It's okay now, right?"

"Hell, no," Jason yelled. "Nothing is okay. I'm out because my grandma bonded her house to raise my bail money. It's the only thing she owns, and she had to put it up for a fucking two-thousand-dollar bond that we can't pay back. And X...he's still inside. His foster parents are done with him this time."

"Foster parents?" Drea said, then remembered Xavier had mentioned that when they first met what seemed like forever ago. "But he used to go to Woodruff, which isn't cheap, so they must be able to afford—"

"No one's coming to his rescue."

Drea didn't speak, realizing her game had been completely off. Except for the tipster in the car, she hadn't read a single thing correctly since she stood under that light pounding numbers into the alarm keypad. And now she remembered what Ms. Vance had said about the scholarships that hadn't quite worked out. That was how Xavier could afford to attend Woodruff, not because of well-to-do fosters.

"Last time X got out, we both said never again. We were going straight for good. Now, getting caught for the B&E and whatever other charges they make...our parole violation...the only good thing about this whole fucked-up situation is neither of us is eighteen yet. They'll have to send us back to juvie."

Drea wanted to remind him that regardless of whether he'd been caught because they had stayed a few extra minutes to hack her grades, they still had been there to commit some crime, something beyond breaking and entering. If they'd really wanted to stay out of jail, they wouldn't have been there. But she wasn't stupid. She just wanted to say whatever the right words were to make him leave.

"Why are you here, Jason? What am I supposed to do?"

Jason stopped pacing and leaned against the wall across from her, looking defeated.

"I don't know. How the hell should I know? It just didn't seem right, you kicking back in this big fancy house, being top of your class or whatever, as if that shit even matters, while X is in jail."

"It does to me," Drea said, wishing she hadn't. It sounded ridiculous even to her; she could imagine what Jason must think. Not that she had to. He'd made it clear what he thought about her.

"If it matters so much, why didn't you earn it honestly?" Then he looked at her as if for the first time since he arrived. "What happened to your leg?"

"I fell."

"While you were leaving us to do your dirty work, I hope."

Drea didn't respond.

"Well, there's some justice, I guess." Jason sneered and headed for the gallery and front door. Before he left, he added, "You need a new alarm system. This one's for shit."

14

Friday, 11:14 a.m.

After Jason left, Drea had tried to go back to sleep, but her guilty conscience would not cooperate. She'd be lying if she said it was only guilt keeping her awake. She was unnerved by how easily her home had been broken into, a house once run by thieves and currently run by a cop—two groups of people who took home security seriously. Worse was the fact that Jason wasn't even the half of the team who claimed he could break into anything. That half was sitting in juvenile detention right now with no one to bail him out and unknowingly keeping a girl he barely knew from getting any sleep.

When she heard the front door open, she was half expecting it to be Jason, but this time it really was Damon, still in uniform.

"Hey, you're awake."

"Yeah, just woke up," Drea lied. "I've been knocked out since you left. Hey, don't you usually change before you drive home? I thought you said it was safer for cops not to wear blue when they're off the clock."

"I wanted to come straight home and check on you. If you've been asleep all this time, why is the security system off? I set it before I left. You must have gone out." Damon dropped a box on the floor, his glare an accusation. "You're supposed to be resting."

"I got a little stir crazy and went out onto the porch. Are you going to arrest me for that? Oh wait—you won't even arrest me for an actual crime, so I guess I'm safe."

Damon ignored her last comment. He probably knew it was only a distraction tactic.

"You must have had a smoke while you were out there. I found this cigarette butt on the porch. You're smoking now, on top of everything else?"

He couldn't really believe that of her. Sure, Damon knew about the shoplifting incident, so Drea wasn't exactly Little Miss Perfect anymore, but that was months ago. Had he ever smelled smoke on her? Since her parents had disappeared and left him in charge of her, Damon had watched her like she was his next mark. If she had been smoking, he'd have caught her in the act or found evidence by now. But she couldn't explain Jason's visit without revealing why he'd been there—to implicate her in his crime—much less that he'd broken into their house, so she just let him finish his lecture.

"At least show some respect for the house. Don't stamp out your cigarettes on the porch and leave the butts like you're on the street."

He sighed deeply while he took off his holster, taking care

to remove his gun first, setting it on the side table before hanging the holster over the back of the love seat, where he collapsed. As though removing his work tools relieved him of his duty of being Drea's disciplinarian, he morphed back into big brother Damon.

"So how's your leg? Are the painkillers working? I should get you something to eat—you're probably hungry."

"I'm not hungry and the drugs are definitely doing the job. Go get some sleep. Don't worry about me so much."

"That's my job now, remember? Which reminds me—I went by your school today."

"Oh yeah?" Drea was glad she wouldn't have to find a way to ask why he'd been at her school this morning without actually asking.

"I told the principal you hurt your leg and couldn't make the last day of school. She let me clean out your locker." He pointed to the box he'd dropped.

"She let you in my locker?"

"It helped that I was in uniform and that I'm a member of the family that donates a ton of money to the school."

"That still doesn't seem cool," Drea said.

"Does something in that box have anything to do with last night?"

"No, it's just weird, that's all. I figured a cop would need a warrant for something like that."

It was true, she had nothing to hide, at least not in her locker, but she didn't like the way Damon's uniform and last name gave him all-access to the one part of her life he didn't already have it.

"What's weird is *you*. I wasn't a cop searching your locker. I was a brother helping out his sister. Like when I described your phone and asked the office staff to call me if anyone turns it in."

"What are we going to do if no one does?"

"Buy a new one," Damon said, rubbing his eyes. "Apparently it was a slam-dunk arrest. I checked it out and the police investigation of the case is closed. No one knows you were ever there. If someone finds the phone on campus, they'll just assume you lost it yesterday during school, just like I told the office lady."

He leaned back into the love seat, relaxing for the first time since he got home. It seemed the weight of carrying her since their parents left had exhausted him.

Drea knew she was being ridiculous not trusting Damon, but after being taught her whole life never to trust a cop, it was hard to let go of the instinct, even if the cop was her brother. But since Jason had broken in and told her about his night in jail, and how Xavier was still there, she'd had time to realize Damon was right. She had been playing games that could have gotten very serious last night if not for him.

"I'm sorry I've been a bitch. You were right last night, at the hospital," Drea said. "They left because they're them, not because you're a cop now. Thanks for keeping me out of jail. I know you're risking your new job for me." Drea didn't tell him that he'd risked a lot more than that.

"It's only a risk if you were there doing something illegal. I mean, besides breaking city curfew. I could have cited you for that since you aren't seventeen."

"I was there because—" Drea finally tried to explain, but Damon cut her off.

"You're welcome. I'm glad you appreciate what I did, but I've been thinking about what you said—what you keep saying—about me letting you off. Now I'm going to do something to fix it."

"Um, so you're going to arrest me after all? Because—"

"It's a surprise. You'll find out on Monday."

"You know I hate surprises, especially when it's something like this. It can't be anything good. You're really going to make me wait all weekend?"

"Stop whining. You could be in a jail cell right now."

Drea thought of Xavier and obeyed.

"Man, I'll be glad to come off graveyards next week. Swing shift means my already feeble social life will be officially dead, but at least I won't feel like a zombie."

Drea thought it funny that before police academy, Damon had spent his nights partying and chasing girls. Now that he didn't have to chase them at all—his field-training officer had warned him about the women who made sport of hooking up with cops—he didn't have the energy. Still, she was glad for the cop groupies. As hard as she worked at being good, it was in her blood to dislike the police, but now that her brother was one, she was grateful there were a few people out there who didn't automatically hate him.

"Maybe you should get some sleep."

"I'm dog-tired but too wound up to sleep. I have my first court appearance this afternoon. Well, as a police officer."

"You don't sound very excited about it."

"Because I'm not. Even after interning for a judge, courtrooms still make me nervous."

"You're one of the good guys now," Drea said without thinking. She could tell from Damon's expression he still had a hard time believing it. "Just remember what Mom always says: 'You don't actually have to be the queen. You just have to convince everyone else that you are.'"

Damon laughed. "You sound a lot like her when you say it. So you're advising me to con the grand jury?"

"This time it won't be a con. No matter what happened last night, you really are a good cop who knows what he's doing. You just have to convince *yourself* that's who you are."

"We'll see," Damon said, which meant he was done with the conversation. "It's after eleven. I could order a pizza. You need to eat."

"And you need to sleep." Drea picked up the little amber-colored bottle from the table and rattled its contents.

"Won't it knock me out? I have court in five hours."

"You sleep hard for three hours, then it wears off. Can't do well in court if you're half-asleep. I'll make sure you're up with plenty of time to get ready."

Damon tried to suppress a yawn, but failed. "You know it's illegal for me to take your drugs."

"Do you have to be perfect all the time?"

"I've never been perfect any of the time. That's the problem."

"I won't tell if you don't," Drea said as she watched him swallow one of the pills. "They work pretty quickly. You probably ought to head upstairs."

113

Thirty minutes later, before Drea headed out of the house for the second time, she stopped at the foot of the back stairway to listen for Damon's loud snoring. She only felt slightly bad for drugging her brother to sleep. It was for a good cause. Two good causes if you counted the fact that Damon really could use the rest.

When the taxi pulled into the seedy strip mall, the driver turned around to get instructions from Drea, by now fully expecting there would be some.

"Lady, I really wish you hadn't asked for my cab number."

Drea felt a little victorious, having moved up in his estimation from *kid* to *lady*. She knew it had everything to do with the tip she'd promised him, but it still made her feel more confident than she really was.

"Sure you are. You already know I'm good for the fare, and then some."

"Yeah, but whatever you're up to, the dispatch records could make it look like I was up to it with you."

"You sure worry a lot, Mister . . ." Drea strained to see the small print on the hack license taped to the dashboard.

"Frank."

"Mister Frank."

"No, just *Frank*."

"All that worrying makes me think you have something to worry about besides me and what I've been up to."

Considering how easy it was to persuade him to do things he had misgivings about, Drea was certain her cabbie had a less than perfect past. Even though he was probably pushing fifty, and in spite of all his protests, she felt certain Frank was still up for a little trouble every now and then.

"I never said I was an altar boy," Frank said, flashing a mischievous grin. "I suppose you want me to wait here while you go inside."

"Yes, please."

Frank dipped his head to get a better look at the storefronts through the passenger window, though he had probably driven this route a thousand times. She watched him take in the pawn shop, the check-cashing store, and the pool hall ("LADIES DRINK FREE!"), among the other places he probably thought were questionable businesses for Drea to be visiting.

"Maybe you'd like it better if I go in there with you. With your bum leg and all."

"No, I'll be fine," Drea said, grabbing her crutches. "I'm getting the hang of these."

Before she could get the door open, Frank was already out of the car and around the other side, opening it for her.

"Okay, after this, straight back home, right?"

"That depends on how things go inside."

"Seems to me you come from a nice family. You live in that big fancy house. Why is a young lady like yourself visiting a place like this, anyway?"

Drea smiled at Frank, glad it was his cab the taxi company sent the first time. *Nice family.* If only he knew.

15

Friday, 3:07 p.m.

Drea had been right about the painkiller. It made Damon sleep hard for three hours, and he had gotten just enough rest to convince himself maybe he wouldn't be a complete screwup on the witness stand. Still, he got to the evidence room early enough to take another look at the surveillance video that had helped him identify and arrest the thief. That bolstered his confidence too, because he knew there probably wasn't a detective in the department, much less another uniform, who would have figured it out. His field-training officer had said as much. The only reason he did was because his parents had taught him their business so well.

When Damon had watched the video for the first time, he had known right away that the suspect was a professional and had cased the store before the day of the theft. She didn't look around for cameras when she walked into the store, and yet she knew how they were angled and where she should stand to ensure they wouldn't record her face. It was also obvious to him that she'd decided on her mark before that day, because she went straight for the salesman when she walked through the door and asked him to show her items from the display case. When she used him to get the stolen watch out of the camera's view and eventually out of the store, the poor salesman had no clue. Damon had confirmed his hunch by looking at video from weeks earlier and found she'd been inside twice to get the camera layout. And now, thanks to the tip he'd received earlier that morning, he could offer the prosecuting attorney more than circumstantial evidence.

Damon arrived at the justice center and found the prosecutor standing in the hall outside the courtroom. If he hadn't already known her, he would have assumed she was one of the first-year law interns who took summer jobs at the court, or maybe a straight-from-journalism-school reporter for the paper. A freshly minted law school grad, she looked no older than Damon, though she had a couple of years on him.

"Angie."

"Damon, wow, you look...great. I haven't seen you in uniform yet."

"You haven't seen me in three years. A lot can change in that time. I'm not that kid who followed you around begging for your number."

"No...you're definitely all grown up now."

"Are you still trying to pretend two years' difference makes you so much older?" Damon asked, though he knew exactly what she'd meant. He remembered she couldn't be charmed like all the other girls back then. Things had changed all right, and in his favor, so he let her off the hook by adding, "Although you *are* an assistant district attorney who now goes by Evangeline."

"I know full well that I look like a kid playing attorney. I figured using my official name would give me the illusion of age and sophistication." She stood a little taller and put her hands on her hips, all grown-up confidence. "Is it working?"

Something was working. But Damon just said, "I think we have them all fooled."

"Who would have thought?"

"Everyone did, because you were a genius, starting law school at twenty. Unless you're talking about me being in a police uniform. No one would have ever thought that. Especially you."

"Maybe so, Officer Faraday, but now I'm convinced. I heard you were the one who caught the suspect. You were the only one who noticed she stole the watch. We wouldn't be here if not for you."

He noticed she dropped her a voice a little when she said the last line. Was she flirting? Damon hoped so.

"So, why are you out here in the hall?"

"The docket's full and the grand jury is running behind schedule. Our case is being pushed to Monday." Angie sounded disappointed, but her face didn't show it. "It's my first grand jury on my own, and while the video is enough to indict, a smoking gun would be better. I hope you'll be a rock-star witness."

"I doubt it. It'll be my first time too. My training officer testified at the prelim hearing, but she retired and moved to Florida last week, so I'm up."

"Perfect," Evangeline said, full of sarcasm.

"Um, thanks?"

"Oh, sorry. I'm sure you'll do great," Angie said, leaning in and touching his arm for just a second too long. "It's just . . . the video only shows she slipped the watch into the salesman's pocket before she lured him to the back room. There were no cameras in the back room when she took it from the guy's pocket. All we have is your conjecture and the salesman's corroboration of your theory. All circumstantial. The suspect should be planning her summer vacation as a free woman."

"Well, I may be able to fix that. Can we talk here?"

Evangeline looked around. They were alone in the hall.

"What do you have?"

"Early this morning I got a tip, followed up today, and got you some evidence that isn't a bit circumstantial," Damon said, holding up an evidence bag for her to inspect.

"Is that what I think it is?"

"Your smoking gun. You won't believe where I found it."

Evangeline smiled. "Officer Faraday—fresh out of the academy and already winning points with the DA's office."

"More like fresh out of the academy and already in trouble."

"Really?" Evangeline said, smiling even wider. "Do tell."

"Nothing interesting, but I'd appreciate it if you put in a good word about this with people who count."

"I can do that."

"Well, if you don't need my testimony or this watch until Monday, I'll check it back into the evidence locker. It'll be there when you need it." Damon headed down the hall, thinking the exchange with Angie had gone so much better than his court testimony would have. He considered turning around to see if she was watching him leave, but decided not to, telling himself he didn't care whether she was or not.

Before he left, Damon decided to make another stop. He had a proposition to make to a judge he knew, and hoped he'd find him in chambers. His preoccupation with finding the judge, and of course, with meeting Angie, was the reason he didn't notice the man standing just around the corner, leaning against the wall, and opening a pack of cinnamon gum. The man had heard everything.

16

Monday, 7:13 a.m.

By Monday morning, Drea had adjusted to life on crutches and the idea that she would be spending her last high school summer break around people who'd made really bad choices. That was the only information she could get out of Damon about the surprise she would be getting today. When she tried to glean clues by asking how she should dress, his answer was a vague, *like you're going to school*, which made no sense because she wore a uniform to school. She decided he'd meant the way she'd dress on the second Friday of the month when Woodruff allowed regular clothes as long as they met the dress code. The only theory she'd come up with was that she'd be doing something at the police department, and she had spent the weekend researching their website, figuring out what kind of work they'd allow an almost-seventeen-year-old girl to do that would put her around bad people and their bad choices.

It wasn't like Drea didn't know anything about criminals; she just didn't know anything about the kind she was soon to spend her summer with. Common criminals. Even among crooks, there was a social order, and the criminals in her world were not even close to common. Her parents may have started out that way, looking to score because they didn't want to spend their nights in a box beneath an overpass when they were teen runaways, and later because they needed to feed Damon. But by the time Drea had come along, those days were long past. Drea had grown up in the big fancy houses Frank the cabbie had spoken of, though she had never stayed in one long enough for it to ever feel like home. She attended only the best schools, even if she never completed a full school year in the same one.

At least that had been the case until this home and this school.

Once Drea began middle school, her parents had stolen or scammed enough furniture, jewelry, porcelain figurines, and whatever else they could sell on the fine-antiques circuit to stop looking for the next score. Then they were just criminals for the sport of it, though Drea preferred to think it was because they didn't know how to be anything else—including model parents. Until their recent disappearance, Drea had believed all the moving from town to town, house to house, was just part of the game. If the police really had been looking for them in every town they'd ever run from, surely they'd have been caught long ago. So what were they up to now, and how long would they be gone?

Drea could see them leaving Damon. Not only was he a full-fledged adult with a job and Responsibilities (the main one being Drea, which really did require the capital *R* despite what the outside world thought of her), but Damon had never needed them in the first place, not as far as Drea could remember. Sometimes it seemed he was the only adult in the house, parent to them all, which is why he hadn't missed a beat when their extended antiquing trip forced him to actually become one. But Drea was not like Damon. She had always needed them. She still needed them.

Over the weekend, she'd had a lot of time to think about her parents—when she wasn't thinking about Xavier. She didn't agree with Damon's take on the situation, that they'd left to save themselves. If that were the case, they'd have run when the big heist was being investigated, not ten months after the fact. People barely talked about it now. They'd gone back to pretending things like that only happened in the city even while they beefed up their home security. Drea didn't think Damon believed his story either, that it had come from the same place her accusation at the hospital had—anger at their parents, and behind that, fear for them and whatever had made them run.

Drea was glad Damon hadn't wanted to know why she'd been at Woodruff that night. That way, like her in-denial-neighbors, she could pretend the whole thing never happened, pretend those kinds of things didn't happen to a girl like her, and start over. From now on, she'd make it as easy as she could for Damon, who hadn't asked to become her parent or to move back home. He always stayed over with Drea when their parents' shopping trips took them away for more than a night, but this time, he'd given up his apartment in Magnolia. Come to think of it, just how long did he think they'd be gone? Maybe Damon really did believe what he'd said last night.

Since their parents had left nearly three weeks ago now, he'd spent each weekend making sure Drea didn't go off the rails like she had last fall, instead of driving down to Atlanta to party like he used to. On Friday nights, his phone would start vibrating with texts from women inviting him out or trying to hook up, and he'd turned them all down despite Drea's protests that she was fine. So fine, in fact, that she was still going out even though he wasn't. She'd returned home from a party at Madeline's to find Damon on the sofa, fighting sleep so he could wait up for her.

So today she had breakfast on the table when Damon walked into the kitchen at precisely 0630 hours. He used military time now. A month ago, her mother would have been the one flipping pancakes, and Damon would have been perfectly happy calling it six thirty. Everything was changing so fast and there seemed to be nothing Drea could do to stop it.

When they pulled into the justice center parking lot forty-five minutes later, Drea was confused.

"I thought we were going to your job."

"Why? I never said anything about the job being at the police department."

"You're wearing a suit, for one," Drea said. "Where else would you a wear a suit except to work?"

"I have to testify in court this morning. Since I'm not on duty until this afternoon, I don't have to wear the uniform."

"But you said I'd be working with people who made bad decisions. I thought I'd be doing some ride-alongs with you, maybe volunteer as a victim's advocate or something."

"Researched our website, huh?" Damon asked, knowing her as only a brother could. "That's most of the problem, Drea. You've always looked at crime from a theoretical point of view."

"What theoretical? My whole family is a bunch of criminals."

"Family doesn't count, especially since our specialty was white-collar crime. Well, mostly. I don't know what you were up to Thursday night, but I'm pretty sure it wasn't white-collar."

"Crime is crime," Drea said, knowing it wasn't true. She'd been thinking the same thing earlier.

"Yeah, right. The result of our family's crime is you living in a mansion and attending a private school they practically own."

"I began learning how to run a con about the same time I learned to talk. There is no *theory* in that. I've seen it up close and personal, thank you very much."

"Learning isn't the same as doing," Damon said as he

found a parking space in a section of the lot reserved for police officers. He hung an official-looking placard from the rear-view mirror.

"So you're bringing me to the courthouse to become a criminal?"

"No, I'm bringing you here to *live* with criminals for a few hours a day. It's the next best thing. I'm pretty sure their crimes aren't white-collar, and I know for certain none of them ended up in mansions and private schools."

"When it comes to criminals there is no 'next best thing.' You'd better start giving me some details, Damon, or I'm getting out of this car and hailing a taxi."

"You aren't in a position to be giving ultimatums," Damon said in a voice he'd never used with her before.

It was deeper, as though it came from someplace in him that even he didn't know nor could he control. But there was no question what that voice was saying: Damon was not one to be messed with. It startled her, and she turned to look at him. His face was hard, with no give in his features. He looked like her brother, but harsher, more inflexible. This must be the Damon who arrested bad guys now, and the one who'd fought them off during his time in juvenile detention. Come to think of it, she had seen this other Damon once before, outside the party last summer when he got in Xavier's face and she thought she'd have to break up a fight. That whole scene reminded her of the promise she'd made herself just this morning, so Drea backed down. "Don't I at least get a warning shot across the bow?"

"Come on, I'll give you a tour." Damon got out of the car. "Let me show you around the campus before we go inside to meet the judge."

Drea reluctantly left the car, feeling strangely like it was the last tie to her old life where summer meant her mother's fabulous garden parties or a week on the beaches of St. Bart's. It was just a summer job. She tried to shake the odd feeling.

"I'm still not hearing words that make any sense, Damon."

"This is where you'll be working this summer as a science tutor—"

"For inmates?"

"Not quite. This isn't the jail. It's the justice center, which houses the county and municipal courts. And Justice Academy."

"Wait a minute. When you went there, Justice Academy was an actual school, even if it was in a strip mall."

"It was *behind* the mall, not part of it."

"I think the relevant point is that it wasn't in a courthouse."

"The judge you'll be meeting decided to move the school here since he allows only a forty-student enrollment. He figures being here is a deterrent for the students, a constant reminder of why they're at J.A. Plus, it's easier for him to run the school."

"The judge runs the school?"

"He's the juvie court judge and the principal."

"Just how bad are these kids, anyway?"

"He was my principal too. You'd know all that if you ever bothered to come to the school when I was here."

"You mean when you were at the strip mall. If I didn't visit the school there, I sure as hell wouldn't have visited you if it was here."

"It isn't prison or juvie. It's just like any other school. When the bell rings at three thirty, they go home to their families just like I did. Just like you do."

Drea heard the unmistakable laughter of girls her age approaching them from behind. She and Damon moved off the sidewalk to let the faster-moving crowd behind them pass. First, there were two men and a woman in suits, all with briefcases, probably lawyers on their way to court. They were followed by a couple of sheriff's deputies. Behind them was the source of the laughter—three girls dressed like the girls at her school when uniforms weren't required. Except the girls at her school wouldn't use so much makeup, jewelry, and perfume. They'd be wearing real Jimmy Choos instead of lookalikes from Shoe-a-Rama, and their clothes would fit well, not a size too small.

"See? They're regular students, just like you."

"No, they're nothing like me."

"Only because the cop who picked you up from the Promenade's security office and who found you at the scene of a B&E is your brother," he said, sounding again like the Damon she'd met for the first time when he got in Xavier's face last summer. "Most have been through the system, but they got early release for good behavior and are serving probation while they attend the academy. It helps them transition from the juvie system to the outside. A few got lucky and haven't been in the system yet. The judge hopes he can keep it that way."

"You said the school only has forty students. Why did these forty get a break?"

"I guess someone—a probation officer, the warden, Judge Claiborne—saw something good in them, so they got a second chance. Sort of like I did for you, except you didn't have to go to juvie first."

Drea was quiet as Damon resumed the campus tour, which was really just walking around the justice center grounds pointing out parking lots and the various entrances, even though she could only use the main one with the metal detectors. Did any of the officers they passed recognize Damon despite his civilian clothes, and assume she was a criminal that he was accompanying? A normal girl, one who didn't grow up among crooks and an ex-felon, would probably never wonder that.

As they approached the back of the building, Drea was startled by the sudden ringing of a very loud alarm, followed by the opening of a metal garage door that led to underground parking. Two sheriff's deputies holding assault rifles emerged from the garage and posted themselves there. One of the guards nodded in their direction. Damon returned the nod.

"Let's keep moving," Damon said, picking up his pace, apparently forgetting Drea was still on crutches.

"Why? What's the hurry?"

"Prisoner transport, bringing the defendants in for trial. A bus must be pulling in now."

As if on cue, Drea heard the motor of the bus pulling in behind them. Drea could hear the hiss of air brakes as the driver parked the bus.

"See? Nothing like a regular school."

"Stay away from this garage, okay?"

"Well, duh."

"I wish they'd moved the school here while I was still attending," Damon said as they came around to the side of the building opposite the place where Drea imagined murderers and rapists in shackles were being unloaded. "Look. The creek runs right along this side. After the judge expunged my record and I spent that year as his intern, I'd come out here on my break and walk along the creek path."

"You make this sound like some kind of treat," Drea said. "It isn't."

"Ask those boys we arrested last week. Compared to where they're headed, I'd bet they would think it's a treat."

Drea didn't want to think about how the boys had spent that night. She hoped Xavier had been released by now and was at least at home waiting for his hearing, wherever home was. Jason had said Xavier's foster parents had given up on him. Had he meant just as far as covering his bail, or had they given up altogether?

"So, you got me a job tutoring summer-school ex-cons?" Drea said when the tour came full circle, back at the front entrance. "Not even the best and brightest of the losers. I mean...no offense."

"They aren't summer-school ex-cons. J.A. doesn't have a summer break. They're in class year-round. It's just fourth quarter for them."

"Year-round school. Harsh. I guess it *is* supposed to be punishment."

"Exactly. Now you can pay penance for whatever you were doing Thursday night that has you feeling so guilty." Damon stopped a few yards from the door and lowered his voice. "You asked if I wanted to know why you were at the school. You pretty much told me it was for something criminal by saying I'd risked my job for you. Were you there with the kids we arrested? I know one of them used to go to Woodruff before he was sent in."

"I didn't know Xavier when he was at Woodruff," Drea said, which was mostly true. "That's what happened, I mean, why he left—he went to jail?"

"If you didn't know him, how do you know which one I'm talking about?" Damon headed for the door and held it open for her.

Inside was nearly as bright as outdoors, thanks to the ceiling made of glass. It was a beautiful building as far as courthouses go, though Drea's experience was limited and even then, they'd clearly had a remodel since Damon's trial. The atrium was full of tall potted trees, and beyond the metal detectors, Drea spotted some kind of tile mosaic in the center of the gleaming floor. She wondered if, like the hospital, the architects thought they could make visitors forget why they were there, if only for a minute or so.

"Thursday night was just a coincidence," Drea lied.

"Some coincidence, but I believe you."

When it came to pretending she was good and true, Drea was playing a trick not only on the world, but on her family, too. She truly wanted to be as good as they all believed she was. "I'm glad, Damon. After the crap I pulled last fall, then the other night . . . it's important that you still believe in me."

"Always," Damon said as they joined the line for the metal detectors. "I'm glad you weren't with them. Those boys will now be at least two-time losers, and whatever you were there to do, doing it with them would have only worsened your situation if the arresting officers had found you there."

As if to prove the point, she spotted a man in an expensive, well-cut suit near the head of the line. She could only see the back of him and he didn't stand out in a line full of suits, except that the man was flanked by two boys: Jason and Xavier.

17

Monday, 7:45 a.m.

It turned out that the judge was just a man. After her brother had graduated from Justice Academy and had begun interning for him, Damon would come home each day with a Judge Claiborne story that made him seem more than mortal. The judge had been a football star at Clemson and probably could have gone pro. He had graduated law *and* med school. He was a leader in the 100 Black Men of Atlanta. His wife was a former Miss Georgia. The judge even donated some of his annual salary to Justice Academy every year. Drea noticed a bottle of water on his desk and half-expected him to turn the contents into wine.

After Damon had introduced her to Judge Claiborne and left her to fend for herself in a building full of criminals, Drea had spent the next twenty minutes feigning interest in whatever the judge was talking about while he gave her a tour of the courthouse. If anyone were to ask her an hour later what he'd said, she wouldn't remember a word of it. She was too distracted wondering which courtroom the boys were in for their initial hearing and hoping the tour wouldn't cause them to cross paths. It was bad enough knowing she was walking around free when she had been trying to do the same thing they were arrested for. She didn't need to see the final act of their crash and burn.

By the time the judge arrived at the classroom—which turned out to be just an unused courtroom—where Drea would spend her first day on the job just observing, she was relieved there had been no more Xavier and Jason sightings. At least not until she walked into the room and found them both sitting in the back row. After the judge introduced her as the new summer tutor, telling everyone that she was the top student in her class at the Woodruff School with an academic career Justice Academy students should aspire to, Drea went to the first row, leaned her crutches on the wall, and took the seat closest to the door, certain the two boys in the back row were silently mocking her, ready to tell the whole room she was a fraud.

Judge Claiborne didn't leave after her introduction as she'd expected, and instead, removed his robe, hung it on a hook, and returned to the front of the class. As he rolled up his shirt-sleeves, Drea wondered whether this was because he was about to get down to business or because the room was so warm. Or maybe it was only Drea who was sweating like she'd just run the Peachtree Road Race.

"Andrea, in case you were wondering why school starts at seven-forty-five, I teach this class before I start my other job. The rest of the day will feel very much like an ordinary high school day," the judge explained. "But my class serves as a daily reminder of why our students are here instead of an ordinary high school, and where they'll go—or return—if they screw this up."

The judge was addressing Drea, but it was clear he was talking more to his students than to her, and he paused a few beats to let his message sink in. Drea imagined his dramatic flair was learned on the bench where he had to play the role of imposing authoritarian while meting out justice. Or maybe that was just who he was. Either way, it worked on Drea. It may have been the way Damon had sprung this job on her, or knowing Jason was sitting a few rows back wishing all kinds of wrath upon her, or realizing whatever had begun to happen between her and Xavier that night probably had been crushed by his arrest, but Drea was certain she was the guiltiest person in the room. Even in a room full of people convicted by the court.

"Students spend this class learning the law and what happens when they break it," the judge continued. "In addition to law studies, we have a weekly talk from an inmate serving time in the county jail as well as show-and-tell Thursdays."

"Um, show-and-tell Thursdays? What is that, exactly?" Drea asked. She didn't want to draw any more attention to herself than the judge had already given her, but she couldn't let that one go without a comment. She imagined kids standing in front of class demonstrating the use of lock picks or switchblades.

Judge Claiborne smiled. "One student shares how they began their life of crime. They give us an honest, no-holds-barred account, in their own words. It's really all tell, no show, but that doesn't sound as good," he explained, to Drea's relief. "The students think I'm forcing group therapy on them, but I believe one person's mistake can be another's lesson. Justice Academy isn't just a way station between jail and freedom. Our goal here is to keep kids from ever going into the detention system, or from ever returning to it if they've already been there."

No matter how Drea felt about spending her summer with felons, it seemed the judge and his school were doing something important, maybe even something good. She felt she should say something deep and profound in response to the judge's explanation, but all she could come up with was, "Oh, okay. Thank you."

"We have fun here too, right?" The judge's tone lightened considerably, but he was barely able to inspire a groan of agreement from the class. "We go on field trips, except at Justice Academy, students observe trials taking place in our courtrooms or meet with victim advocates. Criminals tend to see the result of their actions in terms of what it does to them. Learning how their actions impact victims is a powerful lesson. Oh, and on Friday, we'll visit the county jail. That's always exciting. You're welcome to join us, Andrea."

Drea smiled politely at the judge, but there was no way in

hell that would ever happen. She took a quick look around at her future tutees. They all looked so hard, though not a single one looked afraid. She wondered why there wasn't a bailiff or sheriff's deputy standing guard. If this had been juvie hall there would be guards, and the only reason these kids—no, these *people,* because they probably hadn't been kids for a very long time, no matter what their birth certificates said—weren't in juvie hall is because Judge Claiborne hadn't sentenced them. He had wanted to give them another chance before they went into the system. You shouldn't judge a book by its cover, but that adage didn't apply to Drea. One thing she was good at was judging people, reading the truth behind their lies, and she was certain that no one in the room deserved Claiborne's magnanimity. Herself included.

Today's class was about parole violations and the importance of establishing a good relationship with your probation officers. Drea assumed the lesson applied to at least half the room, including the boys in the back row. After the class ended, the judge put his robe back on and left for his first trial of the day, but Drea didn't move. She was waiting for another teacher to replace him, or for the bailiff she'd hoped was standing just outside the room to enter, but no one came. It was just her and a room full of ex-convicts dressed up to look like high school students.

A few of the older boys began pulling together room partitions that had been accordioned against the walls, creating four smaller rooms. Now she understood why the courtroom, sandwiched between two hallways, had four entrances, one in each corner of the room. The partitions created classrooms, one for each grade.

Drea looked behind her and found that the partitions had separated her from Xavier, and left her alone with the girls she'd seen earlier during her tour of the grounds with Damon. They were all dressed in a different shade of green, and she wondered if green was the color of some gang. She'd only heard of blue and red as affiliation colors, but Drea's gang experience was limited to movies and TV. Or maybe they were mules for Atlanta drug dealers who wanted to extend their business into Magnolia. *Mule* made it sound as though they only carried the drugs, but Drea imagined there was more to it than that. Surely a mule had to be tough enough to defend her cargo, know how to handle her business and herself. The girls were grouped around a table two rows away from hers and they weren't the least bit giggly now. They were looking her over, probably deciding which one was going to kick her ass first, just for something to do. One delinquent Drea was sure she could handle, but three of them?

As certain as she was that Jason wanted her dead, Drea was relieved when he entered her newly created classroom.

"What are you doing here?"

"Um, my brother made me . . . get a summer job, I mean. I'll be tutoring and—"

"Yeah, I heard the judge. I mean, what are you doing *here*? This is the ninth-grade classroom," Jason said, as though she had any idea which grade that quarter of the courtroom had been partitioned into. "The teacher in the junior classroom sent me to get you. The judge just told everyone you'll be observing junior classes today. And you're supposed to be so brilliant."

Drea got up in a hurry, happy to be leaving the gang girls and embarrassed that she'd been terrified of freshmen. In her defense, those girls looked as hard as the upperclassmen. The thought made her less excited to be leaving them. She was about to jump from the pan to the fire.

18

Monday, 11:52 a.m.

After a morning of observing classes, Drea figured she'd done her time and planned on leaving for lunch and never coming back, but just as she tried to make her escape, she saw Xavier at the end of the hall waving at her. She considered ducking into a stairwell and pretending she never saw him, but she heard someone behind her call her name. She turned to see Judge Claiborne standing in the doorway of what she now knew was the ninth-grade classroom. Drea weighed her options and decided Judge Claiborne would be easier to talk to than Xavier. Besides, if he saw her talking to the judge, Xavier couldn't accuse her of avoiding him. What was she supposed to do—ignore the principal?

"How was your first morning, Andrea?"

Drea debated whether to break the news to the judge that it had been not only her first morning but her last. The judge was like a god to Damon, understandable since he'd pretty much saved Damon's life, so she decided her brother should hear the news first that this job was not going to work out for her.

"It was . . . interesting. Some of the students seem really strong," Drea said, and she wasn't just playing nice. She was thinking of a boy in the bio class she'd observed. Once she'd stopped staring at his neck—every inch of it tattooed—and watched him whiteboard Bayes' theorem to calculate carrier status for recessive genetic traits, she'd been blown away. Drea was certain that had never happened in her biology class at Woodruff.

"You sound surprised," the judge said. "Every student at Justice has the potential for academic excellence, or they wouldn't be here. I'm not saying that as some politically correct cheerleader, because I don't have time for that."

"Oh, I didn't mean—" Drea tried to explain, but the judge cut her off, which was just as well because his implication was exactly what she'd meant, and she probably wouldn't have come up with a believable explanation, anyway.

"I gave every kid here a break during sentencing because I know each one of them has what it takes to excel in their studies. I reviewed their transcripts, interviewed their old teachers—they may not be at the top of their class in a place like the Woodruff School, but they're all quite smart in at least one discipline. We have math whizzes, history buffs, science fair winners. There was even a National Spelling Bee contestant a few years back."

Drea hesitated for a moment, wondering how to ask the

question without eating her foot again. "So how did they end up in your court or jail . . . I mean, juvenile detention?"

"They have plenty of brain power. What they didn't have were parents who gave a damn, or who weren't incarcerated, or using meth, or cooking and selling it. In some cases, they made bad choices in friends. Some didn't have enough food and did what they needed to do so they or their siblings could eat."

Drea thought of Xavier and how she had accused him of stealing Skittles when he committed his first crime at age seven, and felt a twinge of guilt, until she thought of her first impression of the Green Gang Girls. Then the twinge became more like a slap across the face.

"So none of these kids are here for serious crimes?" she asked.

"Now, I didn't say that. Some of them just made knuckle-headed decisions; those I gave probation and made them transfer to Justice. Others . . . well, they committed serious crimes and had to do some time, but I gave them shorter sentences and probation. Our goal is to show them there's another path than one of crime. That's why you're here, to help our staff help these kids, not only as a tutor but as an example."

Now the guilt felt like a house that had been dropped on her.

"In fact, there's one student in particular I want you to meet."

Drea followed the judge when he stepped into the ninth-grade classroom where the Green Gang Girls still lingered after the lunch bell—well, lunch *buzzer*—though it was pretty quiet so it wouldn't disturb the rest of the courthouse. He motioned one of the girls to join him.

"This is Tiana Moore."

"But she's in ninth grade," Drea said, unnerved by the way the girl was staring her down. "I thought I was supposed to tutor eleventh graders only."

"Since you're already working at the collegiate level— Damon told me about your summer at Hathaway College— we'd like you to tutor science for all grades. Tiana should probably be in the eleventh grade."

"Oh, I see. You were kept back," Drea said, wondering how she was expected to tutor two years' worth of science in a single summer.

"Not quite," Tiana said, rolling her eyes at Drea. "I'm twelve, and the school system won't skip me that far ahead."

Twelve? She was smaller than the average ninth grader, but between the makeup and clothes, the girl didn't look a day under sixteen. But after Drea got past the fact she'd been afraid of a middle-school kid, she had to admit she was intrigued by a twelve-year-old performing at the eleventh-grade level.

"But we'll change their minds, won't we, Tiana?" Judge Claiborne said.

"They think just because I stole something, that I can't be really smart. But the judge will fight them for me, I just have to pass the exam to test out of tenth grade."

"I'd like you to give Tiana a little extra attention," the judge said after sending the girl and her friends off to lunch.

"And may I suggest some homework for you?"

"Me? But I'm not a student here."

"Not schoolwork. Self-work. Try leaving the judgment at the door," the judge said, adding before he walked off down the hall, "Your brother could probably teach you something about that."

Drea had come back from lunch after all, and had made it through the day without having to talk to Xavier, even though she saw him when she observed his math class. The evil eye Jason gave her every chance he got eventually became less intimidating as the hours went on and she'd begun to see it was his default setting.

As the judge had promised, after his class, the school day for Justice students was like any she'd have at Woodruff, except for the constant police presence in the halls and the inmate transport van that arrived with a new batch of criminals while she sat along the creek and ate her lunch alone. Finally released at the end of the day, Drea was looking forward to getting home to a real meal, since lunch had been chips and soda from the vending machine.

After she made her way out the front entrance, moving like an old pro on her crutches, Drea realized she and Damon had forgotten to make a plan to get her home. Since his shift had begun half an hour ago, she would to have to find her own way.

When she called Frank the cabbie and asked him to pick her up in front of the courthouse, his response was exactly what she'd expected, and made her smile for the first time all day: *Look lady, I don't know what you're up to . . .*

Drea sat on a bench near the curb to wait for Frank and took out the new phone she'd bought over the weekend, resigned to the fact her old one was gone for good. She checked her email, as always, hoping for the message from her parents that never came. There was a message from Madeline asking what was up with her missing the last day of school and whether the rumors were true she'd broken her leg.

She hadn't spoken to Maddy or anyone from Woodruff since the break-in. She felt oddly disconnected from them, as though that night had drawn some kind of line between them. That world was pre-everything: her attempt to commit a felony; Damon jeopardizing his job and more for her; finding Xavier again only to watch him get arrested, possibly because of her; having to spend her summer with juvenile delinquents instead of cruising the mall with Maddy. Even the weirdness of Jason breaking into her house. Not only would her friends not get the reason she'd missed the last day of school, they'd never understand the person she'd become in the few days since she'd last seen them.

But hadn't she been that person all along? In truth, they only knew fake Drea. Did that make them fake friends?

Someone sat on the other end of the bench, but she didn't look away from her email, worried it might be some bonded-out felon taking a break from his trial. She hoped Frank's taxi would pull up before whoever it was tried to engage her in conversation.

"Thank you."

Drea looked up to find Xavier sitting beside her, but quickly turned back to her phone.

"For what? Being the reason you're here?"

"I was already here, and *I'm* the reason. It has nothing to do with you."

"But I thought changing my grade slowed you down. Jason said—"

"Jason's angry. Jason is always angry at something. This week, it just happens to be you. He'll come around."

"It doesn't matter. I won't be here tomorrow."

Drea had spent most of the day, when she wasn't avoiding Xavier, Jason, or the girl gang, figuring out how she would tell Damon she wasn't going to do this. She'd have to pay her penance some other way. She could have dealt with the criminals, and even the gangsters in lip gloss and Steve Madden knockoffs, but she couldn't spend a whole summer avoiding Xavier.

"That's too bad. Science is my worst subject. I could definitely use some help."

"Whoever replaces me will help you, I'm sure."

"Jason says your brother made you get a summer job. Why your brother and not your parents?"

"It's a long story and my ride will be here any minute. Besides—it doesn't matter if I'm never going to see you again, does it?"

146

"I suppose not. But won't your brother be pissed you quit your job after only a day?"

"He'll get over it."

"Is that the guy you were with this morning? I remembered him from that party last summer, when he acted like he wanted to kick my ass. I was a little worried he might be your boyfriend... or something."

"Oh, God no. That was just my brother." Drea was so surprised he'd care whether she had a boyfriend, much less be *worried* that she did, she blurted out what she'd been trying so hard to keep from him.

Good thing Damon had been wearing a suit and not in uniform. Xavier didn't need to know what happened that night after he and Jason were arrested, especially the part about her brother being a cop who made sure she hadn't shared their fate.

"So you saw us?" Drea asked, once she recovered from his question and her blunder. She'd seen Xavier and Jason in the security line, but was sure they'd missed her since she'd been behind them.

"Yeah, I was wondering why you were here. I was hoping if you *were* with that guy, he was a loser on his way to jail, considering his apparent anger issues and all."

Drea remained silent. She didn't want to ruin the moment that she learned he cared about her relationship status by reminding him he actually was, if not a loser, certainly on his way to jail.

"I bet I know what you're thinking, but I'm not going to

jail. I have a great lawyer. That was my next thought when I saw you—that they'd caught you, too, and you were with your attorney. Every suit in this place is an attorney."

"No, I didn't get caught." She wondered if he could hear the guilt in her voice.

"Weird place for a guy to want his sister to work. Especially a girl like you."

"Well, like I said—I won't be after today."

Drea didn't look at him, and hadn't since he'd first joined her on the bench. Keeping a poker face was another skill she hadn't seemed to inherit from her parents. Xavier was getting dangerously close to knowing more about her than she'd like. She was safer looking away from him; a good con can read emotions you don't even know you're feeling.

"Whatever you're reading must be pretty interesting. At least more interesting than I am," Xavier said, but Drea didn't respond. "Well, if I'm not going to see you again, I'm glad I got a chance to thank you. I know it was you who posted my bail."

"Bail?"

"You're the only person I know with that kind of money. Or any money."

"I don't know what you're talking about."

Xavier stood and moved in front of her, forcing her to look up at him. Drea realized it was the first time she'd really looked at him since that night. Even this morning when she'd seen him sitting in the back row, or behind him in his math class, it was barely a glimpse, just long enough to register that it was him, but not long enough to let him see her guilt.

"You're a terrible liar," Xavier said, and then walked away toward the parking lot. She watched him run across the street in time to board the bus that had just pulled up.

Even if he'd stayed, Drea would not have denied it a second time, because it was true. Not just that she'd posted his bail, but that she was a terrible liar. She'd always thought it ironic that she could read people so well, spot a con or a weakness in even the best-told lie, and yet she was one big, walking tell. She showed every hand, telegraphed every play. That's what her father had meant when he said she was good at planning but bad at execution. Or what Damon had said about her being a con only in theory.

She'd always believed that her sense of morality had kept her from being a criminal like the rest of her family, but maybe it really had been this weakness. But she knew that flaw wasn't the real reason. In her heart of hearts, she knew Damon was the only one in the family with any true sense of good, even if he got derailed for a little while. She and her parents shared the same murky sense of right and wrong. Her parents were just much better liars.

19

Tuesday, 12:00 p.m.

Drea hadn't slept much the night before, doing the homework the judge had suggested without even realizing that's what she was doing, tossing and turning in bed until three in the morning. When he'd chastised her, Drea had wanted to point out the irony of a judge asking her not to judge, but didn't have the nerve. Several sleepless hours later, she had gotten over herself—mostly—and had really thought about what he was asking.

The most obvious realization: She was being a total hypocrite in judging Tiana and her gang. Scratch that. Tiana and her *friends*. Drea had almost committed a crime for the sake of her ego, to keep up the charade of being perfect and good, not to feed herself or keep the electricity turned on. The only reason she wasn't facing time at Justice Academy as a student—if she had gotten lucky and the judge deemed her worthy—was because of her brother. And speaking of Damon...he wouldn't be a cop right now if not for the judge and his school. Worse, he might have gotten out of juvie only to continue on in the family business if her parents hadn't gone straight for his sake.

Then there was that. Her parents had made some of the same bad choices as the Justice kids, and they had come from good parents and good homes, at least according to their story, before they had to steal to feed themselves, and later, Damon. And maybe they had to steal to survive at first, but unlike the judge's students, her parents had had options, like going back home, getting jobs, and waiting until they were grown and ready to leave. If their love was so strong, wouldn't it have lasted another couple of years? And okay, so they had to steal a few things at first because they didn't plan very well, but they were obviously brilliant to have never been caught. Why not use those powers for good instead of being criminals for nearly two decades?

That was the thing Drea had come to recently accept about her parents. They actually *liked* being criminals, or at least doing the things that made them criminals. They liked casing the mark, the challenge of conning the target out of whatever it was they wanted from him. Damon's arrest five years ago had scared them straight, but apparently the fear had worn off. She was convinced they had something to do with the Peachland heist. Drea loved her parents, but she didn't want to be them, which is why she returned to Justice Academy the next day after all.

She had been grateful when she learned she'd spend her

second day observing the sophomores' classes. It meant she'd been able to avoid Xavier all morning. She hadn't counted on him waiting outside her classroom at the end of fourth period and asking her to join him for lunch.

Hadn't she spent the first two months of her English Lit class dreaming about this very moment? Now that it was finally happening, Drea was completely unnerved. She was still feeling guilty about the boys' arrest, despite Xavier's assurances that changing her grade hadn't slowed them down.

There was also the way Xavier acted so... well, *close* was the best word she could come up with to describe how he'd been toward her from the moment they'd reconnected. Like the way he'd pulled her close when he'd introduced her to Jason, or how he'd smiled at her before he ran down that hall toward the school office. He acted as though they'd been great friends, or something more, before he'd left Woodruff, and now they were just picking up where they had left off.

"Come on," Xavier prodded, "you gotta eat. Besides, who knows when we'll have the chance again?"

"I've decided to stay for the whole summer semester, so we have about nine weeks' worth of chances. At least that much," she added, because maybe there'd be more time than just the summer.

"That depends."

"On what?" Drea asked, trying to sound flirtatious, thinking Xavier was playing coy with her.

"On my preliminary hearing this afternoon."

"But I thought that's why you and Jason are here. Isn't Justice Academy your sentence?"

"It's obvious you've never been arrested," Xavier said, unaware his statement was sending Drea's guilt into overdrive. "Nothing moves that quickly. I'm surprised the prelim was scheduled so soon. Probably Judge Claiborne had something to do with that."

"Wait—how *are* you here? Even before the B&E, I thought you left Woodruff for juvenile detention." Drea said before she could stop herself.

"How'd you know that?"

"Um, I just figured, you know, since you're here now, it's the reason you left Woodruff all of a sudden. And I know many Justice kids serve time before they come here."

"You're right. I did a juvie stint first."

"So Thursday night was your third strike." Drea wondered if it worked the same for juvenile offenders.

"What makes you think this isn't my second strike?"

"People at school were saying you had been in detention even before you came to Woodruff."

Xavier was quiet for a minute, so Drea tried to fill the awkward silence. "I mean, well, they were just rumors. I probably shouldn't have believed—"

"You make it really hard for a guy to ask you out for lunch. Let's say we not talk about my criminal record. I'm hungry, and one of the best things about going to school in downtown Magnolia is the food trucks."

Drea decided the next half hour would have been something straight out of her old Xavier fantasy world if not for Jason walking toward them, glaring at her. Or the fact that Xavier might have his probation revoked, be found guilty of his latest charges, and be sent back to jail. The thought was like losing him all over again. The worst part was that this time, she knew there was really something going on between them. She hadn't just imagined it.

No, that wasn't the worst part of it, after all. The worst part had just turned left into their hallway about ten yards ahead of them, and was now walking toward the main exit too, in the deep navy uniform of the Magnolia Police Department. The justice center was crawling with cops, but Drea immediately recognized this one even though his back was to them. His shift didn't start for three hours, so why was he in uniform, anyway? She'd known there was a chance of this happening eventually, but not today, not when she and Xavier were about to have their first-and-hopefully-not-last lunch date, even if Jason had to tag along. And it wasn't supposed to happen like this. She'd imagined all the ways she'd explain it to Xavier, but none of her scenarios went like this.

"Hey, it gets crazy busy downtown at lunch time. Let's just grab something here," Drea suggested, trying to get the boys to head toward the justice center cafeteria and away from the main exit and the truth she wasn't quite ready to tell.

"The cafeteria has a decent burger and fries," Jason said, surprising Drea. She'd figured he'd veto any idea of hers. "We only get forty-five minutes for lunch, and I don't want to waste it all walking three blocks so we can stand in those long food-truck lines."

Xavier acted like he didn't hear either of them and kept walking toward the front entrance. Now they were all in the wide-open atrium that led to the security line and the main doors, and Drea was grateful it was crowded with people leaving for lunch. She could only hope Damon didn't turn around, that he'd keep walking and get outside before they did. Maybe she could make up an excuse to stop, say she left something in the classroom, and put some space between them and her brother. But as if the world were conspiring against her, an old woman who'd just cleared security stopped Damon and asked him a question. Drea could tell by the woman's approach and by Damon's hand gestures that the woman was lost.

They were only a few yards away from her brother now. If they could just get past him while his back was still turned to them. Just as they were passing behind Damon, he began to turn in the direction they'd come from, completely missing them. Drea had never felt so relieved, at least until another ten yards later when Xavier stopped abruptly, causing her and Jason to nearly run into him, and turned around.

"You guys might be right. The truck lines are a hassle. We'll stay here for lunch."

Drea looked back, expecting to find Damon and the old woman behind her, but they were both gone. Then she caught a glimpse of the woman through the crowd, heading toward the traffic-ticket bureau, but Damon was nowhere to be seen. She could only hope he'd disappeared before Xavier had suddenly changed his mind and whirled around. As they headed back for the cafeteria, Drea was desperately hoping Damon hadn't decided to have lunch there too; Jason was recounting what was good on the cafeteria menu; and Xavier hadn't said a word.

Once they arrived in the cafeteria and joined the food line, not a cop in uniform to be seen, Drea's pulse finally began to slow to something like normal. In the food line, Xavier offered to carry her tray since she was on crutches—surely he wouldn't have done that if he'd spotted Damon in the atrium—while she found an empty table. When she tried to give him money for her food, Xavier wouldn't take it, reminding Drea he'd asked her to lunch. By the time the boys arrived at the table she'd picked for them, she had finally relaxed, confident her cover hadn't been blown. *Cover.* She'd been around her family way too long. She didn't have a cover. What she had was a lie, even if it was a lie by omission.

"How's your chicken Caesar salad, Drea? Like it?" Xavier asked.

"It's pretty good. Jason was right."

"And your first couple of days at Justice Academy? Not as bad as you thought it would be?"

"You mean besides staying clear of the prison transport bus?" Drea said, adding an uneasy laugh. Something in Xavier's tone made her feel his questions weren't just idle lunchtime talk.

Xavier smiled at her, but it wasn't the smile that made her weak. This one made her feel like a rabbit trapped by the fox.

"And what about your brother? When were you going to tell us he's a cop?"

Jason dropped his fork, which clattered onto his plate so

loudly Drea was sure everyone in the room heard it and had stopped to look at them. She quickly looked around the room and realized no one was watching; it was too loud to hear a fork drop over the din of the busy cafeteria. Nothing had changed in the last second except her. She'd become a traitor.

"Your brother's a cop?" Jason asked, but didn't wait for confirmation. "I told you, X. Told you not to trust her, and I don't know how many times I said she was the snitch. Hell, she didn't even have to call nine-one-one to narc."

"No matter what it looks like, I promise you I didn't call the police that night," Drea said, keeping her voice as low as possible. Not that it mattered, because Jason didn't seem to have much concern who heard them. It wasn't his brother who could get into all kinds of trouble.

"Does your brother know you were there that night?" Xavier asked.

"Of course he knows," Jason said. "He knows we were *all* there because she called him. What was his name, X? How much you wanna bet he was one of the cops who arrested us?"

Both Drea and Xavier ignored his questions. Drea recalled everything her parents had taught her and hoped for once that her genetic disposition to be a great liar would come through for her. Otherwise, Xavier would probably hate her forever, and Jason would report Damon without thinking twice.

"He has no idea who you even are. Woodruff isn't in his patrol zone."

"So now you know the patrol zones of the Magnolia PD?"

"I know my brother doesn't work in the same zone my school is in."

Xavier was silent for a second, and Drea knew he was trying to decide whether she was telling the truth. While she may not have sold the lie completely, she'd mustered up enough acting skill to keep him from reading it outright.

"I wonder what he'd think if he found out his little sister was a burglar?" Jason asked. "Or worse, what his boss would think."

Drea looked to Xavier for support, but could tell by his expression she wouldn't be getting it.

"If you weren't the snitch, prove it. If you don't, your brother might get an anonymous tip," Xavier said, his tone so sinister it frightened her a little.

"You guys must be crazy. How could I possibly prove that? What about the other person who knew you were there—your client? How do you know that person didn't call the cops?"

"Because he'd have as much to lose as we do. More to lose, actually," Xavier said, watching her face with such scrutiny that she felt Magnolia's best detective couldn't unnerve her as much. "You're a con, Andrea Faraday. I can feel it. You may have had everyone at Woodruff fooled, but that's something we have in common. The only difference is I act on my instincts. You're too afraid to act on yours. You're only one crime away from being here as a student instead of a tutor, just like Jason and me."

"She almost did the crime until you offered me up to do it for her."

"It's okay, Jason, because Drea's going to get us out of the charges."

"How am I supposed to do that?"

"Your brother can help us," Xavier said. "And you know the judge. I saw you in the hall talking to him yesterday, looking all chummy. You have connections."

"I only met Judge Claiborne yesterday, and my brother is a rookie cop just two months out of the academy. Those aren't connections."

"We don't like the police for obvious reasons, but we always suspected we could be so much more effective if we could afford to buy one," Jason said, sounding hopeful. "A con and a cop joining forces? It's a powerful thing."

"You think my brother is going to help you guys?"

"*Someone* set us up that night," Xavier said, clearly suggesting that someone might be her. "He's a cop. Isn't he supposed to find the truth?"

"Yeah, this is about good versus evil," Jason added.

"Do you guys even know the difference? If you consider yourselves the 'good' in all this, I'm thinking you don't. Whether someone set you up or not, you do realize you're actually guilty, right?"

Xavier ignored Drea's questions and continued his sales pitch. "You're a criminal who hasn't come out of the closet yet, at least not completely. You were trying to that night, but lost your nerve."

Drea sat a bit taller and squared her shoulders, trying to make herself seem, and feel, more imposing. "I didn't lose my nerve. Maybe I was the better con that night. I got you to do my job for me, didn't I?"

"All the more reason to help us," Xavier said, though Drea was certain he didn't buy her attempt at swagger. "My prospects don't look good at this hearing today so trust your instincts, use your brother's access, get in good with the judge—whatever you need to do to figure out who set us up. If it really wasn't you."

"I swear to you, Xavier, it wasn't me."

Xavier stared right into her as he threw down his challenge. "So prove it."

20

Wednesday, 7:27 a.m.

The next morning, Damon ignored Drea when she told him she could get to work on her own (Frank the cabbie was already on her favorites list). Now, as he pulled into the justice center parking lot, he insisted on walking her into the building.

"It's almost seven thirty. You just had to toast another Pop Tart for the road," Damon said, sounding peeved.

"What's the big deal? I have ten minutes until first bell. Anyway, it's enough that you drove me here. Don't you want to go back home and get some sleep after that long shift? You can just drop me right here at the front entrance," Drea said as Damon drove past the entrance and down a row of parking spaces.

"What kind of brother would I be to make you take a cab to work when I've got the day off and can drive you myself? Or let you hobble up those steps without some help?"

"First off, they have a ramp, by law. No hobbling required. Second, you'd be the brother you've always been, the one who taught me not to depend on anyone but myself because no one will be more loyal. What happened to that guy?"

"That guy had a change of heart after his parents bailed on his sister."

"Seems like them bailing would make you believe even more in that advice."

Damon didn't respond, just checked himself in the rear-view mirror after he put the car in park.

"What's up with that?"

"What?"

"The mirror. And the shower when you got home."

"I've been on the street all night."

"And if you're just going home to crash after you drop me off, why the nice T-shirt instead one of your ratty old concert shirts? You live in those off duty. And those are your Saturday-night, hope-you-get lucky jeans." Drea leaned in and sniffed. "You're wearing cologne!"

"Maybe *you* should have gone to police academy." Damon got out of the car. "I work with those people in there. I can't look like a bum."

"Which is why you should have dropped me off at the front entrance and kept moving." Drea hopped out before he could come around the car and treat her like an invalid. "Speaking of moving, look how well I get around on these crutches now. I think I'll be able to give them up sooner than the doctor said."

Drea sped ahead of him through the parking lot and had made it up the ramp to the main entrance by the time Damon caught up with her.

"Why are you trying so hard to keep me out of that building?" he asked, opening the door for her.

"Why are you trying so hard to get *inside* that building? And on your day off."

Not only did Drea not receive an answer, Damon followed her inside, joining her in the security screening line.

"Seven thirty on the dot," Damon said, distracted by something, or someone, in the employee line. Drea followed his gaze to the employee line and saw a pretty girl with dark hair.

"Is she the reason for the cologne?"

"Just go. It's your turn through the metal detector."

"So pushy," Drea said as she handed over her crutches to the sheriff's deputy manning the detector and hopped through on her good leg.

After the deputy returned her crutches, Drea figured out why her brother was being so pushy. Their arrival on the other side of security coincided with that of the girl Damon had been watching. The meeting itself was clearly not so coincidental, even though Damon wanted the girl to think so as he *accidentally* bumped into her. Drea played along. She owed Damon that and more.

"Evangeline. Funny running into you."

The line was so lame that Drea thought he was working a con on the woman, though she couldn't imagine why he wouldn't run his usual Casanova game to get a girl.

"You wouldn't happen to be here with any more last-minute evidence for another case, would you?" she asked, leading them all away from the line and farther into the atrium.

"I'm not here in an official capacity. Just wanted to drop my kid sister off at Justice Academy. This is Drea."

Kid sister? Now Drea saw what was going on. Evangeline wasn't just a conquest. Damon *liked* her, and apparently when he actually liked someone, he became as nervous around them as she did. This was going to be fun, especially since Drea got the impression his crush would not be an easy catch.

Evangeline may have looked young, but it was clear she was all business, and not just from the firm handshake she'd given Drea, or the suit and briefcase. She had that same thing Xavier had, that presence. Her eyebrows were perfectly arched, and she had that looks-natural makeup thing down to a science. It was all Drea could do not to ask her for hair tips. Evangeline's hair was far curlier than her own, kinks and coils springing from her head in defiance, and yet they looked as polished as her expensive suit.

"I have a summer job tutoring," Drea added in case the woman got the wrong idea from Damon's incomplete introduction.

"Well, I'm glad you're here as a tutor and not a student. I'll be handling some of the DA's juvenile cases, and I wouldn't want to ever have to prosecute you," she said to Drea, but she was looking at Damon the whole time. "I'd better get to court. Nice meeting you, Drea. Try to keep your brother out of trouble."

Damon stared at Evangeline until she boarded the elevator.

"She's cute. Totally your type."

"I don't have a type."

"Yeah, you do. You like them when they don't take any crap from anyone, especially from you. I can tell she won't."

"She clerked for one of the judges a couple of summers. I knew her when I interned with Claiborne, and that was it," Damon insisted, blushing.

That was new. Her brother was Mr. Smooth when it came to women, and because he was so charming, almost all of them were willing to take his crap. Clearly there was more to this particular woman than he was letting on.

"All I'm saying is I think your crush is mutual."

"It's not like that. Besides, crushes are for kids. I'm a grown man." Now that Evangeline was long gone, he was back to his usual cocky self.

"Well excuse me, *grown man*. And what's up with the 'kid sister' thing? You never call me that."

"What?"

"Oh, I get it," Drea said, putting it all together. "She's a lot older than you."

"Two years. Not that much older."

Drea spotted Xavier coming through the security line just then. She turned her back to him, hoping he hadn't seen her. He already knew about Damon, but she didn't want her worlds to collide by having them meet again. Maybe Damon wouldn't even remember Xavier. It had been almost a year since their little run-in at the fund-raising party.

"Okay, you had your accidental meet-cute with me as your prop. Shouldn't you be going now?"

Apparently Xavier had noticed her after all, because he made a point of walking past them and saying hello. Fortunately, he kept on moving.

"Is he the reason you didn't want me to come inside?" Damon asked.

"What? No way!" Drea hoped her protest wasn't too much, and added, "He's just one of my tutees."

"I saw the way he looked at you. Justice kids aren't all bad, but if you're talking to some dude, I'd rather it not be an ex-con."

Drea was relieved Damon didn't recognize Xavier as the valet who'd ticked him off at the party last summer. There couldn't be that many Asian guys named Xavier running around Magnolia, so she hoped Damon wouldn't remember the valet's name was the same one on the B&E arrest sheet, either.

She was heading for Judge Claiborne's class—ten minutes early thanks to Damon having to stalk the cute lawyer—when Xavier sidled up alongside her all stealthlike. He didn't say anything until they had reached the hallway leading to the court/classroom.

"Did you tell your brother about our conversation?"

"I can't believe you really think I set you up," Drea whispered even though the hall was empty.

"We need to talk. In here," he said, holding open a door that led to a rarely used stairwell.

As she passed through the doorway, she felt his hand on the small of her back, but only for a second, as though he'd thought better of it. This boy really knew how to take some liberties, though she had to admit she was a little excited by the thought of . . . well, whatever he intended doing once they waited for the air-spring door to close completely. Still, she held her position right next to the door while he leaned against the stair railing.

"It's mostly Jason who thinks that." He stared at her, hard. "He kind of hates you."

"Yeah, I sensed that. Are you saying you don't believe I set you up, because if I remember right—and I do—you also threatened me and my brother."

"Jason believes it. Since he's the one who can rain down all kinds of cyber wrath on you, he's the one you need to convince."

"You didn't answer my question," Drea said, staring back at him just as hard. She had a strong feeling he was about to tell her a lie, but then he pulled it back.

"No, of course I don't believe it. But I do need your help. The DA showed probable cause at my hearing yesterday, so I'm going to trial."

"Oh wow, I'm so sorry," Drea said, and meant it.

"Not like I didn't expect it, right?"

It was true, she had expected it too, given his record and what she remembered of Damon's arrest. But hearing Xavier's

167

news that he might spend the next who-knew-how-many months—or years—in a cell was too much. She felt both heartbroken and guilty.

"Hey, now," he said softly, stepping closer and brushing a wayward curl from her face, "I'll be okay. I have a great lawyer and—"

Drea backed away. "No, it's just . . . I'm just wondering how I or my brother can help, that's all."

"No, that isn't all. I'm a thief—a *reformed* thief—and good thieves can read people. You and I have that in common. You're hiding something about that night, but being a snitch isn't it. I hope you trust me enough to tell me what it is." He stepped right up to her then, his face so close to hers she thought he might...but he didn't. He only said, "But if you don't, I'll figure it out eventually."

Then he opened the door and stepped back into the hall. So did Drea—after she took thirty seconds to compose herself—and followed him into the classroom. He'd already taken his seat in the back row next to Jason. He smiled at her as she entered the room. She looked away, but was certain his eyes were still on her as she stood behind the podium and pretended great interest in the tutoring schedule she was going to discuss before Judge Claiborne began his class.

As she explained her availability during each grade's study hall, Jason stared her down, so she focused on him instead of Xavier. She wanted Jason to know she would not be intimidated by him, that he couldn't just Bogart his way into her house any old time he wanted. But he was also the easier boy to deal with right now, despite the death rays he was shooting her.

Until she realized that Xavier had been only partly right. They were both good at reading people, but no one could read a liar the way she could. She'd been honing her gift since she'd learned she had one. How many times could she have told on the real culprits of some playground offense and saved herself trips to the principal's office? She never did. Jason was wrong. She was no snitch, though she could have been a damn good one if she wanted.

So while she knew Xavier had told the truth about not believing she'd set them up and that he'd eventually figure out what she was hiding, what he didn't know was Drea had detected he was hiding something too.

21

Wednesday, 11:55 p.m.

During lunch, Drea was waiting for a taco salad from the food truck parked along the north side of the justice center when Xavier appeared beside her. She thought it odd the way he crept up on people, magically appearing from nowhere, until she remembered his criminal specialty.

"So I guess you really are going to stay."

"I made a promise to my brother and the judge. Once I make a commitment, I keep it, no matter how unpleasant it is," Drea said.

"It could be worse. You could be one of us."

"One of you?"

"A Leaguer, a student here." He paused a second to place his order before explaining, "That's what we call ourselves. You know, like the Justice League?"

"You guys are the exact opposite of the Justice League."

"My point is, we don't get to decide whether we'll be here or not. It's this or the detention center."

When their orders appeared in the window at the same time, Xavier invited Drea to join him. Considering she'd held out on him about Damon being a cop, Xavier seemed pretty forgiving. Certainly more than she'd have been in the same situation.

"No, thanks. I want to work on my tutoring schedule over lunch."

"You can't avoid us forever," he said, nodding in the direction of the park across the street, where she recognized Jason, with his mass of blond curls, sitting at a table. Xavier grabbed both their orders and started heading that direction. "I have your food. You have to follow."

Drea did follow, moving on her crutches as though she'd always used them. As in most things she attempted, she'd mastered them quickly.

"Why'd you bring *her?*" Apparently, Jason could hold a grudge longer than his friend.

"She couldn't carry her food and use the crutches at the same time," Xavier explained as he pulled food from the bag.

"That's not true. I could have put it in my backpack," Drea said, but Xavier didn't seem to hear her.

"Aw, man," he was saying. "They screwed up my order. I asked for chicharrónes and they gave me chicken. Jason, play nice while I go fix it."

Jason turned away from her, stretching his legs out along the length of the bench and looking out into the park. Drea didn't want them to be alone any more than he did. The last time it had happened was when he broke into her house. She sat across the table from him anyway and said what she'd been wanting to say since he'd threatened her and Damon the day before.

"You can't actually believe I called the police that night. Why would I? You were in there doing me a favor."

"*X* was doing you the favor." He sounded angry, as though he'd been waiting just as long to have this conversation, but he still wouldn't look at her. "I don't know your reason, but it had to be you. We were working a job. We were careful. Four minutes passed between when you left us and the police caught us. Someone who knew we were there called the cops and told them right where we'd be. They came straight for us."

Drea didn't admit that she was still there when the cops nabbed them, up on the hill behind the school, watching. She didn't tell him about the tipster across the street. But Jason had it exactly right.

"If you were still inside when the cops arrived, how do you know they went straight for you?"

"I mean, I know it's dead in Peachland and the cops have nothing to do, but how are they gonna show up, get inside the school, and come right to us in only four minutes?" Jason asked. "Were they just hanging around on the next block, waiting for a crime to happen at Woodruff?"

She had wondered the same thing, but Drea wanted to stay focused on the part where she had nothing to do with the police finding them so easily. "If I set you up, why would I bond Xavier out of jail?"

"I don't know. Guilt, maybe. If I hadn't come to your house—"

"*Broken into* my house . . ." Drea reminded him.

"Whatever," he said, turning toward Drea but still refusing to look her in the eye. "If I hadn't planted the idea, would you have helped him?"

It was useless to argue. Jason had made up his mind about her the night of the B&E. It wouldn't matter if she explained that of course she wouldn't have known Xavier needed to be bonded out if Jason hadn't told her.

"Jason, I know you hate me, so I'm especially grateful you didn't out me to the cops. I'm sure you wanted to."

"I don't narc, at least not until I met you," he said, picking at a splinter of wood that was fraying from the table. "I sure as hell wanted to bust you."

"Well, thanks for not."

"I didn't do it for you," Jason said.

She turned around for a second to look in the direction of the food truck. "You and Xavier are pretty close."

"I'd do anything for X."

Drea wasn't sure if the *anything* he was referring to was not snitching on her, or helping Xavier break into the school. It was already clear who ran the partnership, so she assumed Xavier had been hired for the job they kept talking about that night, and he subcontracted the tech part to Jason.

"You've been working together awhile?"

"Not until the other night. Even though I'd asked a million times, he'd never let me work with him. Said he didn't want me caught up in all that, though he never really explained what 'all that' meant. The school job was the first time he ever needed me. He didn't have to ask twice."

"You guys seem so close. Did you grow up together?"

"You could say that."

Jason stopped picking at the splinter and looked at Drea for the first time since she sat across from him. He was gangster at staring down people from the back row of a classroom, but up close and personal, the only person she'd ever seen him look in the eye was Xavier. Maybe she'd been wrong in her conclusion that, if Xavier weren't around, Jason would defer to no one. Even when he'd broken into her house, he had avoided her eyes. Until now, he had either stared past her or around the park. Drea knew he was only looking at her now to either check her reaction or figure out whether he could trust her.

"Last year, we landed in juvie on the same day and we did a whole lot of growing up while we were in there. We had to. Xavier had been in before, but it was my first time inside and I was already piss-myself scared just being there. These guys were about to give me a beat down just for the hell of it until X stopped them."

"What did he do?"

"What do you think? He sure as hell didn't debate his way out of it. Juvie ain't the Woodruff School. X is seriously badass," Jason said, looking past her again. "I know you like him, but don't let his game fool you. And don't think you're the only one he's running it on."

Drea ignored his implication and asked, "What did you go in for?"

Jason looked up at her for the second time, but now he was smiling. Another first.

"Oh man, it was a righteous score. I hacked into the system all the travel agencies use, got some round-trip tickets and luxury hotel rooms for me and nine of my closest friends."

"To where?"

"San Diego. Comic-Con."

Drea almost laughed at the cliché of it, but didn't interrupt Jason's story.

"One idiot couldn't keep his mouth shut, had to brag about how he didn't pay a dime for his first-class ticket or his penthouse suite because his friend was the best hacker on the planet. He was right about that last part, but the rest fucked me up. Got me arrested."

"Hey, I got us free food."

Xavier had returned and, as usual, she never even heard his approach. But she now saw him in a different light. Despite his warnings, Jason had made her like Xavier even more. In the few minutes it had taken him to sort out his order at the food truck, Drea was certain his shoulders had become just a little broader, the muscles in his forearms more defined. And his smile, oh my God, she could just stare—

"What, is there something in my teeth?" Xavier said, putting down the taco he'd started on as he walked from the food truck, looking genuinely mortified.

"No, I um . . ."

"I told her how we met and now she thinks you're Superman," Jason said.

His comment threw Drea for a second. Clearly she and Xavier weren't the only ones at the table good at reading people. She should have expected it. It was a skill every con had better be at least decent at.

"Help me eat these fries they gave me for screwing up the order," Xavier offered.

He acted as though he hadn't heard Jason's assessment, but Drea noticed him smile a little, and now she was the one who felt mortified. She regained her composure by throwing the attention on Jason.

"There's something I've been wondering about. I had to volunteer in Woodruff's front office for three days before I could get a look at the registrar's password as she logged into the system. But you hacked my school account *after* you were released on bail."

"Yeah, so?" Jason asked, taking advantage of Xavier's offer and digging into the fries.

"If you can hack the system from the outside, why did you even need to break into the school?"

"We didn't just hack the system," Xavier said.

"There was another reason to be there?"

He didn't answer her question, just unwrapped his second taco.

"Being inside made it easier to hack," Jason explained around a mouth full of fries. "I didn't have time to break down the firewall."

Drea wasn't sure she believed Jason's explanation, but asked, "Why not? Was the whole crime just a spur-of-the-moment whim?"

"No, not a whim," Xavier said. "A *job*. We told you that already. My . . . the client gave us zero notice."

Drea thought about this as she stabbed at her taco salad without actually eating any of it. Being falsely accused by Jason had ruined her appetite.

"Couldn't you have just told the client to go to hell? How much did he pay you? I hope it was worth it, or at least enough to cover your legal fees. I don't imagine that lawyer I saw you with is cheap."

Jason bristled. "You got a lotta nerve getting all righteous on us. Better watch your step or I'll—"

Drea didn't get to hear Jason's threat because Xavier cut him off.

"Oh, so it's okay for us to get busted doing your dirt, but you're judging us for being there to do someone else's? Don't worry, you'll get your bail money back."

"That's not what I meant. And you don't have to pay me back," Drea said before realizing she had just copped to posting his bail.

Xavier angrily crushed a food wrapper into a ball. "Grab the fries, Jason. Let's find another table," he said as he stood to throw the paper ball into the trash can a few feet away. His shot landed perfectly.

Drea stood too, and grabbed his arm. He looked down at her hand, and it was clear from his expression that touching him was something people didn't do, even though he'd had no problem touching her more than once. She let go.

"You guys misunderstood what I was trying to say. Give me a chance to explain myself better, will you?"

Jason was about to protest, but a quick look from Xavier stopped him, and they all took their seats again.

"About what you guys want me to do. Let's pretend I can actually help you. I need a little background information."

"Like what?" Jason asked.

"I need to know everything about that night—why you were there, who hired you for the job. You said there was a client. High school kids, even those with a record, don't generally have *clients*. Unless they're drug runners or in a gang, juvie criminals commit crimes for themselves—they want the clothes or the car, so they steal them. They need to get high, so they jack somebody for their meth." Drea paused, then added, "Or they're hungry, so they steal some food."

"Let on you know her brother is Five-0 and she starts sounding just like one," Jason said, actually looking a little amazed.

"We're not exposing our client," Xavier said after finishing his second taco. "Or our business, for that matter."

"Then how am I supposed to help you if you won't tell me anything?"

"I liked you from the start," Xavier said, "but trust is earned. Even then, con artists generally trust no one, especially not another con."

"Especially not one with a cop for a brother," Jason added. "Unless . . . is your brother dirty?"

"Didn't you hear me say he's fresh out of police school? Of course he isn't dirty—he hasn't had time to be," Drea said, certain they could hear the lack of conviction in her voice. She knew Damon would never be a dirty cop, even if he did cover up her involvement in the B&E. That was different. That was family.

"So you're saying he has the potential of being dirty, given a little time or incentive," Jason said after noisily drawing on his straw to get the last of his soda.

"No, that is not what I'm saying, and could you please keep your voice down? What I'm saying is my brother isn't dirty, and I'm not a con."

"We don't care how you get the job done, we just need to know you're going to do it. Otherwise . . ."

Xavier didn't complete his threat, but he didn't need to. Both boys remained quiet. It was one of the oldest tricks in the book—using silence to give the mark some time to think about the consequences of going along with the con or not. How could she possibly be crushing on a guy who'd blackmail her? Xavier was so smug, thinking he knew her well after only a few days. She would never admit that he had called her right on just about everything, including being a criminal at heart, even if she'd never actually done a job. It was in her DNA, just like green eyes and high cheekbones. She'd also never admit that in spite of the whole blackmailing thing, he would still be the last thing she'd think about before she fell asleep that night.

22

Thursday 7:49 a.m.

Now that she had her tutoring schedule posted and had met with the science teachers to learn more about what each of her tutees needed, Drea didn't really need to show up at school until the first study hall of the day, which didn't happen until second period. So she surprised herself when she arrived by first bell, in time to join Judge Claiborne's class. When he announced who would be giving this week's show-and-tell Thursday talk, she was glad she came.

"Today's speaker has managed to avoid giving his talk for months, claiming illness, family emergencies, or conning other students into switching their scheduled dates with his," the judge explained, drawing some laughter from around the room. "Okay, everyone, remember the rules: no interruptions and no judgment."

As Xavier replaced Judge Claiborne at the front of the

room, Drea noticed a sheen of sweat on his forehead despite the overly air-conditioned room. The sheet of paper he was holding—freshly ripped from his spiral notebook (everyone heard him do it) just before he walked up to the podium—trembled slightly in his hands. He cleared his throat several times. For the first time since Drea had met him, he was not cool and collected. In that moment, he was no longer a masterful con artist. Drea felt his discomfort, even felt a little bad for him, but she was eager for him to begin. Finally, she was going to learn something true about Xavier Kwon.

I was born in South Korea, came here when I was seven grew up on the south side of Atlanta, always broke because my father had a chronic illness that made it hard for him to keep a job, so I learned how to steal. When I was ten, eleven, something like that, he got sick enough he had to stay in the hospital for a few months. It was just me and my dad. My mother died when I was, like, a toddler or something—long before we even left Korea. A lot of you know how it is when you first come to this country—either you already have family here or you join a church or a community center with other immigrants and you make yourself a new one.

Not us. Atlanta is full of Koreans, mostly on the north. That's why we lived south—my father didn't want people in his business so he kept to himself. That's just how he was. I didn't have any family in the States, blood or made, so when my dad went into the hospital, Social Services fostered me out to some rich people who wanted to help a poor kid. I found out they really didn't, but I gave them something to talk about at their dinner parties, when they'd trot me out for five minutes, long enough for their guests to ooh and ahh over their good deed, before they'd send me back to my room.

But it was cool because they put me in their neighborhood school for a semester—no way were they driving me twenty miles south to my old school. That's when I began stealing for a reason other than need. For the first time I could remember, I didn't need anything other than my dad to get better.

I stole stuff like skateboards and bikes, things I'd never have stolen in my old neighborhood from kids like me, the ones who lived in the projects or close enough to them that they may as well have been project kids. They never had anything worth taking, anyway. I only hit the kids I thought deserved it. The assholes who had so much they didn't even care whether they lost something since Mom and Dad would just score them another one, a bigger and better version of whatever I took. It never failed. I'd lift their bike, and the next week they'd have an even better one for me to steal a month later. Then I'd take the bus to a more middle-class neighborhood, find playgrounds, sell what I stole.

After a while, I ran out of customers. You can only hit so many playgrounds so many times before people start suspecting maybe this isn't really your stuff you're selling, even if your customers are kids. So I moved on to shoplifting or stealing things off people like wallets and watches. I mostly worked in Buckhead because I figured those people had plenty. Losing a few hundred dollars wouldn't keep them from making the rent.

It wasn't like I used the money to buy games or concert tickets or stupid shit like that. Most of it went to helping out my dad with the bills. He came home from the hospital that first time, but he was on disability and it barely covered food and rent, much less the doctor bills Medicaid didn't cover. My dad never asked any questions about the money. I told him I helped out at this market after school, just to make him feel okay about it, but he knew the deal. For one thing, I was like . . . twelve. In the projects, even when you try to stay under the radar, everybody knows everybody's business like one huge dysfunctional family, so there's no way he believed I was working at some market even if he was too weak to leave the apartment to verify it.

Then he died, and I went into foster care permanently. My next foster family wasn't rich, but they had enough money to pay the bills without my contribution, not including the monthly check they got from the state for taking care of me. I kept stealing, though. That's when I had to admit I didn't do it for some noble cause like I'd kept telling myself. I stole because I liked it, liked the thrill of not getting caught. That's something I could never figure out. Rich people steal for the thrill, broke people steal for a living, but I've never been rich, so go figure.

Xavier stopped his story there and walked back to his seat. Drea had thought he was going to talk about the arrest that took him away from Woodruff and possibly her parents away from her, but apparently, that wasn't how show-and-tell Thursday worked. Students only shared why they took the wrong path, not the path itself. That was a story she'd have to talk him into sharing herself.

23

Thursday 9:15 a.m.

Drea was sitting in the small meeting room off the judge's chambers, which he'd designated for tutoring sessions until he could find better accommodations. The justice center had already given him a whole courtroom to use as a school, and as persuasive as he was, he hadn't yet convinced the facilities people to give him more space. He'd promised her it was a momentary problem. Not that Drea minded. The table was big enough to accommodate four students, which was probably the most she could effectively tutor at one time, anyway. But for her very first session, there would only be one student.

Tiana arrived just as the second-period bell buzzed outside Judge Claiborne's office. Drea had already begun to stop thinking of her as a member of the Green Girl Gang, not only because the girl had so much more to recommend her, like being a genius according to the judge, but also because neither she nor her gang had worn green since Monday. They all wore the same color each day of the week, but Tuesday it had been blue, and today, Drea had seen them all in different shades of yellow.

Drea had meant to start the session with something more professional, like asking Tiana which of the sciences was her favorite, but instead opened with, "So, you're really only twelve?"

"You really rich?" Tiana asked, but didn't wait for an answer. "Must be if you go to the Woodruff School. Wish I could go there. Then I know I'd get me a scholarship to college. Are those charms real gold? My friend Monique says they is. The minute you walk into the room, she starts fiendin' for 'em."

Drea realized Monique must be the girl who always looked at her like she was sizing her up and, Drea had assumed, figuring out a way to do her harm. But it turned out the girl wasn't interested in her at all.

"She wants my bracelet?"

"Oh, don't worry. Monique ain't no thief. She won't mess with you. She just looks scary because in juvie, you have to look scary or people will be all the time in your face. It ain't like she'll jump you for your bracelet or nothing. She just likes to set stuff on fire," Tiana explained matter-of-factly.

"That's . . . reassuring."

"Not random stuff. Just boys' stuff, when they do her wrong. At some point, they all do her wrong. At least, according to Monique. The last time, she stole this boy's backpack and lit it up on the sidewalk in front of his house. With all his crap in it and everything," Tiana said, pausing just long enough to realize an error in her assessment of Monique. "Hmm, I suppose she might steal, after all. But only in order to set it on fire, and she likes your bracelet way too way much to do that, so you're safe. I think."

Drea wondered how she was going to get a single word in with Tiana, much less enough to figure out what tutoring help she needed, but Tiana had that covered too.

"I brought this to show you," she said, pulling a book out of her bag and sliding it across the table to Drea.

"*Light and Lasers?*" Drea opened the thick textbook, which clearly was not obtained from Justice Academy or any other high school.

"I checked it out from the library. I'm really interested in the use of lasers to study the electron motion within molecules and atoms. I've also been reading about the Schrödinger equation—I'm not sure I really understand it, but it seems so fascinating."

Drea wanted to again ask Tiana if she was really twelve, but feared looking like an idiot in front of a genius because the judge's assessment was clearly accurate, except that thing about her operating at the eleventh-grade level.

"Wow," was all Drea could manage to say.

"I can't decide if I want to study quantum mechanics or optical science when I go to college. You think maybe I could study both?"

"If anyone could, it's probably you. And I don't think you

need a place like the Woodruff School to help you get a college scholarship."

"I don't need to know it for the exam to skip tenth grade, but will you help me with that equation and maybe the concept of wave function?" Tiana asked, truly expecting Drea could.

"I'm afraid you may be out of my league, Tiana. If anything, you should be tutoring me," Drea said, meaning it as a compliment, except the girl looked crushed, and then angry.

"So I'm wastin' my time messin' around with you," she said, struggling to return to her backpack the textbook that seemed about half her weight.

"I didn't say I couldn't help you. Well, *I* probably can't help you, but I know someone who can," Drea said. "My physics professor from Hathaway College is spending his fall sabbatical at Georgia Tech in Atlanta. I'm sure he'd love to meet you, but until then, I'll help as much as I can this summer."

"Seriously?"

"Seriously. But now I have a question for you."

Tiana took her seat again, but looked wary. "You want to know why I'm at Justice, right?"

"No," Drea answered, though it wasn't exactly true now that she knew the girl was brilliant. "But I'm wondering why you talk the way you do—at least when you aren't talking about electrons. Then, your grammar is perfect."

Tiana's expression suddenly turned about as hard as her friend Monique's when she'd stared down Drea on her first day, but only for a second. Now Drea could see the twelve-year-old behind the bluster.

"It's what I know."

"Yeah, but it isn't all you know. Why switch back and forth?"

Tiana looked at Drea as though she was carefully choosing her next words. "I talk the comfortable way with my family. I talk the other way around people who might judge me."

Drea was about to protest, to explain she only wanted to understand, but decided against it. Maybe she still had lessons to learn.

"Besides, I don't want them saying I'm stuck-up and trying to act white. They already think I'm trying to be better than them because I want to try for a science scholarship and go to college."

"Whoever 'them' is, they're wrong. Grammar isn't a race thing. It just is."

"Maybe when you're rich. I bet you live in a mansion on a street full of white people," Tiana accused. "You don't know anything about it."

"I know the great thing about language is you don't have to be rich or white to own it."

"Maybe," Tiana said, leaning back in her chair as she seemed to consider what Drea had said. "But where I'm from, words—the wrong words—can get you hurt. They won't like me if I act all sadity like you."

"Who won't like you?"

"Monique and Sharon. That's my other friend. Not friends—more like family. They're the only one I have. That's why we always wear the same color, so people know we're family and not to mess with one of us or you mess with all of us."

"Where's your real family?"

"I told you where my *real* family is," Tiana said, rolling her eyes. She was as good at doing that as she was at talking lasers. "But if you mean the people who disappeared when I was a little kid so eventually I'd have to live in a group home with my *real* family, then I have no idea."

"Real family should like—no, love—the *real* you, no matter who you are," Drea said, immediately feeling both like a fraud and as though she'd found a kindred spirit. "You may be underestimating Monique and Sharon."

"You think?"

"I do. You should give them a chance."

"Sharon does like to read a lot. She writes the best stories. Maybe she's only faking like it ain't cool—*isn't* cool—to sound stuck-up like you."

"Probably," Drea agreed, ignoring the stuck-up comment. "The judge told me every kid at the academy is here because they excelled in school before they got into trouble. Your friends may not be future Nobel Prize winners in physics like you, but I bet they're hiding some of their smarts from you, too."

"Maybe so," Tiana said, but didn't sound convinced. "Well, I guess if you can't tutor me, I should just go back to study hall."

"You don't have to. We still have another twenty minutes left. You could tell me about the Schrödinger equation, and I can try to keep up."

Tiana laughed at that, but headed for the door, anyway. Before she left, she said, "It was books."

Drea looked at the girl, confused.

"The books at my old school were boring, so I stole some from the science section at the bookstore," Tiana explained. "See? Monique isn't the thief in my family—I am. That's why I'm at Justice. So why are you?"

Apparently it was a rhetorical question, or Tiana didn't care to hear the answer, because she walked out before Drea could give her one, which was just as well. Drea wasn't exactly sure she had an answer, but she was getting closer to one.

24

Friday, 8:03 a.m.

On Friday morning, not only had Drea stood her ground when Damon tried to veto her decision to leave the crutches at home (okay, she compromised and left *one* at home), she also refused to join the school field trip when he lectured her on being a team player. Drea had no intention of accepting Judge Claiborne's invitation to visit the county jail with the rest of the school, but she went to work anyway, despite having no one there to tutor. She told herself it might be an opportunity to start working on that project Xavier had assigned her, perhaps make some of those contacts he and Jason were convinced she had, but the truth was, she was beginning to enjoy her job. Or maybe she enjoyed who she could be at Justice Academy— her true self. No one, including the judge, had any expectations of her other than to be an excellent tutor. She didn't have to work at proving she was perfect or good. If she ever had the nerve to reveal that she, too, had criminal tendencies, the kids here probably wouldn't judge her. Without knowing it, they were teaching her to do the same.

Drea wanted Judge Claiborne to know she wasn't really the judgmental girl he'd met on Monday, or at least, that she was working on not being that girl, which was why she was holding a basket of muffins when she arrived at his office door. When the judge's assistant motioned her into his office, Drea was surprised to see a girl from Woodruff, star of the drama club, sitting in the chair across from him. The judge really was trying to turn Justice into a normal school if he was bringing in an acting tutor. Of course, she could just as likely be there as a student, considering the first time they'd met, the girl had been trying to steal Drea's jewelry. It was very likely she *had* stolen the chinoiserie box she'd kept the jewelry in, though Drea had been in no position to tell that to the police when they'd come to her house to take a report.

"I didn't mean to interrupt—I just wanted to give you some homemade muffins, Judge Claiborne."

"I thought you weren't coming today, but your timing is perfect. This is Gigi, and she's joining us for a while, but the rest of the school has already left on the field trip. Since you're here, perhaps you could keep her company and fill her in on where the senior class is on the syllabi."

"Um, okay, I suppose I could—"

"I don't need a babysitter," Gigi interrupted. "I know the drill."

"Of course you know what's expected of you here," the

judge said, "but it's always nice to have a friend in a new place. I understand you both attended the Woodruff School. Do you know each other?"

"Not really," she answered before Drea could. Gigi was watching Drea the way a boxer sizes up his opponent before the start of a match. "We didn't run in the same circles."

"No, I don't imagine you did."

Drea read the meaning in the judge's words, and understood that their academy roles had just been cast. Gigi definitely wasn't there as a tutor. Playing the thief's friend wasn't what Drea had hoped to gain when she walked into the judge's office, but she figured this was better, doing him a favor.

It was probably a small thing to the judge, but it meant he owed her something, even if he probably forgot about it the minute she and Gigi walked out of his chambers. And it wouldn't be a small favor, Drea was already certain.

"What happened there?" Gigi asked, wagging a finger in the direction of Drea's walking cast and crutch.

"I fell."

"I figured that. *How* did you fall?"

"Not much of a story. I was running down the stairs, turned my ankle—fell."

"You're right. That *is* a lame story."

A couple of cops were walking toward them, and Drea moved behind Gigi, single file, to give them room. Drea noticed Gigi change her stride slightly and toss her hair a couple of times, treating the corridor as though it were her runway. It worked. She definitely got the officers' attention, even though they tried to pretend they hadn't noticed her.

"If it wasn't for the muffins, I wouldn't have believed it was you who walked into that office."

Drea didn't have to ask what she meant about the muffins.

"Since there's no class, I could use some breakfast," Gigi said, heading for the front door without asking if Drea minded the detour. She was supposed to be doing the judge a favor and putting him in her debt, not skipping out with Justice Academy's newest delinquent. When Gigi crossed the street toward the breakfast burrito cart, Drea reluctantly followed.

After Gigi placed her order, she turned to Drea, looked her over again, and said, "Top of the class. Most Likely to Do... well, All Things Good, I suppose. Who would ever think you'd be serving time, even if it's here. *Quite* shocking. But the muffins? Ever the teacher's pet."

Drea had finally escaped being cast as Little Miss Perfect, at least at Justice Academy. She wanted to set Gigi straight, but decided not to. It would be interesting to see if her own acting would be good enough to fool the drama-club queen, even if her "acting" was really just not admitting the truth. So she didn't correct Gigi's assumption, just followed her again, this time toward the park across the street after she paid the vendor and grabbed her burrito.

"Let's just get it out of the way, shall we? First off, the judge should have said I was *rejoining* the good folks at Justice Academy. I've been here before, pre-Woodruff."

"Why?"

195

"Men are so gullible, believing everything they read on the Internet. How is it my fault a few guys convinced themselves they were in love with me and offered to pay my way out of my war-torn country?" Gigi asked as they stood on the corner waiting for the light to change. As if to corroborate her story, a guy in a beater went by and called out "Hey girl!" to her, but for his trouble, all he got from Gigi was a lip curl of disgust. "Like I have time for losers in hoopdees."

"War-torn country? Ha, arrested for running a sweetheart scam and you call me lame. That one's older than my parents. But I guess if it ain't broke."

Gigi turned to give Drea her full attention. "You know more than you let on, *Miss Priss*, though I'm not all that surprised."

"Everyone at school thought you weren't around after midterms because something bad had happened to your family," Drea said, wondering what she meant by that last comment. "A couple of kids saw a cop car take you away."

"Nope. Turns out I was in *jail*." Gigi paused for dramatic effect, but when Drea didn't give her the reaction she was probably hoping for, she continued. "I started that rumor about my family. As I was being led away by the police, I managed to tell the drama club's resident busybody. I knew the *whole* school would hear the story by the end of the day. It helped that the officer who arrested me didn't use cuffs."

"You showed back up at Woodruff for the last week of class. How did you get clear of the charge?" Drea asked. The light changed, and they crossed the street.

"I didn't. My bond was eventually posted. Now I've been *indicted*, but I'm still out on bail until trial, on condition I'm enrolled at Justice until then. As for Woodruff, money and power make questions go away, I guess. No one asked about my six-week absence, though they said I'd have to *redo* the semester. They don't think the Magnolia County Detention Center's curriculum was on par with Woodruff's. A whole *semester* to make up six weeks, so now I won't graduate until December. Can you *believe* it?"

"Nope." Drea kept her answer short in an effort to keep Gigi talking. Maybe she'd divulge useful information about her involvement in the Peachland heist, or where all that money and power came from that got her back into Woodruff.

"What were you arrested for if you don't mind me asking?" The girl wouldn't mind. Anyone else would have begun to feel interrogated by now, but Gigi clearly loved talking about herself as much as she loved an audience.

"Turns out it's just as illegal to con people out of stuff as it is to con them out of money."

Gigi went quiet for a moment as they crossed the grass, heading for the picnic tables. She focused her whole attention on trying not to sink into the ground, still moist from a morning shower. Drea had already moved behind Gigi after she had tried to lean against her for leverage. It took some nerve to use as a crutch the girl who was negotiating the wet ground in a walking cast using an actual crutch. Drea found it comical watching Gigi tiptoe her way to the table, red soles flashing

197

with every step. Who wears five-inch leopard-print stilettos to school, anyway? Even if they are Louboutins.

"So your main line of work is grifting. After our first meeting, I'd only figured you for a thief."

"Oh, I have many talents," she said, having made it safely to the same table where Drea had shared lunch with the boys earlier in the week. "For one thing, I'm fluent in seven languages."

"Wow. That's a lot of languages," Drea said, feeling less impressed about the three she spoke fluently. "I was wondering what your superpower was."

"My what?" Gigi said as she stood on one foot while using a plastic knife to scrape mud from the shoe on the other.

"Judge Claiborne said everyone at Justice is here because they were brilliant in at least one school subject."

"Oh, you mean learning Mandarin, Russian, and Farsi? All that was for professional development. I'm not ethnocentric when it comes to young, rich, and gullible men. I'm all about equal opportunity," she explained before putting her hands on her hips and staring off into the distance, as though she were a model striking a pose. "But *this* is my superpower. I mean, look at me. Why *wouldn't* I use all this to get what I want? I can talk my way in and out of practically *anything*."

"Except an arrest, apparently. Twice."

"Touché."

"So what did you con someone out of this time around?" Drea asked.

Gigi didn't respond right away. Up to that point, Drea had

been surprised the girl was willing to talk so freely about why she was at Justice, especially considering she and Drea had said maybe ten words to each other the whole time they were at Woodruff, even though they'd had neighboring lockers.

Along with Xavier, and just as she'd promised at the back-to-school gala, Gigi had been the other new kid at Woodruff during the just-ended school year, though she had managed to make it almost eight months before returning to a life of crime, instead of two. Gigi had put a lot of effort into making friends when they'd run into each other at their adjoining lockers, which Drea never quite understood. That whole thing of catching Gigi in the act of stealing Drea's ring and jeweled comb kinda made friendship impossible. After a month of trying, Gigi had backed off. Unless she was on the stage, or flirting with some boy, she was mostly quiet at Woodruff and pretty much kept to herself.

It occurred to Drea that they had something in common, besides the criminal background. They both pretended to be different people. Of course, that's what grifters do, but Drea didn't get the feeling Gigi was 'on the job' right now. This girl who was so willingly telling Drea her story was a totally different person than the one she'd played at Woodruff, which made Drea wonder which was the real Gigi.

"Just a little trinket for my crush, although I hate that word—*crush*. Sounds so sad, doesn't it? Now that I think about it, the word is *entirely* apropos, because that's exactly what he did when I gave it to him. He crushed me."

Drea was about to ask what Gigi meant by a "little

trinket," but giving their history, she had a good idea. "Let me guess—jewelry?"

"I cased my mark for *two weeks*. Convinced him I was an investment banker, wore Fendi suits and carried a Louboutin bag to look the part, always on my phone pretending to make deals, as if Magnolia is just a *hotbed* of mergers and acquisitions. Even made sure I had an alibi for fifth and sixth periods—my drama and study hall teachers both thought I was cleaning out our *wreck* of a costume and set room," Gigi said, stopping long enough to take a bite of burrito before resuming her story. "Of course, I was the one who'd spent the last two weeks slowly turning it *into* a wreck so when I volunteered to clean it, the drama teacher was more than happy to get me a pass out of study hall, too. I got back with fifteen minutes left in sixth period and I was like a *madwoman* trying to make that place look like I'd been working on it the whole two hours."

"And after all that, he didn't like the gift?"

"No, he loved it, but couldn't accept it. Turns out it was *me* he didn't like, at least not the way I liked him. He said he was flattered, *blah, blah*, but the gift was too much."

As she talked, her hands doing as much talking as her mouth, Drea thought maybe it was Gigi who had been too much, like the way she had to put emphasis on at least one word out of every ten. She couldn't possibly talk like this all the time. It had to be a performance.

"After you told him how you really felt, did you stay friends?" Drea asked, her curiosity not limited to Gigi's story.

She'd been wondering if what they said was true about taking a friendship to the next level, especially when the friendship was new and tenuous at best.

"Would you believe he *dumped* me? Altogether—said he wanted no relationship of any kind."

"Wow, harsh."

"It *really* was, and I hated him *completely* for weeks. Sitting in a jail cell for something you did out of love, only for your love to throw it in your face, gives you a lot of time to grow a nice strong hate. But now I've forgiven him."

"Really? Why?"

"He did me a huge favor—*huge*—that made my life much easier than it could have been. He helped me get back into Woodruff. Did you feel that? I think it's starting to rain."

"I didn't feel anything."

"My hair *cannot* get wet. I have a date after school. You know, get back on the horse and all that." Gigi got up and started walking across the grass—more like picking her way across it in her cleatlike heels—toward the justice center. "Ugh, this stupid mud. It's ruining my shoes."

Drea followed her, despite not having felt a drop of rain yet. She wanted to ask if by "date," Gigi really meant *mark*, but decided that could wait for another conversation.

"Your crush goes to Woodruff? That's what you meant by power and money? His family must be on the board or he's crazy rich," Drea said, mentally running through the yearbook trying to figure out who the mystery man was. "Sounds like you might still have a shot with him if he was willing to do that."

"I know, right? But we agreed we work better as friends. At least, I *pretended* to agree. He's sort of the reason I'm here instead of in juvie. He posted my bail."

"That was nice of him, considering he'd broken your heart and wanted nothing to do with you."

"The way you say it sounds so *horrible*. It wasn't quite that bad, and we're friends again. *Just* friends. I don't love him anymore, but I don't *hate* him, either. Things work out in the end."

Drea wondered if that was true. Would she be as okay about it as Gigi if things worked out the same between her and Xavier? She'd find out soon enough if she didn't come up with a way to save him.

"You've had a tough time of it since you left Woodruff. You could still go to jail, and yet you seem pretty upbeat." Since the girl had begun telling her story, Drea had been wondering if she was on some kind of happy pills, because she truly seemed not to mind at all that her life was like a bad soap opera.

"Because I have *the* best lawyer in the world, and he says the prosecution's case is pretty weak. The evidence they *claim* they have against me is either make-believe or they planted it, because I don't leave evidence."

Drea lowered her voice as they entered the building. "But you just admitted that you—"

"Enough about me. I knew the *moment* we met you had a felonious side," Gigi said, a little too smugly. "That's why you didn't call the police on me like you threatened, had to protect your own secrets. So what did Miss Perfect do to end up here?" Gigi asked as they waited in the security line. "I've been *dying* to ask since you walked into the judge's chambers. I can't imagine I could come up with a script better than the truth, though I have my theories."

Drea ignored her question. "Based on what? You don't even know me."

"Don't like to talk about it, huh?" Gigi asked. "I can understand that. It must be hard to fall from grace."

"Who talks like that?" Drea said, suddenly angry.

"Like what?"

"'Touché.... Apropos.... It must be hard to fall from grace.' Who talks like that? It must be hard to forget you aren't onstage all the time."

"So sensitive. I guess you hate the Miss Perfect thing, huh?" Gigi held out her hand and said, "I suppose no one can call you that now that you're here. Truce?"

Drea shook her hand, but it didn't mean they were friends. Gigi hadn't told Drea a single lie as she recounted all the details of her grifting-for-love story, but that didn't mean she wasn't capable of it. Drea was just lucky she would be able to see right through it when Gigi finally did lie. In a way, *actor* was just a nice word for *liar*, and Drea had had enough of those in her life. She had seen Woodruff's winter production of *Taming of the Shrew* with Gigi in the title role. One thing Drea knew for certain—Gigi was a very good actor.

25

Saturday, 1:14 p.m.

If someone had told Drea a year ago that she might fall for a boy who'd blackmail her, she'd have told them they were crazy. But a year ago she hadn't known Xavier Kwon, she'd had the highest GPA in school without needing him to change her grades for her, and he hadn't yet saved her from being arrested. Now she just needed to get Jason to like her. Or to at least tolerate her. She didn't believe Xavier would actually follow through on his threat to tell Damon or the police that she'd been at Woodruff that night, but she had no doubt Jason would eventually.

He deferred to Xavier in almost everything, but Jason hated her as much as he worshipped his friend. After all, he had broken into her house and threatened her, something Xavier still didn't know anything about. She'd hoped by not telling Xavier about it she would score some points with Jason, but now that he knew Damon was a cop, he was back to being completely obsessed with Drea being the snitch. Jason had made it his mission to set Xavier straight about her.

But she wasn't going to let Jason or a possible guilty verdict for Xavier ruin whatever was starting to happen between them. By some miracle—okay, by some criminal karma—Drea had reconnected with Xavier and discovered he might like her, too. No way was she going to lose him again. She had no idea how she was going to save him from juvie for his third strike or prove she wasn't the one who set them up, even though she'd thought of nothing else since they'd given her the ultimatum. She decided to focus on the second part of the task—proving she didn't call the police on them—the easiest part. After all, the charges were legitimate—they had broken into the school and were caught in the act. How was she supposed to get them out of that? She may be the smartest person in her class, but even a genius couldn't disprove facts. It occurred to Drea that Xavier and Jason were pretty smart themselves, and for them to ask her to do this meant there must be facts she didn't know.

That was why she was in the back of Frank's cab the next afternoon, idling in front of a house that was the nicest one on the block. That wasn't saying much when half the houses looked abandoned with their boarded-up windows and front yards that were mostly weeds and dirt, along with the drug dealer who did a brisk drive-through business near the stop sign at the end of the street. The little green bungalow Frank parked in front of had a recent coat of paint, and every windowpane was accounted for and gleaming. Not only was there actual grass in the lawn, hydrangea bushes were blooming in front of the porch.

When he'd breached her alarm system and broken in on a sleeping Drea that day, Jason had told her about this house. It was the one his grandmother had offered up for his bail collateral, and the home she'd offered up to Xavier, at least part-time, anyway. It turned out Xavier's foster parents hadn't given up on him after all, hadn't sent him back to the group home as Jason had believed, but they were more than happy to let him crash at Jason's place this weekend. Their disappointment in him had made the past week awkward for everyone in the house, especially Xavier. He'd told Drea that, last weekend, after he'd returned home thanks to her posting his bail, they were too angry to even yell at him.

But now she was waiting for him to join her in the taxi. He was on the porch telling her nemesis something Jason didn't look too happy to hear—probably that he hadn't been invited. Drea was certain she could get more information about why they broke into the school that night and for whom if Jason wasn't there convincing Xavier not to trust her.

"Who is this guy, anyway?" Frank asked.

"Just a boy."

"They're never 'just a boy,' especially not in this neighborhood. Your folks know about this boy?"

Since Frank had become Drea's personal driver over the past week, he apparently had taken her loyalty to his cab as permission to act like a surrogate dad. She did like Frank, but mostly because he stayed out of her business. She didn't like the direction their relationship was taking.

"If my parents don't care, neither should you."

"I'm pretty sure they care."

"I'm pretty sure they don't." Drea met Frank's gaze in the rearview mirror, and she made sure her expression showed she meant business, and if he didn't back up, he'd be missing out on the nice tips she always gave him. It worked, because Frank didn't ask another question.

By then, Jason had been talked back into the house and Xavier was opening the door opposite Drea.

"A taxi?"

"I'm down to one crutch, but still can't drive," Drea said, pointing to her walking boot. "How are you? Are your fosters still angry?"

"I'm just giving them some space for a couple of days, but that's as much as I can stay away. My probation officer would go off if he knew I was spending the weekend at my accomplice's house."

Drea caught Frank's eye in the rearview just as he was about to turn around and give his two cents. He was probably planning to throw Xavier out of his cab, but she gave him another *don't mess with me* look and said, "Frank, do you know this area?"

"I sure do know this area, which is why I was saying—"

"Great. Can you take us somewhere close for lunch, something nice?"

"I can promise you food and close, but it won't be nice."

"That's not cool, Frank." Drea wasn't sure if this was also Xavier's neighborhood, but it was his best friend's. If she wanted to make Xavier trust her, the cabbie's comment was a bad way to start.

"No, he's right," Xavier said. "That's what happens when you go slumming, Drea." No one in the taxi said another word until Frank pulled in front of a place called Fat Daddy's Fish and Wings three minutes later.

26

Saturday, 1:20 p.m.

When the taxi pulled into the strip mall, Drea realized she was already familiar with the area, though she'd never been there until a week ago. Three doors down was the bail bondsman who took her two thousand dollars in exchange for Xavier's temporary freedom.

"Nice enough for you?" Frank asked, but didn't wait for a response. After Drea and Xavier got out of the car, he added, "I'll be waiting right here. Sit at the front window, miss, if you don't mind."

"What's up with Dude?" Xavier asked while he held the restaurant door open for Drea.

"Frank? He's okay."

"Exactly. Most people don't know the cab driver by their first name, and most cabbies don't act like they're driving Tony Soprano."

Drea smiled at that. She loved *The Sopranos.* They had something in common other than crime, even if it was a reruns-only TV show about crime.

Fat Daddy's Fish and Wings was the kind of place that made Drea suspect the owner was paying off the health inspector. The only scent she could detect, and it hit her the minute they got out of the cab and long before they reached the door, was hot grease that was probably older than she was. The menu behind the counter was handwritten on the kind of poster board she'd used for grade-school science projects, most likely a decade ago since the magic marker had nearly faded to illegibility. The poster boards had the same yellow glaze of grease that covered every other surface in the place. Three menu items were spelled incorrectly. No one was behind the counter to greet them when they came in.

They'd been standing there nearly a minute when a tiny old woman emerged from behind the wall the menus were hanging on. Clearly she wasn't Fat Daddy. The woman smiled when she saw Xavier, scowled when she saw Drea, then smiled again when she said something to Xavier in a language Drea didn't know but guessed was Korean since he'd told the class during his presentation that he was from Korea.

Since he'd immigrated to the States so young and spoke English without any hint of an accent, Xavier surprised Drea when he spoke back to the woman effortlessly, like he'd been speaking it his whole life, like it was his native language.

"She wants to know what you want."

"Just iced tea, please." Drea gave her order directly to the woman, who scowled at her again. She wondered if she'd

210

have had to go thirsty if Xavier hadn't been there to translate.

"You should order food."

Drea just wanted to start the conversation that was the whole point of this trip, so she looked over the menu again and ordered the only thing that wasn't fried. "I'll take the side salad."

The old lady did not approve, and told Xavier so.

"She says it's a *side* salad. You should order something else with it."

"I'd like it on the side of some fat-free dressing."

Now Xavier was scowling too. "Do you really think this place has fat-free anything?"

"Then just the tea."

The way the woman was giving her the evil eye, it was clear she'd understood every word Drea had said. She decided that unless the tea was somewhere behind the counter where she could see it being served, she wouldn't even be drinking that.

A few minutes later, as Xavier carried their tray to a table, Drea asked, "Okay, my turn. What's up with her?"

"Yeah, I don't think she likes you."

"She should join ranks with Jason." Drea propped her crutch against the wall behind her and took a seat in the booth. "What did I do to her? Does she know you?"

"Never been here in my life. She likes me because I speak the language. A lot of kids born here don't. Which makes her dislike you even more than she normally would, I guess."

"But why? Did I offend her by not ordering some fried grease?"

Xavier looked at her for a second, like he was trying to figure out what to say next.

"She thinks we're together, and you know...she's old school. A lot of the *halmonis*—the grandmothers—they aren't so progressive. I'm not supposed to be with a brown girl."

"It's only *lunch*," Drea said, ignoring the fact that if she could wave a magic wand, they really would be an *us*, except at some place other than Fat Daddy's. "And it was kind of rude of y'all to speak Korean, especially when she was giving me looks like she wanted to poison my drink."

"What makes you think it was Korean?"

The menu was all Southern soul food, but the old lady was Asian, so she just assumed...Had she made some kind of culturally insensitive assumption? He'd said in his show-and-tell that he was born in Korea, but maybe he was like Gigi and fluent in fifty million languages.

"I just thought, I mean—"

"Relax. You're right, it's Korean. I just wanted to mess with you."

"Why?" she asked, relieved she hadn't made some cringe-worthy faux pas but also not caring whether she sounded a little angry.

"Why what?" Xavier asked, shaking hot sauce onto his fish. Apparently he didn't notice that he, or maybe it was the old lady who was still behind the counter giving her the side-eye and probably cursing her, was beginning to piss her off.

"Why do you want to mess with me? Why are you threatening to turn me in and report my brother?"

"Report your brother?"

"I meant reporting *to* my brother that I was there."

Xavier put down the hot sauce and stared at her, the fish plate forgotten. "Hmm, I don't think that's what you meant at all."

"Look, I just don't get why you'd . . . that night at the school I thought we were . . . Never mind. If you don't believe me, then I really don't care whether you think I narced or not. I guess trying to talk to you was a mistake," Drea said, getting up to leave.

"Whoa, wait a minute." Xavier looked as embarrassed as Drea had a second ago. "You're right. I'm not a game player. Not usually. But you have me all messed up in the head and I guess . . . I guess I don't know how to handle it. Will you stay? Please?"

Drea looked at him, then out the window at Frank, who had seen her get up from the table and Xavier grab her arm. He was already out of his cab, but Drea waved him off and took her seat again.

"I know you didn't turn us in. I just needed a way to make you help me, and I figured a girl like you wouldn't give me the time of day."

"A girl like me?"

"A girl whose family can throw a party and the richest, most powerful people in town show up. The kind of girl who is friends with a judge and has a cop for a brother."

Xavier was being truthful with her. She wanted to be just as honest by telling him she wasn't the girl he thought she was. Most of Drea's energy was spent proving to the world she was superlative in all things, but she wanted him to know the real her. The first time they'd met at the valet stand, she'd put on her usual act, but that was before she fell for him. By the time they'd found themselves together at Woodruff the other night, both there to do something wrong, she longed to show him her true self, but didn't know how. He'd even made it easy for her when he said he knew that down deep they were more alike than different, but she was still keeping up the act. She was all those things he'd just said, but she wasn't Little Miss Perfect. Even being rich wasn't exactly true. What would he think if he knew her family had made their money by doing the same thing he and Jason did, just on a much grander scale? But she wasn't going to tell him, at least not just yet. Besides, she suspected he already knew, if not everything about her family, enough.

"But why hold out on me?" Drea said, focusing on the reason she'd asked him to lunch. "You committed the crime. You wouldn't ask me to help you avoid going to jail if there wasn't more to the story, if you didn't think there was a reason—a *legal* reason—for the charges to be dropped."

"Not dropped. Reduced maybe, at least down to a parole violation. I was so close—out of juvie, going to Justice, and I wouldn't even be *there* next year. My parole would have been over, and I could have done senior year at a regular school."

"Like Woodruff again?"

"No, probably Magnolia High. Woodruff...well, that was just a one-time thing."

Though she had a theory, Drea hoped he might explain what that meant, and how a boy like him—the complete opposite of the kind of girl he thought she was—had ended up there in the first place. But he didn't, and she didn't ask.

"But now I'm facing a whole new set of charges, another

214

trial, another sentence. The only good spot in all of this is I'm seventeen—at least, for another eight months—and still in the juvie system. That . . . and seeing you again."

Drea had been looking into his eyes the whole time he talked, trying to pick up any hint of a lie, and there was none. But his last sentence made her look away. If not for her brown skin the old woman had been hating on, he'd be watching her blush right now. Maybe he noticed it, anyway. She stuck with business and tried hard to ignore how warm she felt as she returned his gaze.

"If you want me to help you, tell me why you were at the school that night," Drea demanded.

"I can't. It isn't just about me."

Something else that made them more alike than different—they couldn't be honest with each other for the exact same reason.

"If I can help you, it helps Jason, too."

"It isn't just Jason, either. If I'd known this was all you wanted to talk about, I wouldn't have come. I thought you were worried about me."

"I was. And I also wanted to thank you for not telling the cops I was there that night. I don't think I ever told you how much I appreciate—"

"Stop thanking me, will you? I have something for you." He pulled something from his jeans pocket and placed it on the table between them. When he moved his hand, Drea was surprised to see her old phone.

"I thought I'd lost it that night. You found it?"

"Sort of."

Drea remembered how he'd pulled her close to him the minute they'd met, his arms around her shoulders, his fingers trailing down her back. "You *stole* my phone?"

"I'm a thief," Xavier said, as if that was enough explanation. When she said nothing, only glared at him, he offered more. "When I took it, I had no idea why you were at the school that night, didn't know anything about you really, except that... Well, let's just say I needed insurance."

Drea lowered her voice to a fierce whisper and leaned in. "Do you know how freaked I was thinking I'd dropped it and the cops had found it that night? I fell and sprained my ankle looking for it."

He punched something into her phone. "Listen," he said.

It took ten seconds of audio before she realized he'd recorded their conversation that night, but not that long to realize it implicated her in their crime. He was as good at extortion as her family was at stealing.

"But when? How? It has a password."

"I recorded you on my phone. Through the magic of Jason, the recording is now on yours. Proof not only that you were there, but that you recorded it yourself."

"I can't believe you would—"

"I won't. Take it. And don't worry about there being any copies, because there aren't. I erased mine, and Jason knows better than to use the copy I gave him against you."

"Why?"

"Because I want you to trust me."

Drea slowly slid her hand across the table and grabbed the

phone, snatching her hand back as though she was expecting it to be some kind of trap.

"The police must have heard it already, when they found it on you during your arrest."

"You'd think so," Xavier said. "I've been arrested a few times, and nothing about that B&E arrest was right. No pat down, no handcuffs. When I got to intake, they didn't confiscate any of my personal belongings, so your phone was never out of my possession. That's what I'm saying—someone set me up, and I think the arresting cops were in on it."

Drea thought about it for a second. "I thought it was weird that night how they went straight to your location. I could tell from the way their flashlights moved through the building."

"So you believe me?"

"I want to," Drea said. "Tell me whatever it is you're holding back."

"That would mean I trust you."

Drea wasn't sure why Xavier would care about her trusting him if he wasn't able to do the same for her, but she was going to let it slide—for now. Her parents were criminals, but she hadn't become one until recently, and even now, she was still playing make-believe. Despite what she'd learned from her parents about always keeping her guard up, she was still able to give people the benefit of the doubt, especially people who looked like Xavier Kwon and stayed on her mind 24/7. She got it. He was a true criminal, and it would take a while to earn his trust, especially after she'd held out on him about Damon being a cop.

So she told him, "It's okay if you aren't ready to tell me

who hired you, but you will eventually if you want my help."

"Why does that matter? It isn't like the client set me up—that would defeat the whole purpose of me being there."

"True, but it's like reading a book with pages missing. It won't make sense unless I know everything." When he appeared unmoved by her analogy, she added, "It's like planning a heist when you have only half the building's blueprints."

"Yeah, I hear what you're saying, but no."

"Okay, so tell me what happened to make you leave Woodruff?"

Xavier leaned back in the booth, arms crossed. "You already know."

"Juvie records are sealed, and I didn't hear a whisper of a rumor about your last arrest, couldn't glean the tiniest clue from Atlanta news reports or the *Magnolia Times* crime blotter. I'm not the only one with friends in high places because someone did a good job of keeping it below the radar, so I know you were arrested, but not why."

"Can't tell you that, either."

Drea stared at him and said, "Because that second arrest and the B&E are related, right?"

Xavier said nothing, just went back to working on his fish platter. Now she wished she'd ordered something after all. It would have given her something to do to fill the nothing that was happening between them. After a few minutes of staring out the window, and trying to smile the old lady into smiling back when she came over to check on them (it didn't work), Drea spoke again.

"If you can't talk about your client or your second arrest, can you at least tell me why you went to jail the first time?"

"I thought Jason told you."

"Jason only told me why he went in and how he met you there. Besides, that was for your second offense, the one that made you leave Woodruff." She almost added, *and me*, but it was still too soon for that. "It's only fair you tell me about your first time, since you know all about mine."

Xavier smiled and said, "Do I?"

"I'm talking about the school break-in. You were right about that being my first. So now you owe me the story of your first arrest."

"I suppose I can tell you that," he said, putting his empty basket on the tray and pushing it to the edge of the table. "This could take a minute. What about Frank out there?"

"He'll wait."

"If you want me to tell it like that, you have to agree to stay quiet until I'm done—no questions, no judgment."

He turned around and said something to the old lady, who'd been watching them the whole time, either because she'd had no other customers since they walked in, or more likely because she wanted to make sure Drea didn't get her clutches into the nice Korean boy. A minute later, she brought them refills on their drinks, even though Drea hadn't taken a sip from her first glass. Xavier thanked the woman, finished off his first soda, and began his story.

27

Saturday, 1:51 p.m.

I never planned the boost. It was totally random, mostly because I'd never stolen a car before, and by the time I was fourteen, I'd run out of new things to steal. I already told you—and everyone else at Justice thanks to Judge Claiborne—how I started out stealing bikes and stuff like that, and how I'd run out of places to sell my loot.

One day, I come up north to scope out Magnolia, looking for fresh hunting ground where no one knows me, when I see this red Ferrari. I'd never seen one in real life—not that many two-hundred-thousand-dollar cars show up in the neighborhoods I lived in. So something just comes over me and I have to boost it. I already know how to get into a locked car since I'd been stealing sound systems out of them for a while, and I'd been messing around with hotwiring—not taking the cars, just trying to see if I could start them. Nobody was as surprised as me when I got the car started on the first try, including the dude I stole it from.

It's my first car, I'm only fourteen, so while I was a good enough thief to steal it, I didn't know enough to steal it well. So I drive to the Promenade where all the really rich people shop, and park the car in a space right next to the valet car section because I figure no one will notice a Ferrari next to all those other fancy cars. I'm in the food court trying to figure out what to do next—it isn't the kind of thing you can take to a pawn shop—and this guy sits down at my table. He's a little dude, maybe five six on a good day, kinda old—like fifty or something. Like somebody's grandfather. So I'm thinking he's trying to cruise me. When you hang out in malls as much as I did, you learn that kind of thing happens all the time.

"Jesus, you're just a kid," he says. "Probably don't even have your license yet."

"Look perv, I'm not your average kid hanging out at the food court. Keep scamming on me and you'll find out," I tell him. It wasn't an idle threat, because I could handle myself even then. At least I could in a fair fight, which I could see this wasn't going to be when two more guys joined us, taking a position behind the guy's chair, on either side of him. They were the total opposite of Old Dude, and looked like twins except for their faces. Both over six feet, not much older than me, built like every minute that they weren't scaring people for Old Dude, they were at the gym overdosing on steroids between sets. All tatted up the neck like they didn't give a damn if anyone suspected they were trouble. Old Dude clearly wasn't some perv on the make. I look around the food court, trying to figure out if I'd be better off running or making a scene.

Old Dude smiles and says, "I don't doubt it. But what you can't do is steal from me and expect to get away with it."

I stared at the guy, trying to figure out if I'd ever boosted from him. I'd stolen a lot of wallets by then, but I don't forget a face, and his wasn't ringing any bells.

"When you steal a car, you have to disable the GPS if you don't want to be tracked. You have to check for security cameras around the car before you steal it. You don't do those two things, and people like me will find you and then people like my friends show up looking to hurt you."

"Look, man, nothing's wrong with the car. Not a scratch—everything is the way it was when I found it," I tell him, about to shit myself I'm so scared. "Check it out for yourself. It's in the valet section of the parking lot."

"I know where the car is. One of my men is delivering it to its owner in Florida as we speak."

"Aren't you the owner?"

The man leans in, lowers his voice, and says, "I was when you stole it. Some people flip houses. I flip cars."

"You mean you steal them and turn them around." I wasn't an idiot. But the guy already knew that.

"And now you will steal them for me."

"Who says?"

"The scary men standing behind me."

"So you're saying I steal for you and you don't hurt me?"

"No, I'm saying, work for me and I don't kill you." And I know he's not kidding. "No one will think twice about a kid hanging around a Ferrari who hasn't had his first shave yet. But me? I couldn't give a shit how old you are. The minute you stole from me, you became a man."

Not only wasn't I feeling like a man, I wanted to yell for my mother, and I barely remember her. It was all I could do not to cry like a baby right there in the food court. But it turns out he was right, even if I didn't know it at the time. I grew up right then and there. That was the moment I figured out there was no one left on the planet who cared about me more than I cared about myself. So I went to work for him. Not like I had a choice or anything. My foster parents were cool enough, but from that point on, they became part of my cover. They made me look like a regular high school freshman, and no one knew my extracurricular activities included boosting high-end cars on the weekends.

It was going pretty well for about six months. I'd probably stolen a few million dollars' worth of cars by then. Old Dude had taught me a lot—and no, I'm not going to tell you his real name. How to case the right car, the right getaway route, what to do if the owner caught you in the act. We worked in pairs, and there was always a lookout with me while I got through the security systems, disengaged the GPS, and got the cars started. The whole process took under a minute, but we weren't about hurting people or getting arrested, so we'd walk away from a mark before we'd hurt him.

But some of the marks weren't just regular rich assholes. Some were bad guys, worse than us, and I had to know how to handle myself. By then, I was already a big kid, five eleven and one seventy-five, all muscle. My father was old-school. When we were still in Korea, he made me learn tae kwon do from birth practically. I was a natural, so good that, by the time I'd talked my first set of fosters—the rich ones—into sending me to the best dojang in Atlanta for some formal training, the instructor classified me as a black belt even though I was still a kid. So when kids stepped to me talking some stereotype bullshit, they were always surprised to find that in my case, the stereotype was truer than they'd ever hoped. But Old Dude taught me how to apply my martial arts class-learning to the streets. Less Karate Kid, more mixed martial arts cage fighting. For the whole six months I'd been working for him, I never had to use it, even though after six months of being a professional thief, I thought I was a badass, so I was actually hoping I'd get a chance to. Until the day I did.

My partner and I had cased this Tesla and thought it was the perfect mark: There was no dog and the house didn't have much outdoor lighting, but it did have a thick stand of trees on either side of it so nosey neighbors wouldn't see us. So I get to work, expecting to be out

224

clean in about thirty seconds like we always did, when I hear my partner say, "What the fuck?" We had a code word for abort because we thought it made it feel more like James Bond—and "What the fuck" wasn't it, but the way he says it, I know the whole thing has just gone bad. I get out of the car ready for whatever is about to go down, but it isn't anything I'd ever prepared for. I was expecting the car's owner had somehow sneaked up on us, or his security people, or maybe we had been wrong and the guy had a rabid Doberman.

But out of nowhere, two cops had appeared. They weren't security people. These were real Atlanta PD in uniform, which didn't make sense because we had cased the place and even if someone had made us, only a minute had passed between when we arrived at the mark's house and when these cops found us. I knew before the cop cuffed me that I'd been set up. That's what I'm saying—I know a set-up when I see one.

So I'm sitting in jail waiting for some public defender to show up. By then, I'd lucked into my second set of fosters. They weren't as cool as the ones I have now, but better than the Richie Riches because they actually gave a damn about me, even though I was doing my best to screw it up. But I'm expecting a public defender because I figure my understanding foster parents are probably going to draw the line at grand theft auto. Instead, this lawyer shows up who clearly doesn't work for the government. I know how to make a mark, and this guy's shoes alone cost a couple thousand.

"Maddox Cray," he says, taking the seat across the table from me, "but my clients call me Mr. Cray, and that's what you will call me."

"Did my foster parents hire you?" I ask, even though there was no way they could afford him. Even his name sounded expensive.

"No. I'm doing this pro bono."

You know how half the people in Atlanta aren't actually from here? This guy was not only a native but he had that Southern drawl only old-money Georgians have, the one actors try to copy even if they're playing a high-school dropout. You know—like they own the whole state or something and they're just letting you borrow a piece of it. And he looked like he may have been out of law school maybe a minute, so he had to be rich or powerful or both to have the attitude he did. He was big-time.

"Seriously, who put you on this case? It must have been Old Dude."

"Hardly. You need to forget about him and start saying you stole that car on your own, not in service to your boss." Cray goes quiet for a second before he adds, "Unless you plan on turning state's witness against him, which I'm here to advise you to do."

"Bust Old Dude? Hell no. If that's the kind of advice you're giving, I'll just take my chances with the public defender. You can call the guard, because you're done here."

"Look, you're not even fifteen, with no record yet

even though I know you didn't start stealing yesterday. That means you're a smart kid, smart enough not to get caught."

"At least not until yesterday. And even then, it was a set-up."

"It wasn't a set-up. The Feds have been building a case against your boss for nearly a year. They've been watching you."

"The Feds?"

My heart almost stopped when he said that. Felt like the room had suddenly gotten smaller. I had to stand up for that one to sink in. The guard came into the room, but Cray told him everything was fine. He was lying because absolutely nothing was fine about my world in that moment, but the guard went back outside and closed the door behind him.

"When you steal cars in one state and sell them in another, it becomes a federal case. I can tell from the look on your face you know exactly what that means."

"State juvenile laws don't apply."

"Exactly. That's why you need to turn for the Feds."

"I'm fourteen and didn't use physical force against anyone during the commission of the crime, so the Feds won't try me as an adult, even if the case is in their jurisdiction. Where's the incentive to snitch against a guy who might kill me if he found out?"

The lawyer smiles because I've just blown his mind with that legal knowledge I dropped on him.

"I knew you were smart, but that was truly impressive. With that kind of brain power, you know the deal I'm offering is your best bet."

I'd been pacing around the room that whole time since the guard went back out. I figured most lawyers wouldn't want their clients roaming around loose, but Maddox Cray wasn't the least bit afraid of me. I guess old-money dudes feel they run everything and own everybody, even in jail.

"Take a seat. I don't want the guard coming back in here."

I did what I was told and asked, "So I wouldn't get any time if I narc?"

"I'll see what I can do, but can't make any promises. Worst case, I can get you reduced down to a few months in juvenile detention, with a year of parole."

Cray looked at his phone like he had something better to do, but he just wanted to make sure I grasped that information before he told me the best case, knowing full well a few months in juvie wasn't the worst case at all.

After about a minute, he says, "Best case, you get no time and I get you into this second-chance high school they have here for kids like you. You picked the right county to steal a two-hundred-thousand-dollar car."

"And if I take my chances with a trial?"

He put away his phone and stared at me, making sure this next part really sunk in. "You could be an adult when you get out, or even get transferred into the adult system if the sentence is long enough."

"Can I think about it?"

"I don't know what there is to think about, given your options. But go ahead, think about it. Until tomorrow morning. That's when the offer expires," he says, then drops his card on the table before he leaves.

I called him before he could even get back to his office.

Drea had kept her promise and hadn't asked Xavier any questions while he recounted his story, but she had about a hundred of them by the time he finished.

"So you went to the Feds, then?"

Xavier took a few seconds to answer, and Drea got the feeling he still felt bad about turning on Old Dude even if the guy was a very bad person.

"Yeah, and I still had to do six months in juvie, but it was a lot better than what I'd have gotten if I hadn't turned."

"And this rich and powerful lawyer just decided to handle your case for free, out of the blue?"

"I guess I got lucky. That's what he told me that day—that he just randomly picked my case out of a huge stack only because he had to meet his firm's pro bono caseload quota."

Drea wasn't buying it. She didn't believe in that kind of luck. Her parents had taught her that luck almost never happened, and any con who relied on it would wind up in prison or dead. But she didn't sense that Xavier was hiding anything from her. So maybe he was the rare lucky one.

"So you did your six months in juvie, then went to Justice?"

"When Judge Claiborne sentenced me, I guess he saw something good in me. He was the first...since my dad. My last fosters and the current ones, they *want* to believe in me. I can't blame them if they really don't. But the judge, he didn't even give me the full six months, and after I finished my time in detention, I did most of tenth grade at Justice."

"And then Woodruff for your junior year? How did that happen?"

"I told you—I'm not going to talk about that," he said as he got up to take his tray to the counter.

Drea wanted to remind him that he said he couldn't talk about the arrest that made him leave Woodruff, not how he got there in the first place. But she was beginning to sound like she was interrogating him, which she was. And if she was being honest, she'd have to admit she wasn't doing it just to get background to help her figure out a way to help him. In truth, she just wanted to know. *Needed* to. But she wasn't going to find out today because instead of returning to their table, he stopped at the front door just long enough to tell her he'd walk back to Jason's house. By the time she'd gotten her crutch and managed her way out to Frank's taxi, Xavier was already out of sight.

28

Monday, 7:05 a.m.

Xavier had stayed on Drea's mind for the rest of the weekend. She'd known he was a thief, but hearing the details made it real to her, made it a lot less easy to romanticize. He stole from kids. He stole from rich people. Though he justified it by saying he needed the money for his dad, or that his victims were assholes, it didn't change the fact he was a crook, just like her parents. Except Xavier was probably more dangerous. At least her parents didn't deal with common street thugs. It was funny how all the people she loved walked on one side of the law or the other, dangerously close to the dividing line.

Not that she loved Xavier. But she did like him. A lot.

Since last week, Drea and Damon had already developed a morning routine: He made coffee, she made something her mother would have deemed too decadent for breakfast. This morning, it was from-scratch chocolate cupcakes with cream-cheese frosting she'd made the night before. Maybe it was the cupcakes waiting for her, or maybe it was Xavier finally telling her something real, but Drea felt almost happy, a first since her parents had left. She came downstairs without the remaining crutch, feeling out her ankle with just the boot. It took her a bit longer, but she could tell that once she got used to it and gained confidence that she wouldn't keel over without it, she'd soon be moving faster.

She and Damon ate while reading the local paper, something they thought so old-fashioned every time their parents renewed the subscription. Maybe they did it because Peachland was the first time they'd stayed anywhere long enough to renew an annual subscription. But she hadn't decided whether she and Damon had adopted the habit because it truly was a better way to read the news, as opposed to reading it on a three-inch screen, or because it was a way to keep their parents in the kitchen with them every morning.

"You think we're turning into those siblings you read about who never leave the house they grew up in, never start their own families, and instead grow old together like some kind of weird married couple?"

Damon looked at her like she was crazy. "I don't know what your life plans are, but I've got a date tomorrow tonight."

"The girl you were trying to accidentally run into at the justice center last week?"

"Her name is Evangeline," Damon said after polishing off a cupcake.

"I thought you had a shift tonight. Do you plan on taking her to a donut shop during your break?"

"I've been on the force two months and haven't had a donut yet. We're having an early dinner before my shift starts."

An assistant district attorney who worked juvenile cases would be an asset if Drea was going to help Xavier. "I don't know if that counts as date-level dining."

"Yeah, you're probably right," Damon said, suddenly looking a lot less excited about his date. Normally he'd just brush off her teasing. He must really like this girl.

"So where are you taking her?" Drea felt a bit guilty for using Damon, but it was for his own good. He needed to make the most of this opening with Evangeline. "Pick the right place and even two o'clock can feel like a dinner date. Maybe L'Auberge? Or do they go dark between lunch and dinner? I'll check for you."

"Don't worry about it. She's taking me. You were right—it isn't officially a date—though I appreciate your interest in my love life, even if it's a little weird. She just wants to return the favor after I dug up some last-minute evidence that helped her win a case."

"I remember y'all talking about that during the accidental meet-cute. You left off an important detail of this story, Damon. She's using the old don't-want-to-ask-a-guy-out-so-I'll-tell-him-I-owe-him-one method of asking you out. It's a date, even if it's during an hour only senior citizens would hit the streets looking for a good time."

"So you think she's interested?" Damon said, looking hopeful.

"Totally."

He didn't say anything for a few seconds, and when Drea looked up from the paper, she found him staring at her.

"What?"

"You've already given up the crutches—almost a week earlier than the doctors said, by the way."

"They were annoying. I'm fine." She still couldn't drive because of the boot, but at least her bruised armpits would get a rest.

"Soon you won't need the walking cast anymore, and you'll be able to get yourself to the courthouse. I might miss this morning routine."

"See. I told you. Weird old sibling couple in the making."

Drea was quiet for a second, then figured it was a good time to ask one of the questions she'd been wondering about all weekend.

"Damon, is it true that if a local case becomes federal, that local sentences are superseded by federal sentences?"

"Now there's an abrupt change of subject. Where'd that come from?"

"Some kids at school. Hey, you're the one who made me work with a bunch of delinquents. I'm just trying to get to know them better."

"That sounds about right, but I can ask Angie tonight, if you want. She worked in her law school's juvenile justice clinic."

"*Angie* is it, now?" Drea said, getting in a last bit of teasing. "She's probably put a few of my tutees in jail."

"No, that case I found the evidence in is her first in juvie court."

Drea hoped Damon's date went well tomorrow, and not

just because her brother was obviously smitten. Angie could prove a useful contact in her efforts to help Xavier, even if she still had no clue how she'd prove a guilty boy innocent.

Drea had Damon drop her at the courthouse fifteen minutes early to advance that very cause. She hoped her brother would soon score an ally in the prosecutor tomorrow, and in the meantime, she would work on Xavier's trust issues. Last Friday, Judge Claiborne had announced he had a schedule conflict and wouldn't be available to teach his class Monday morning. Despite a unanimous vote to start school late that day, he made it an extra study hall period instead. On the ride to work, Drea had sent a text to Xavier to meet her in the judge's chambers for an impromptu tutoring session. She was surprised when he actually showed up.

"I didn't think you'd come."

Xavier took a seat right next to her, unlike her first tutees last week, who had all sat on the other side of the table. She'd had to encourage them to move closer, but not Xavier.

In fact, he seemed especially close. Or was that all in her head?

"Why wouldn't I come? You're the tutor, and I could use some help with chemistry. I'm great in math, so the formulas don't give me any trouble, but—"

"Xavier—"

"I told you, my friends call me X."

"So we're friends now?" Drea said.

Xavier smiled. "I see what you did there. And I hope so. I did tell you my life story."

"Not all of it. That's really the reason I asked you to meet me."

He rolled his chair back away from her, and suddenly it seemed they were miles apart.

"Wait. Hear me out. You wanted me to trust you, right? Trust needs to be mutual, or I won't be able to help you."

Xavier didn't say anything, but he didn't leave the room, either.

"Believe me, I know how difficult it is for a con to trust people. You know that, because you know who I am, don't you? I mean, who I *really* am."

"You're Andrea Faraday, rich girl, socialite, member of one of Peachland's top families," he said, his face revealing nothing.

"The reason you can't tell me about the charge that took you away from Woodruff, or whether that arrest and the B&E are related, is because both are somehow tied to the big Peachland heist last summer. That's why you said you owed me when you offered to change my records."

For the first time since he'd walked into the room, Xavier didn't look her in the eye, and instead, crossed one leg over his other knee and began playing with the frayed hem of his jeans. "I don't know what you're talking about."

It didn't matter. Drea would know when he was lying even without that tell, but its existence still excited her. Xavier was a good con. That he even had a tell meant he had a difficult time lying to her.

Someday, she would get him to admit the reason he had a

hard time telling her lies when lying usually came so effortlessly to him, but right now, she needed to say what she brought him here to say, or she might chicken out. Discussing it before would have meant exposing her parents. But now, it might mean saving them, even if she didn't know what from. And she really did trust Xavier, even if he didn't trust her.

"If you were involved in the Peachland heist—"

"I was in the gym with you when that went down. You know that because you were watching me the whole time."

"You were watching me, too, but we both know that doesn't matter. Any decent criminal always has an alibi," Drea reminded him before she continued her thought. "And if you were part of that heist, then you know my parents were somehow involved. You know they're on the run, and you probably know why."

"Drea... I can't," he said softly, and she believed him. But she still didn't know why he couldn't.

"You know that by me revealing my suspicions, I'm exposing the people I love. I'm doing it not just because I need to know why they ran and how I can help bring them back, but also because I need you to trust me."

Now Xavier pulled his chair close again, right up to hers, and took her hand. "It isn't that I don't trust you. It's so much the opposite of that."

"Then what is it? What can't you say?"

Xavier let go of her hand and pushed away from the table, this time for good. As he stood up to leave, he said, "I'm not telling you for the same reason your parents had to leave. To protect you. So don't ask me again. Please."

And then he was gone.

29

Monday, 12:07 p.m.

It took her a few minutes to get her wits about her, but when she did, Drea went looking for Xavier in the eleventh-grade classroom, but he wasn't there. Between his classes and her ninth- and tenth-grade study hall tutoring sessions, she checked the classroom every period, and by lunch, realized he must have cut school to avoid her. It was so not the thing to do since he was already on the judge's bad side given the pending B&E trial. She considered texting him again, but if he was willing to get into deep trouble with the judge just to avoid her, she decided it was best to leave him alone—for now.

Drea took a seat on the bench outside the classrooms as they emptied for the lunch break. She was contemplating whether she too, would cut and run, at least for the rest of the day so she could process what Xavier had said about her parents needing to protect her, when Jason took a seat next to her.

"Who was the girl I saw you with last Friday?"

"Hello to you, too."

"Whatever. So what about that female?"

"You aren't one of those guys, are you?" Drea asked. "The kind who call girls females?"

"You *are* females, aren't you?"

"When guys use it that way, it sounds vulgar for some reason. Or like we're the prey on one of those animal shows on TV."

"Does every girl think that?" Jason asked, looking truly puzzled, as though this had never occurred to him.

"Yes, every one of us, including the girl you saw me with. Just a heads up, since you're clearly interested."

"How do you know—is she a friend of yours?"

"I wouldn't call her a friend, but trust me. She's a senior and two years older, so you already have that working against you. The *female* thing will just take you out of the running before your charming personality ever has a chance to."

When Jason smiled at that, it surprised her as always. Well, all two times she'd ever witnessed it.

"So why was she here?"

"She's Justice Academy's latest student."

"Sweet."

Drea shook her head, not a bit regretful that she was judging.

"What? It isn't my fault she's here, and if she has to be at Justice, I might as well take advantage of the situation."

Drea considered warning Jason that he probably had no chance, and even if he did, Gigi would eat him alive, but she figured it was best to let him find that out for himself.

"Is Xavier around?"

"He had to meet with his lawyer all morning."

"Did something happen?" Drea asked.

"No, just the usual pre-trial stuff."

That was something she still hadn't gotten used to, the things that were considered business-as-usual at the school, like getting a pass from class to meet your lawyer.

"I'm glad. I was afraid he'd cut."

"Why would he do some stupid shit like that?"

"We had a conversation this morning that...well, I thought maybe I'd upset him."

"So much he'd jeopardize going back to juvie when the judge gave him a break and let him stay at Justice? You must think you're one dope female—I mean, *girl*." Jason said. "You need to get over yourself and get moving on that job X gave you. There's a rumor going around that some douche is trying to overthrow the judge."

"No way. It isn't even an election year."

"That's why I said *overthrow*. He's trying to get a special ballot going, claiming Justice Academy is bad for the community. He wants to shut it down."

"That isn't true, is it?"

Jason stopped talking as a couple of judges still in robes passed them. "Not here." He stood and headed toward the other end of the hall. Drea followed him into an empty meeting room and closed the door behind her.

"He's claiming recidivism rates are bad, that kids who land here tend to end up back in the system anyway, so it's safer and cheaper to just send them straight to juvie and keep them there."

"Is he right?"

"How the hell would I know?" Jason asked, sitting on the edge of the conference table as Drea took a seat at the end of the table with only a view of his profile. She would rather look him in the eye, but that made him uncomfortable. "But I suppose X would be a prime target for this asshole, whoever he is. X went to juvie, got a pass into Justice after a year, finished his probation and even went to your fancy school for a semester, and now he's back here. And if Justice closes and Claiborne loses, this guy could rescind our probation and send about half the Leaguers into the system to finish our sentences."

"How do you know so much about this guy but you don't know who he is?"

"I know a reporter at the *Magnolia Times*. She's working on the story but it hasn't been published yet. She didn't include a name—I'm guessing dude went to her all confidential-like before he was ready for her to break the story."

Drea looked at Jason skeptically. "Seriously, you know a reporter at the paper?"

"Okay so I don't actually *know* her. She usually covers finance stuff, analysis on publicly traded companies, IPOs, that kind of thing. I've been hacking her computer for a while now, trying to get a jump on trading before she publishes her articles. I guess she's trying to break into political stories."

"So you're a stock trader now?"

"You think I'm just a crook, but I have other interests." Jason stroked his chin in an apparent effort to look thoughtful and earnest. "I want to branch out into more white-collar situations."

241

"You mean white-collar *crimes*. You're practically in jail now for hacking. Are you crazy? You'll be adding to this guy's recidivism theory—not that I believe this whole judge-over-throw story is accurate."

"I know what I read. It's happening. And you're wrong if you think Justice is anything like jail. We didn't even want to come back *here*, and we sure as hell ain't going back to juvie. X is sitting on some information he could probably trade for a lighter sentence, but he won't do it."

"What information?" Drea asked, afraid she already knew the answer.

Jason jumped up from the table and began pacing the front of the classroom. By now Drea recognized it as his method of keeping himself from getting too wound up. Past experience had taught her that it didn't work so well.

"That's not your business. You need to stop worrying about conversations with X and daydreaming about having his baby. Just work on getting our charges dropped so he won't have to use it."

Drea sighed, the hopeful feeling she woke up with this morning long gone. "I still don't know how you guys expect me to do that."

"You're the genius. Figure it out. Or your brother will find out you were at the school to do the same thing we were." Jason stopped pacing and stared at her. "Wait—he already knows, doesn't he?"

"Not unless you told him," Drea said, growing uneasy. "Did you?"

He took the chair next to hers and got right in her face. "Your world is about to go to shit. Your snob school will find out you didn't earn the GPA you plan to include on your college applications next fall. You'll be going to juvie right along with me and X."

"You can't prove any of that without implicating yourself." Drea stood and now she was the one pacing the room. "You hacked my grades. And no one knows I was even there. Xavier returned my phone, and I trust him when he says there are no copies."

"Your phone? What are you talking about?"

"Oh, he didn't tell you about that?" Drea said, beginning to feel she might finally have something on Jason for once. "Maybe he didn't think it was important to tell you. Or he doesn't trust you with anything important."

The anger rose in his face, then it shifted to worry. Drea believed Xavier when he said he was trying to protect her. She was about to land another blow on Jason by telling him she knew he was lying about Xavier using information against her. But before she could, Jason's expression turned to something altogether different, a mix of fury and triumph.

"At least when *you* get busted, you'll be going to juvie," he said.

"I'm not going to jail because I didn't commit a crime."

"But what about your brother?" Jason said, pulling a flash drive from his pocket and dropping it into her bag. "Do you have any idea what they do to cops in prison? Well, it's even worse for dirty cops."

"I told you my brother isn't dirty," she said, but Jason just sneered at her and walked out.

Drea followed behind him a minute later, leaving the building and slowly limping through the parking lot, wishing she hadn't given up her crutches so soon. She crossed the street to the park. She didn't want to be anywhere near the justice center when she plugged in the flash drive Jason had given her and opened the only file on it, called *Gotcha!*

The video quality was excellent, thanks to the top-of-the-line security equipment her parents had chosen for the school. Jason must have pulled footage from a camera mounted on the roof's edge, angled down onto the front parking lot and Magnolia Street. Clearly, Drea hadn't known as much about the school's security system as she'd thought. She hadn't realized the camera was even there. It wasn't visible from the ground, and it hadn't occurred to her to climb up on the roof to check things out.

Anyone who knew them could clearly identify Damon helping an injured Drea to his patrol car just minutes after the boys had been arrested and taken away. Any decent cop would want to know why he didn't bring her in for questioning to learn whether she'd been part of the B&E. The story about Damon going home and being there when she fell down the stairs would never hold up. Jason was right—she had been gotten.

30

Monday, 4:18 p.m.

At first, Drea was relieved to see the video because it meant the information Jason said Xavier might use to get a lighter sentence wasn't his knowledge of what her parents used to do for a living, or that they'd come out of retirement for the Peachland heist. The video meant Xavier knew all about her family, but that he probably hadn't shared it with Jason. She trusted Xavier, but was certain his sidekick would turn them all in if Xavier ever lost his loyalty.

But her relief lasted only a moment. If she'd learned anything during her first week at Justice, it was that she couldn't assume anything. Xavier may have told Jason about her family, on top of what he had discovered on the surveillance video.

Drea had no idea whether Jason had shared the video with Xavier, because Xavier never showed up for afternoon classes or her chem tutoring session. She assumed the meeting with his lawyer had either gone very long or very wrong. But she was facing a bigger problem—how to tell Damon about Jason's video. Damon was off work tonight, so she didn't have any excuse not to get it over with.

But when she got home from school and headed for the fridge, she heard Damon speaking on the landline phone in the kitchen and forgot all about her Xavier worries. "Ms. Faraday isn't here, sorry. What can I do for you?"

She hadn't heard either of her parents' names spoken since they'd left—only Mom or Dad—and hearing Damon say her mother's name now meant they weren't on the other end of the line. Was it the local police looking for them because the Peachland heist had finally caught up with them? Or was it the authorities in some lawless country where cops could be bribed, telling Damon their parents were being held for ransom? Or worse?

"No, Ms. Fitch, I'm sure they'll be back in time for my mother to begin planning the next gala. I think they're just having too much fun and have forgotten how long they've been gone, but I'll give her your message next time she calls."

"I'm pretty sure Fitch wouldn't want Mom within fifty miles of the next gala if she knew the truth about the last one," Drea said after Damon hung up.

"Who said it was the truth? Right now, it's only your speculation."

Drea slung her backpack over a kitchen chair. "Oh, come on, Damon. You're thinking the same thing I am."

"No I'm not, because if I were, it would be my duty to investigate it and let my superiors know."

"How about you do just the first part?" Drea asked as she leaned against the counter. "At some point, we'll need to stop telling people one of Peachland's richest couples is on an around-the-world antiquing trip. Use your resources and all that training they gave you at the academy and figure out where they are, even if you don't want to know for sure why they left."

"All right," Damon said, looking guilty. "I have something to tell you, but don't freak out."

"Well, of course I'm gonna freak out now."

"They told me why they left. Not the details but . . . they aren't running from the police. And for the record, the fact they told me that means they aren't afraid of me having to arrest them. I can't believe you'd think I ever would."

"Okay, duly noted," Drea said, beginning to pace the kitchen. "So tell me why they left."

"They're on a job, or scouting one anyway. They wouldn't tell me what it is, just that they owed someone a favor."

"What kind of favor could they owe that would make them come out of retirement after nearly five years?" Drea asked.

"No idea, but they told me it was better I didn't know, I guess because of my job."

"You think it's related to the Peachland heist?"

"Maybe, since I'm pretty sure they'd gone straight up until last summer. And even then, with the Peachland thing—I believe they only set up the marks for someone else, maybe for this person they owed a favor to. I don't think they actually stole the stuff."

"Yeah, I always wondered about that. Cars aren't exactly their thing," she said, joining him at the kitchen table. "But what could they be setting up now, away from home base? They made a point of cutting ties in every city we ever lived in."

"I don't know. I just hope they haven't done something stupid."

Drea was thinking that ship had sailed if they were back in business, but this whole thing was getting to be too much. Drea couldn't see a way to figure any of it out right now. "Let's not talk about them anymore," she said, taking a page from Damon's book of how to deal. If you can't control it, screw it. Or in Drea's version, screw it until you can figure out how to control it. "So are you getting excited about your date?"

Damon brightened, straightening up in his chair. "Angie called me today and said a perp in one of our cases might take a plea because of some last-minute evidence I found. Basically I've helped her win her first case."

"That should score some points outside the courtroom," Drea said, deciding to let Damon have this one bit of happy tonight. After everything got so heavy a minute ago, telling him about the video could wait. Jason wasn't going to the police anytime soon. He needed to hold the video over her to get what he wanted.

"So tell me about the case. I'm hungry. You want

something?" Drea asked, but it was a rhetorical question. Considering Damon couldn't cook to save his life, unless boxed mac-and-cheese and ordering delivery counted, he was always hungry. Drea got up to check out the fridge.

Damon seemed reluctant to tell his little sister about a police case, but only for a second. He knew she'd never tell anyone. The secrets they already shared were ancient and ran so much deeper than some investigation.

"Until last week, all the evidence in this case had been circumstantial and Angie wasn't feeling too confident, especially because it's her first trial case. It didn't help that the crime scene was over forty-eight hours cold by the time I took the call. The store employees had no idea there had even been a theft until a couple of days after the fact."

"Why does it take two days to figure out something's been stolen from your store? It must not have been that valuable," Drea said, still standing in front of the open fridge. Sandwiches would have to do. "And you need to hit the grocery store. Like, today."

"No, it was definitely valuable. A single item worth over twenty thousand."

"Wow. Was it a car dealership or something? I hope it didn't take them two days to notice a car had been stolen."

"It wasn't a car dealership," Damon said as he watched Drea pile bread, pickles, olives, deli meat, and cheese on the counter. "The reason they didn't notice anything missing was because the thief replaced the stolen item with a fake good enough to fool people trained to spot a fake."

"I guess you'd know something about that, living in this house," Drea said.

"Yeah, and I also know the fake added on a felony charge of theft by deception that makes it even worse than just the theft."

"Listen to you, sounding like a cop. So how do you work a cold crime scene?"

"There wasn't much I could do except take witness accounts—which were strong thanks to the suspect's mark being a salesman with a serious jones for her—and watch the security-camera footage. After I saw the woman on tape, her outfit just as described, I knew it was her."

"Because she was stylish?" Drea asked as she spread mayo and mustard on bread whose freshness was debatable.

"Because she was *too* stylish. She'd told the guy she was in the finance industry, and I thought the scarf and glasses were a little glamorous for a banker on her lunch hour, but she was also wearing gloves. Who wears gloves in the middle of June?"

Damon had a point, especially in Georgia.

"The sales guy didn't think anything about the gloves?"

"He thought it was just part of her look—expensive. Like her jewelry—they could have been fakes, but the guy was pretty certain the black pearls she was wearing were the real thing."

Slicing tomatoes, Drea nearly took a finger off. She knew a thief who had a fondness for black pearls.

"This theft was at a jewelry store?"

"Good guess. The guy said when she first came into the

store, she was wearing a black-pearl necklace and bracelet, and said she was in the market for a ring to match."

"I bet," Drea said, recalling how she'd thwarted the theft of her own black-pearl ring.

"Huh?"

"Oh, nothing, just that every girl likes a complete set. So what happened next?"

Damon continued, "At some point, her interest shifted to a twenty-thousand-dollar Rolex."

For a brief moment, Drea considered telling him that deducing his case was a jewelry-store theft was more than a good guess. But the minute she told him she knew the thief, he'd stop talking.

"But beyond the disguise and gloves, there wasn't much to go on from the videotape. She comes into the store, spends a few minutes at the counter mostly flirting with the salesman, asks to use the employee bathroom, then leaves."

"So she got out clean?"

"Yeah, and it was only after I slowed down the video that I saw her make the switch. Almost done? I'm starving." He got up to grab the jar of olives, and took it back to the table before continuing. "So I studied more of the tape and figured out how she got the watch out of the store using the salesman as her unwitting accomplice."

"With such a great disguise, how did you know what she looked like and whom to search for?"

"She had a tell, a mannerism that gave her away, but one I couldn't see on video. When I interviewed the store clerks, I asked them to tell me anything they could think of that was different about her. The guy could only talk about how gorgeous she was, but one of the women noticed she had an annoying habit of emphasizing every other word."

"Oh yeah, it's totally over-the-top dramatic," Drea said, getting so into the story that she forgot for a moment that she wasn't supposed to know anything. "I mean, it sounds like it would be. But how did that help give you any clue to her identity?"

"I recognized that tell, her weird speech pattern, in a Justice Academy kid who was there for a while when I interned for the judge. She would have been in tenth grade then. I pulled her sheet and found she was a perfect fit for my suspect, from physical characteristics to her criminal history. We searched her apartment and found the complete outfit."

"That's not very bright, holding on to the clothes, although I wouldn't ditch a Louboutin bag, either. Provolone or cheddar?"

"Both. Did I mention the kind of bag?"

"No...not just now, but a while back, you asked me whether a girl my age would wear certain designer labels, and I figured it would have to be the same case. Isn't it?" Drea hoped he would buy her explanation, mentally patting herself on the back for coming up with it so quickly.

"Oh, that's right. But here's where I scored some points with the DA—the evidence was still circumstantial because I couldn't find the watch, until I received an anonymous tip."

Gigi had accused the prosecutor of manufacturing some

last-minute evidence to present to the grand jury. Maybe her accusations weren't as far-fetched as Drea had thought. Except she knew her brother, and he'd never doctor up some evidence. Well, at least not for anyone who wasn't his sister.

"Who tipped you off?"

"The tipster claimed she was the perp's friend. This girl really made some bad life choices, including choosing friends who'd bust her."

Drea could relate to the accusation of being narced on by a friend, but in this case, it appeared to be true. She wondered if Gigi knew she had a backstabbing friend.

"Who needs enemies with friends like that?"

"So the tipster tells me to check the girl's school locker. Apparently the thief was a show-off. A lot of bad guys get caught because they can't help bragging."

"So the snitch friend was a classmate?"

"Even better. She had the locker next to the thief's."

Drea nearly dropped their sandwiches on the floor as she carried the plates to the table. *She* was the only girl with a locker adjacent to Gigi's. Boys were in all the others. Drea wondered who the caller could have been.

"Did you ever meet the tipster?"

"She phoned in anonymously. Once I found the Rolex inside the thief's locker, just like the tipster said I would, I didn't need to track her down."

"Because that would be an easy thing to do, tracking her down, I mean. The school could tell you who was in each locker."

"Yeah, but I didn't need to know, and getting a full locker list from the school would have meant getting another subpoena. The one I had only included looking in the suspect's locker and checking her attendance records."

"A tipster just calling out of the blue, right before the case went to the grand jury—didn't that seem a little too kismet?" Drea asked. Had Damon checked his source, he'd have found the tipster was a fraud and the evidence suspect.

"I know, especially since the caller sounded older than a high school girl, definitely not a Woodruff-educated one. I guess I was just so excited to prove to my sergeant that I'm a good cop."

"Prove it to your sergeant or to Angie?"

"Maybe both," Damon said, looking a little sheepish.

"Wait a second. Did you say your subpoena included checking the thief's attendance records?"

"That was the other big piece of information the tipster gave. She said she didn't see the perp in school after lunch the day of the theft, which was about the same time the watch was stolen. Her attendance records confirmed it."

Drea could see the pieces of the puzzle coming together in her head. But there was one more thing she needed to know about the case, at least for now.

"When you found the watch in her locker, was it just the watch, or was there anything else?"

"No, just the watch in a Magnolia Jewelers' box. Why?"

For some reason, she thought there'd be more. If you make the effort of hiring someone to set up an already guilty person, wouldn't you plant something else to make sure a conviction would be a done deal? But the actual stolen item was pretty incriminating all on its own, even without finger-prints, especially something as exclusive and expensive as a Rolex.

"If she stole it, how did she get a box?" Drea asked. "I'm pretty sure she didn't request gift wrapping on her way out with the stolen merchandise."

"I don't know. She'd been casing the store. Maybe she bought something on one of her earlier visits."

Damon had already wolfed down his sandwich and was about to take Drea's other half until she smacked his hand away.

"She would have had to go in on a day that flirty sales guy wasn't there, because he remembered every transaction he'd had with her, and he would have told you if she'd actually paid for something. It would have helped his case with his man-ager, and explained why he never suspected she was a thief."

"I interviewed all the other employees. They all recog-nized her, at least what she let them see of her—she always wore huge sunglasses and a scarf tied over her head in a way that covered her face in profile—and no one but the guy had helped her. I never thought about the box. What, you think she didn't actually steal the watch?"

The thief was channeling Audrey Hepburn in her look, hitting up a jewelry store, and seducing gullible salesmen. There was no Tiffany's in Magnolia, and she preferred the lunch hour over breakfast, but given what she had to work with, it sounded to Drea as though the drama queen had done the best she could in recreating the part.

"No, she definitely stole it," Drea said before realizing she sounded way too confident making that statement. "I mean, from everything you've told me, it sounds like the theft was real."

But the evidence? Not so much.

31

Tuesday, 3:40 p.m.

Even though Justice Academy only had forty students, Judge Claiborne had tried hard to make it feel like a regular high school, if you didn't count the field trips to the county jail or the all-day excursion to the state prison he had planned for later in the summer. Or how there were only four classrooms and the bell was really a quiet buzzer. Half the time they couldn't even hear it, so kids had to rely on their phones to tell them when class was starting, but it was the thought that counted. Just like the way the judge had thought to add a row of lockers—twenty up, twenty down—along one outside wall of the courtroom. Drea found that especially helpful the next morning when she slid notes inside the lockers of her new delinquent friends. She didn't have Gigi's number, but even if she did, she wouldn't have left an electronic trail. Drea was as cautious as any good criminal.

Just as she was heading for the meeting she'd requested, Tiana and her family—today, they were all dressed in various shades of purple—waylaid her in the hall.

"Drea, I want you to meet my play-sisters. This is Monique," Tiana said, referring to the hardest-looking one of the bunch, the one Drea still suspected of worse crimes than stealing books or setting fire to her ex's backpack, "and this is Sharon."

"Nice to meet you, but I really have somewhere—"

Monique stepped in Drea's face and asked, "You can't take a second to answer a question?" in a way that made it clear she thought that perhaps Drea could.

"Well, maybe just a minute."

"I know the judge say you here to help with science," Monique continued, "but Tiana says we need to step up our game vis-à-vis our vocabulary, grammar, and whatnot. You know, learn to conversate better."

Drea was about to point out that *conversate* wasn't actually a word, but didn't want to get sidetracked from her mission or ruin Monique's attempt at détente, even if it wasn't the most diplomatic.

As if reading Drea's mind, Tiana offered, "Monique is really smart in math. She's trying to get the counselor to let her skip Algebra Two next fall and go straight to Advanced Algebra. But she needs some help in biology. And maybe Language Arts."

"No problem," Drea said brightly, and she meant it. If she could help Tiana—and her now slightly less scary friends—she was up for the task. But at the moment, she had a more pressing engagement. "I'll mark you down in my tutoring schedule for tomorrow, but I'm running seriously late for an appointment," Drea added, half-expecting Monique to continue blocking her path, but she finally stepped aside.

When Drea reached the meeting place—the picnic table in the park that had unofficially become their spot—the boys were already there. They were also good criminals, knowing that whoever arrived earliest started with the upper hand. Getting there first meant scoping out the place, planting some backup in case things got ugly, and taking the most advantageous seat. That was where the boys were when Drea arrived, both on the same side of the table, their backs against the sun. While she appreciated Tiana spreading the word about her tutoring skills, that brief conversation had put Drea at a disadvantage even before the meeting began.

The first thing Jason said didn't surprise her at all. "Notes in the locker? Seriously?"

"I didn't want to leave any electronic evidence."

"While I appreciate the paranoia," Jason said, which also didn't surprise her, "evidence of what?"

After Drea looked around the park to make sure no one was in hearing range, she took a seat on the bench across from them. "There have been some developments in your case."

"Don't tell me unless they're positive," Xavier said. "I could use some good news. When I met with my lawyer yesterday, not only did he refuse to take on Jason as a client, he dumped me."

"Why? I thought you'd been with him awhile, since your first arrest."

"He gave some half-assed excuse about his workload being too heavy."

"Well, I don't know if my news is good, but it's progress," Drea said, digging her sunglasses out of her bag. She was committing one of her pet peeves—people who wore dark glasses and forced her to have serious conversations when she couldn't see their eyes—but she hated having the sun burn out her retinas even more. "I have to admit I wasn't fully convinced about your claim of being set up, even with the cops arriving on scene so quickly, or how they knew right where to find you. I mean, those are big red flags but still—I was there. I knew you committed the crime."

"And you're convinced now because . . . ?" Jason said.

"Because of the new girl. Oh, here she comes now."

Of course Gigi had to be nearly ten minutes late—how else could she make an entrance? Apparently that was more important to her than being a good criminal. She already had the kind of looks that made people stop what they were doing to watch her approach, but that wasn't enough for Gigi. In addition to the perfectly-timed toss of impossibly shiny hair, she also had a walk that accentuated the curves, over-the-top like the rest of her, that she'd decked out in high-end designer clothes. That she'd traded flats for stilettos to make the walk across the grass didn't lower her volume a bit. Drea had to admit the girl had moxie, wearing clothes that she'd probably stolen, knowing that she'd stand out in a tiny school where "no-name" and "knockoff" were the labels of choice. She either had moxie or she was stupid, and Drea didn't believe for a second Gigi was stupid.

"Jason and Xavier, meet the new girl—Gigi," Drea said, not really liking how Xavier was just as awestruck as Jason. Neither of them said a word, couldn't even get it together enough to say hello. *Boys.* So much for Xavier Kwon being smooth in any situation. "I'm sure we all have somewhere we'd rather be, so let's get right to it. You boys claim you've been set up."

That seemed to break Jason and Xavier from their reverie.

"Don't talk about our business in front of strangers," Jason warned.

"Are you crazy? We don't know her," Xavier said, then took another good look at Gigi—not in the hormones-on-tilt way, but more like a glimmer-of-recognition way. "Do we?"

"Oh, I think you do," Drea said. "It's the costume that's throwing you off—Gigi's skilled at using wardrobe to change her whole persona. Imagine her in a gray plaid skirt, button-down oxford, and navy blazer with a crest near the left lapel, hair in a ponytail. Or maybe you'll remember her in a white shirt and black pants, carrying a serving tray, though your paths may not have crossed that particular day."

"Wait a minute . . ." Xavier said, realizing he did know the new girl, after all.

"Besides, there is nothing original about a criminal crying set-up, right?" Drea asked.

No one said anything.

"Well, is there?"

After all three shook their heads in silence, chastised, Drea continued.

"Gigi is also claiming set-up. She says all the evidence in

her case was circumstantial until last week. That cop who arrested you, Gigi? I know him pretty well."

"Are you kidding? He gets around for a guy who just joined the force, doesn't he?" Xavier asked.

"You don't know the half," Jason said, shooting Drea a look.

"Anyway, last night over dinner he started talking about your case, not realizing I knew who his suspect was since you'd just told me all about your arrest on your first day back at Justice."

Gigi had been standing at one end of the table since she'd arrived, presumably to give the boys a minute to take in all that was her. She finally took a seat next to Drea before asking, "Over *dinner*? You're dating a cop? He's cute and everything, but no way I'm messing around with a cop."

"It's her brother." The look Jason gave Drea said *that'll teach you to tell our business.*

She ignored it and was about to continue when Gigi nearly yelled, "Wait a minute. That was your *brother*? I didn't even know you had a brother."

"Why would you know anything about my family? I mean, besides stealing from us?"

Jason looked at Xavier and smiled. "This is getting good."

"I should have known. How many Faradays can there be in Magnolia? I guess the apple doesn't fall far from the tree."

"I'm telling you," Drea said, pointing a finger in Gigi's face, "stop talking like you know so much about me and my family."

"Look, Miss Priss, you need to get a clue because," Gigi

hesitated, as though she'd decided to change course midsentence, and continued, "your brother's a *dirty* cop."

"See, I'm not the only one who thinks so," Jason said.

"I don't think he is," Gigi practically yelled. "I *know* he is."

"Oh, right. He set you up. And yet you told me the whole story of how you stole that gift for your crush, asking how could you not 'use all of this' "—Drea slid out from the table and imitated Gigi's hands-on-hips move from yesterday—"to get whatever you want."

"Yeah, I see how she could do that," Jason said.

Drea thought she heard a slight emphasis on Jason's *she*, as though Drea could not "do that," but she didn't comment and just took her seat again, but this time she straddled the bench, all the better to see Gigi's face when the girl told Drea the lie she was surely concocting.

"Your brother arrested me two months ago on nearly all circumstantial evidence, couldn't even find the thing I *allegedly* stole. But the day before my indictment hearing, he makes it magically appear. That's because he planted *fake* evidence in my locker."

Drea watched the boys' expressions change as they looked at one another.

"Besides," Gigi continued, "that isn't the only way he's dirty. He looks the other way for some of his arrests—as long as they're pretty girls."

"Whoa, I don't know where you're getting that from, but you're way off base." Drea said. She knew Damon was a player, but there was no way he'd do something like that. He wasn't even actually a player in the truest sense of the word. He was always honest and told the girls straight off what he was about. Even though he'd made some mistakes in the past, and broke the law to protect her after the break-in, Drea was certain there was no way he'd do what Gigi was accusing him of.

Gigi turned to Drea. "My *lawyer* told me so. He has proof." Not only did Gigi put emphasis on the word *lawyer*, she also punctuated it with a simultaneous eye roll and neck swivel. She may have been wearing a thousand dollars' worth of clothes right now but she had just revealed her true self, the one Drea remembered from their first meeting in her bedroom when Gigi had made that ominous remark about knowing Drea wouldn't call the police despite her threatening to do just that. Gigi was an around-the-way girl. And she was getting pissed.

"Proof? Well, he's lying," Drea said, almost shouting as she stood up from the table again. She was pissed too, and while she may have never had to do battle with hardened juvenile delinquents, Damon had, and he'd long ago taught her to take care of herself.

"Oh man, there's about to be a girl fight," Jason said, looking way too excited about the prospect.

Drea sat back down. She may not be Miss Perfect, but the last thing she wanted to be was *that* girl. Especially not with Jason watching her performance and grinning like all he needed was popcorn.

"How does your lawyer know anything about my brother?" Drea was surprised by how calm she managed to sound considering she was about ready to pop this girl.

"Oh, he *knows* stuff. Plenty. He's powerful."

"I bet he is," Xavier said. "What's your name short for, anyway?"

"Nothing," Gigi said, apparently feeling a sudden need to dig through her Kate Spade tote. She pulled out her makeup bag, from which she pulled a smaller case. Drea expected her to produce some kind of evidence, like a birth certificate or something. But when she opened the case, it was just an assortment of makeup brushes, which Gigi began evenly lining up inside the little elastic holders. Okay—weird.

"My name isn't short for anything. It's just Gigi."

"Oh wow, I don't believe it," Jason said. "Like hell 'it's just Gigi.' Your name is Georgia Garcés. "

"See where I'm going with this?" Drea said to the boys. She turned to Gigi and added, "You're lying about something. I just haven't figured out what it is yet."

Gigi kept playing with her makeup brushes, staying silent for about ten seconds, before throwing them and the makeup case back into her tote and yelling, "I'm not going to sit here and be insulted by *you* of all people, especially when you're related to that sleaze cop." Then she slid out from the picnic table, did a model's pivot, and walked off.

32

Tuesday, 3:51 p.m.

Drea got up to go after Gigi, but thought better of it, returned to the table, and told the boys, "She needs time to digest it, but she'll come around."

"She's a little dramatic, huh?" Xavier asked.

"I like it," Jason said, watching Gigi walk toward the justice center parking lot. Well, less walk and more sashay.

"It can't be a coincidence that you both landed at Woodruff at the same time last fall. What was that about, Xavier?" Drea asked. "Were you in together on some client-sanctioned job?"

"I didn't know anything about Gigi when I was at Woodruff. I have no idea whether she works for the client, and only vaguely remembered her when she showed up today."

"Then you need your eyesight checked, bro," Jason said.

"The client put me there to case the rich kids." Xavier explained. "You know, find out who'd make the best targets,

266

when their families would be on vacation, that kind of thing. And then—"

"And then you'd steal from them," Drea said, finishing his story. "You got caught during one of those jobs and that became strike two, right?"

"That's why I wouldn't tell you about it."

"Wow. Cray really is one helluva lawyer if he got you only probation and another trip to Justice after that," Jason said.

Xavier looked at Drea, she assumed waiting for her to say what he was thinking. When she didn't, he just put it out there. "All right, so now you know why we couldn't just hack the attendance records from outside the school—because I also had to break Gigi's padlock combination to plant the watch in her locker. So the client wanted us to set her up. But why? And whatever the reason, I know he didn't set *me* up."

"At some point, you'll have to stop calling him 'the client' and tell us who he is, Xavier," Drea said just as Jason pointed across the table at her. "Oh snap. Can you get into that reporter's email again? Maybe she—"

"Has a name by now? I'm already on it." Jason pulled a tablet from his bag and started typing. "And you know where Gigi got that idea about your brother letting off cute girls, don't you?"

"Okay, that whole thing is just gross, though I appreciate you thinking I'm cute."

Without looking up from his screen, Jason told her, "Calm yourself. I didn't say all that."

"What's going on between you two?" Xavier asked.

"Normally you can't stand the sight of each other and now you're finishing each other's sentences?"

"Okay, I'm in the reporter's email and—"

"What reporter?" Xavier asked. "Seriously, one of you guys need to let me in on the inside joke."

Jason ignored Xavier's question and said, "Yep, it's him. The lawyer who's running for juvie court judge and trying to shut down Justice Academy is Maddox Cray."

"What? No way." Xavier said.

Drea thought for a moment before deciding it was time she started telling the truth, at least some of it, since the boys had been straight with her. Mostly.

"Jason, go ahead, show him the video from the Woodruff camera."

Jason looked up at her. "You sure? He's never seen it."

"Thanks...I appreciate you looking out. But it's time Xavier knows everything."

"What everything?" Xavier asked, looking more than confused.

Drea didn't answer, only asked Jason to focus on Magnolia Street in front of the school once he'd pulled up the video. He paused it on the image of a man inside a car, and then enhanced the tipster's face. She used her spiral notebook to shield the screen from the sun, and the man's face still wasn't very sharp even after Jason worked his magic, but it was clear enough for Xavier to recognize him.

"I know that guy. He works for my lawyer, does his investigation work."

"Looks like he does more than that," Jason said, about to shut down the video.

Drea said, "No, let him see the rest."

Xavier looked at them both, then at the screen. Drea watched the expression on his face go from interest to confusion to anger. "Is that your brother helping you to his squad car?" He looked up at Drea, reading her, looking for the lie. Or maybe the answer to why she had lied. "He was there, and knew all along that you were?"

"I'm sorry, Xavier. I should have told you, but I was scared for my brother, for myself, and well . . ."

"You didn't trust me enough."

"Believe me, I wanted to." Drea reached across the table, about to place her hand on Xavier's arm, before she caught herself. She remembered how he'd responded the first time she'd done that.

"It's okay. We'll call it even. I didn't trust you, either, back then."

"And I still don't," Jason said.

His voice startled Drea. For those few seconds, it had been just her and Xavier at the table. She recovered and said, "Oh Jason, you know you love me."

"Whatev. So now X knows everything. Do the soap-opera crap on your own time. I don't need to see it."

"Right, okay," Drea said, getting back to business, but happy Xavier took it much better than she'd expected. She hoped Damon would take it as well when she told him all of this later. "So the tipster-slash-investigator probably learned

Damon's identity by checking his squad-car number, and recognized it from Gigi's arrest report."

"Cray must have someone in the police department," Jason said. "That's how those cops got to the school that night and found our location so quickly."

"Or Cray's investigator does," Xavier said. "He's a retired cop, worked for Magnolia PD forever before he started doing Cray's dirty work."

"He probably assumed I was some girl Xavier hired as part of his crew, along with Jason, but that I didn't get caught when you did."

Jason laughed.

"What?"

"Like we'd ever have a girl as part of our crew."

"You and I weren't even a crew until the B&E. Besides, looks like we already have one." Xavier smiled at Drea, and she was momentarily sidetracked. But of course, Jason was there to keep them focused.

"What I don't get is why he wants to be a judge so bad. He makes more money as a lawyer."

"Maybe it isn't about the money," Drea offered.

"Yeah, and Christmas isn't about the presents," Jason said. "It's *always* about the money."

"Jason's right, but Cray doesn't want the job for himself. He's doing it for *his* client. My boss," Xavier said, clearly believing it all now. "See, Cray gave me the job, but he was probably just working for my boss."

"And who exactly is your boss?" Drea asked. "When you

270

told me about your first arrest—wait, does Jason know about that?"

"Go ahead, you can talk."

Drea continued, "You helped the Feds put that guy in jail, so did he get out and you went back to work for him? I'm confused."

"Because I didn't tell you everything. Or you," Xavier said, looking at Jason. "I didn't find out until later that Cray hadn't picked my case randomly as a pro bono. His client—the man I work for now—sent him to help me. I snitched my first boss, Old Dude, out of business and into jail so Cray's client could eliminate his competition and take his best car thief in the deal."

They were all quiet. Drea assumed Jason was thinking the same thing she was—not only did Xavier snitch, but by doing so, he helped replace a bad criminal with what turned out to be a much worse version. Drea was right—she and Jason were thinking the same thing—because at the same time that she blurted, "Xavier, you didn't know," Jason said, "You were looking at adult time, X."

If Xavier was expecting judgment, he wasn't going to get it from them. He looked relieved. "That's when I figured out everyone's a con in the crime business. Even the lawyers have angles."

"Don't take this the wrong way," Drea said, knowing there was really no other way to say it, "but is that why you're so broke? I mean, most thieves who aren't doing it just to survive have money. They like the thrill, but the thrill always comes with stuff, which they also like."

"How do you know so much about what thieves like?" Jason asked.

If Jason was trying to bait her, she wasn't falling for it. She ignored his question and continued her own. "Is it because Cray's client—your current boss—takes everything you steal in exchange for Cray keeping you out of an adult sentence years ago?"

"Pretty much, except that I *am* doing this to survive. The boss isn't the kind of guy you pay your dues to and then walk away from."

Everyone went quiet while Xavier's words sunk in. They were outside on a perfect early-summer day, hearing the faint laughter of a group of kids on the other end of the park playing Frisbee. That's what they should have been doing—enjoying the summer, even if it included Justice Academy, and having a good time. Instead, they were contemplating a world without Xavier in it if he ever defied the criminal he worked for.

"But that's what you're going to do," Drea said, trying to shake off the melancholy that seemed to have infected them all, "because we're going to figure out how to let you walk away."

Xavier looked over at Drea, put his hand over hers, and held it for a few seconds.

"You guys—" Jason started, but Drea wouldn't let him finish.

"Not *you* guys. We are going to figure this out together. At some point, you're going to have to trust me, Jason."

"I was gonna to say," Jason started, but didn't finish his thought. "Never mind. So what do you propose we do?"

"Get out of here, for starters." Drea got up from the table and headed toward the edge of the park where a taxi was parallel parked. "A crew needs a proper base of operations." When she looked back and realized the boys were still sitting at the table, she pivoted around, hand on one hip, cocked her head, and stared at them without saying a word.

Drea was surprised when the boys got up from the table and walked toward her, as if under a spell. The judge had been right—no matter who you were, how rich or smart or perfect people thought you were, there were lessons to be learned from everyone. Even a conniving, designer clothes–obsessed grifter.

33

Tuesday, 4:17 p.m.

When the taxi pulled into the circular drive in front of the house, Drea hoped she hadn't made a mistake bringing the boys not only to her house but into her life. That was against the family rules, aside from the perfunctory fund-raising dinners and the occasional garden parties thrown just to ensure the neighbors, if ever questioned by the police, would never describe them as *quiet—mostly kept to themselves*, which everyone knew were the kind of people that eventually drew suspicion.

"Are your folks here? You want I should wait and drive the boys home when you're finished with whatever you're up to?" asked Frank, who apparently wasn't ready to trust Xavier and Jason just yet.

"No, they aren't, but you don't have to wait. I'll give you a call when they're ready for a ride home," Drea said as she paid the fare and ignored the side-eye her self-appointed protector was giving her. She would not be surprised to look out the window in ten minutes and find Frank still waiting in the circle despite her instruction.

As they walked up to the front door, Jason looked a little in awe. Drea reminded him that he'd been there before.

"Yeah, but I was under a lot of stress at the time."

"Because you were busy dismantling my alarm system and breaking into my house?" Drea asked.

"He did what?" Xavier's tone made it clear he wasn't aware of Jason's little stunt and that he was about to go off on his friend. While Drea appreciated that Xavier now had a sense of loyalty to her, she didn't want their first meeting as a team to get off to a bad start, so she intervened.

"He did it to help you, Xavier, and we've worked it out. Right, Jason?"

"Yeah, we're all good now."

Xavier cut his eyes at Jason and didn't look entirely convinced, but let it go.

"When I was here last time, I wasn't able to take in the whole thing. You live in a fucking castle," Jason observed.

"Not quite," Drea said, feeling slightly embarrassed as she opened the door into the foyer that would surely undermine her rebuttal.

Her parents had the house built in a French chateau style, and being her parents, had spared no expense. The circular foyer, which led to the pass-through gallery into the grand salon, had a thirty-foot ceiling and a ballroom staircase. Jason

275

had seen it before, even if he hadn't quite taken it all in, but it was Xavier's first time inside the house. At least, she assumed it was, until his response confirmed it.

"Compared to what Jason and I are used to, it really is a fuc— I mean, it's really nice."

Was Xavier watching his language for her? It couldn't possibly be for Jason, who didn't seem able to form a paragraph without at least one profanity. Drea thought the gesture kind of sweet. When she entered her code to keep the alarm system from going off, she didn't even block the view of the keypad. She'd reset the codes since Jason's last visit, not that he couldn't just hack the system again, but she hoped they'd notice and appreciate the gesture.

"I'll give you a tour if you want," Drea said, hoping Xavier would understand what she was really offering.

"It's cool you'd let me into your home like this, but we should probably get to work," Xavier said. When Jason headed for the salon, Xavier leaned down and whispered in Drea's ear, "I'm glad you trust us, though."

"I'm guessing this is expensive," Jason said when they followed him into the room and found him holding up a porcelain figurine.

"That's a Meissen, so yes, very expensive," Drea said.

"How did your family make enough bank to afford all this?" he asked.

Drea looked over at Xavier, surprised. So Jason hadn't been trying to mess with her when he asked how she knew so much about thieves.

"Did you really think I'd tell him?" Xavier asked her. "It wasn't my secret to share."

"Tell me what?" Jason asked.

Drea took a second to pray to the gods, or God, or the patron saint of thieves—whoever might be listening since she didn't really believe in any of them except in moments like this when she was just a little terrified—and told Jason the truth. "The same way you'd make your money if you had the right business plan and a good boss."

"The only way I've ever made any money is...wait, get the hell out!" Jason said, losing interest in the Meissen figurine he was manhandling and making Drea even more nervous than she already was.

"Um, Jason, that figurine is not only expensive but very rare."

"I get it," he said, gently returning the figurine to its spot on the French country sideboard. "So you're a thief?"

"Not me. My family. And I wouldn't have told you if I didn't trust you."

"Why tell me, then?" Jason asked. "Why's it so important that I trust you?"

"Because I need your help to take down Xavier's boss," Drea said.

Jason walked over to where the Hassam painting had been before the day that half of Peachland was ripped off. He ran his hand over the still-empty space. Every day since it had been taken, Drea had always wondered why her mother hadn't put something up in its place. Maybe it was a reminder to her parents of how they'd fallen off the wagon after so many years of playing straight.

"Something's missing here."

"We had a painting stolen," Drea explained. "Can you stop roaming around for a second? We need to make some plans." Drea led the way by sitting on the sofa, where Xavier joined her. Jason continued to pace.

"Not that. I mean, this whole thing. We asked you to help clear our names—"

"You mean *blackmailed* me?" Drea interrupted.

"Anyway, I know you got hormones for X, but this can't just be about saving him, or about saving the school. And I know you don't give a damn about saving me, so what's the deal?" Jason said.

Drea looked over at Xavier, who was smiling like he just won the lottery or something. "Is that true?" he asked. "You have hormones for me?"

She thought she'd feel embarrassed by Jason's assessment, but she was pleased to discover the truth didn't bother her at all. She smiled back at Xavier. "You're right, Jason. I really do care about...those things, but my stake in this is bigger than Xavier or Justice Academy. See, I have this theory."

"Wait, this is getting good," Jason said, holding up his hand to stop her. "But I think better with food. Where's the kitchen?"

The old Drea would have responded with, *You must be crazy if you think I'm going to let you wander around my house alone,* but she was still working toward a whole mutual-trust thing with Jason. She was about to answer when he said, "Never mind, I remember where it is," before leaving her alone with Xavier.

Ever since they'd sat beside each other on the sofa, Drea's right hand and Xavier's left had shared the middle ground between them. Slowly their hands had inched closer until their pinky fingers met, barely touching. She'd wondered if Jason had noticed it, or if Xavier could detect from that tiny bit of contact how warm she was growing. It was just a little thing, but just that slight touch made it so she couldn't think straight. Maybe that's why she'd done something as cataclysmically stupid as telling Jason about her family. Maybe that's why—

She never finished the thought because now Xavier was kissing her, and after all those times she'd imagined how perfect it would be when—if—it finally happened, in real life it was nothing like that all. It was so much better. She hadn't even seen it coming, but in a single movement, he had turned toward her, leaned in, and just by touching his lips to hers, made her feel like someone else. No, like who she really and truly was. She'd had boyfriends before, but with Xavier she felt so many incongruous things: safe but dangerous; beautiful but flawed; perfect, and not at all perfect, because with him, she didn't have to be. So many opposites, and yet they all felt so good.

34

Tuesday, 4:20 p.m.

And just when she thought so much good would prove to be more than she could handle, it was over, thanks to Jason's approaching footsteps. By the time he returned with a six-pack of soda and a bag of chips, Xavier and Drea were on opposite ends of the couch trying hard to pretend they were the same people they'd been just a minute ago. But Jason was a criminal and suspicious by nature, not to mention a good people reader.

"Now see, back at the park, before you interrupted me, I was going to say, 'You guys need to make out, hook up, whatever, so both of y'all can think straight. So I'm glad that's out of the way." Jason made himself comfortable on the same love seat he'd taken when he'd broken into her house, distraught that Xavier would have to spend a night in jail, which now seemed so long ago. "So what's your big theory?"

"It's about Xavier's boss—" Drea began.

"That reminds me, X," Jason said, this time interrupting her, "so who is he? What's his name?"

"I don't know. I've always just called him 'the boss' and Cray always referred to him as 'the client'," Xavier explained. "I've never met him. All my directions from him—what to steal, who to steal it from—came through Cray's man. He uses kids to do most of his work, from stealing to drug-dealing to . . . well, I try not to think about whatever else he's into."

"You knew this lawyer was dirty and you tried to get him to represent me?" Jason asked.

"He's dirty, but he's good at what he does. He mostly works criminal defense cases for rich kids who can afford him, and he usually gets the charges dropped, pleas them down, or gets them the lightest sentences, worst case," Xavier explained. "People think he's a good guy because he takes on some random juvie cases for free. What they don't know is the boss pays him a lot of money under the table—way more than his usual fees—because those random kids are part of the boss's crew. I guess as a judge, Cray can make the sentences even lighter, or maybe not at all."

"Sure wish you'd told me all this *before* you asked me to help you with that B&E. First time you ever bring me in on a job, and it's a shit storm."

"I do, too. Sorry, man."

"Um, can *you two* do the soap-opera crap on your own time?" Drea said, but flashed Jason a smile. Something had changed between them today. She was certain he smiled back, just a little. Or at least it wasn't a scowl. "Dirty or not, it's too bad my family didn't know about Cray five years ago. Maybe my brother wouldn't have been convicted."

"Your brother is one of us? See, I always said he was—"

"If you suggest my brother is a dirty cop one more time, Jason, I swear I'll have the taxi driver come in here and hurt you," Drea threatened, certain Frank was still sitting in front of her house. "And he can do it, too. I'm pretty sure he was 'one of us' in a past life."

"Do you consider yourself 'one of us' now?" Xavier asked.

Drea didn't say anything for a moment, but got up and walked toward one of the front windows, where she found she'd been right about Frank. Finally she said, "I always have been, it's just now I can finally admit it. But it doesn't mean I have to use my powers for evil. After you showed me that surveillance footage, I recognized Cray from my parents' party, the one where you and Gigi worked to set up the Peachland heist for the boss."

Xavier popped open a soda. "For one thing, I didn't know anything about Gigi. If she works for the boss, he sent her without me knowing anything about it, but I doubt it because I know everyone in his crew. At least I thought I did."

"Gigi told me she didn't work for anyone, but she must work for the boss. I'm guessing Cray put her in there as a one-time thing to work the crowd, to figure out who planned to attend the gala or would be otherwise engaged during the heist," Drea theorized, trying not to be distracted by Xavier resting his arm along the back of the white sofa, grape soda in hand. "Or maybe to lift house keys off the people who had the sense to remove them when they handed over their cars to Xavier."

"You mean people like you?" Xavier looked at her mischievously.

"People gave you their cars?" Jason asked. *"That's* the job you should have asked my help on."

"They gave me the *keys* to their cars. My job was to play valet," he explained to Jason before turning to Drea. "And for your information, I took pictures of the keys."

"Pictures?" Drea asked.

"Send a photo to a locksmith on the payroll, abracadabra, brand-new key. There's an app for that."

"Really? Because that's just scary," Drea said.

"No, that's technology. Beautiful, isn't it?" Jason asked as he tore open the bag of chips.

"You gotta catch up, Drea," Xavier said. "It's not like I go around with a key press. Do you know how heavy those things are, or how loud?"

Drea ignored his lesson on key-making as a thought occurred to her. "Cray was smart sending you to the gala—it gave you an alibi during the heist."

"Yeah," Xavier agreed. "He used other people from the boss's crew to handle the actual car thefts and home burglaries."

Jason whistled. "Your boss is evil. All those kids he's screwing over."

"That's why we're going to use our special powers for good. To take him down," Drea said.

Xavier finally moved his arm from the back of the sofa, to Drea's fleeting relief, because it was only to set his soda on the coffee table. "You know, if you commit a crime to do a good thing, it's still a crime."

"I've recently decided I'm from the Machiavellian school of thought," Drea said, going to the sideboard to find coasters for their sodas and thinking her mom would have a fit if she found them in her salon, sitting on the white silk upholstery, eating Cheetos. "The ends justify the means. And if your boss is the reason my parents came out of retirement to do a job—wait, do you know where they are, Xavier?"

"No, but your theory isn't a stretch if he was able to get them to help set up the Peachland heist."

Drea didn't need to sense Xavier's lies anymore because she now trusted him implicitly, but she knew he was telling her the truth.

"I'm still missing something here," Jason said. He draped himself across the love seat, getting comfortable. "Like, *all* the details of this Peachland heist y'all keep talking about. Your parents ran it?"

"He doesn't know about that, either?" Drea asked as she placed coasters under their drinks and handed them napkins.

"I told you—not my story to tell," Xavier said.

"They didn't run it, just set it up for Cray and the boss: determining the marks, establishing opportunity to hit them, stealing from themselves so they'd appear to be victims too. They even let Cray pick what he wanted from our house," Drea mused, thinking back to the Hassam painting she'd seen

Cray standing next to as he spoke with her father. Gigi must have asked him for the jewelry box and its contents, save the black-pearl ring, which she probably left behind just to taunt Drea.

"But for now, let's stay focused on you guys and Gigi, and come back to my parents," Drea said as she circled the room, thinking aloud. "So all of you actually committed the crimes you were charged with. But the only reason you were caught was because Cray made sure Xavier and Gigi were. Jason, you were just a bonus second-striker in his plan to build a high-recidivism case against the academy and Judge Claiborne."

"Yeah, so?" Jason said.

"So that means Xavier had a slimy lawyer but you're still going to jail, no matter if he did set you up. The only way out of this is to give the police a bigger fish than yourselves."

"Give them Cray?" Jason asked. "Hell yeah, let's do it."

"I don't know . . ." Xavier clearly wasn't going to be convinced as easily.

"You help the cops take him down in return for immunity from your own charges, or at least plea down to probation. Even better if we can take down the real mastermind behind all this."

Xavier stiffened, sitting up on the edge of the sofa. "You mean narc on my boss?"

"After the way he screwed us over, it ain't snitching, X."

"Maybe, but we could be signing our death warrant."

Drea could see she wasn't going to convince Xavier to go that far, at least not today. "Forget about your boss then. I think giving the police a dirty lawyer who is probably doing far worse things than railroading clients and tampering with an election will be plenty."

"And you don't think that will piss off the boss too?" Xavier asked.

"Not if we do it in a way that doesn't connect us to his takedown. We take a cue from my parents—make all of you look just as much the victims of the sting as Cray, at least until we can bring down the boss, too." Drea stopped in front of the wall where the Hassam once hung. "Xavier, if my parents don't do whatever job the boss has forced on them, do you really think he would hurt them?"

"Or worse," Xavier said. "Or you."

"That's why they did all this, to protect Damon and me. They'd gone straight for all those years before the boss made them do the Peachland heist."

"Apparently not," Jason said.

Drea shook her head. "I know when people lie, the way you know exactly where a firewall is weakest or the way Xavier knows the sound of lock tumblers clicking into place. They were straight. I don't think they owed the boss any favors. He found out who they are—who they used to be—and put them to work for him, using Damon and me as collateral.

"This dude is scary as fu—," Jason said before catching himself. "Why wouldn't they just run with you guys instead of doing the job?"

"The boss has reach," Xavier explained. "You can't run

286

from him. And you can never get out from under him, either."

Drea stopped pacing and returned to her spot on the sofa next to Xavier. "You mean . . . like the mafia or something?"

They were all quiet for what seemed forever, until Xavier said, "We really need to take him down."

"I know just the cop to help us do it."

"You mean your—"

"Say it, Jason, and I'll hurt you myself." Drea even paused a second to give him a chance to call her on it. When he didn't, she continued, "I can enlist an assistant DA to join us, and I have a plan, but we'll need Gigi's help."

"Yeah, good luck with that. I'm pretty sure she hates the Faraday family," Jason said, ever the skeptic, but this time he was probably understating the situation.

"Let me worry about Gigi. In the meantime, we've got a con to plan."

35

Wednesday, 5:25 p.m.

When Drea arrived at the address Jason had pulled from Gigi's school records, she was surprised to find an apartment building with a doorman. It was in downtown Magnolia, just a few blocks from the justice center, in an old five-story shoe factory that had recently been turned into overpriced lofts for people who wanted to feel like they lived in the big city. Even with all the designer labels Gigi wore, Drea had expected something else, something a little less expensive.

She had expectations based on what she knew of her other two favorite juvies, which admittedly wasn't much, but what she did know was so different than this. Judge Claiborne would say she still had some work to do about judging, especially when she came from a family of criminals who not only didn't live on the poor side of town, but gave financial support to a fantasy town where the poor side didn't even exist. Clearly

Gigi was a crook who lived more like the criminals Drea was used to, which made Drea wonder why she stayed in juvie all that time instead of posting her bond.

"What are *you* doing here?" Gigi demanded as soon as she opened her door, but her attitude didn't deter Drea. There was a reason Gigi had let the doorman send her up when he'd buzzed the intercom to get the okay. "I never told you where I lived."

"I have my ways. You didn't come to school today, so I thought I'd check on you—you know, after our conversation yesterday."

Gigi looked at her skeptically and said, "I'm not buying your Little Miss Perfect, baker-of-muffins routine anymore. You're as much a criminal as your delinquent boyfriends."

"All right, so I didn't come to check on you. We need to talk." Drea tried to walk into the apartment, but Gigi blocked her way.

"We don't *need* to do anything. You should be lucky I haven't dropped a dime on your skeezy brother."

"There's a reason you haven't. You had a day to think about it, and while you know for certain someone set you up, you're also just as sure it wasn't my brother."

Gigi didn't respond, but stepped aside, allowing Drea into her apartment.

It was a fifth-floor corner unit with high ceilings, glossy hardwood floors, and tall windows that looked out onto Magnolia Square. Definitely prime real estate. Considering how over-the-top Gigi was in just about everything else, Drea was surprised by the restrained but elegant décor, everything in shades of gray and yellow against white walls. She also had great taste in art. There were several original paintings on the living-room walls, none by artists Drea recognized, but she was certain she would one day. She'd have to tell her mom to keep an eye out for a potential rising star. Yet another iteration of Gigi Garcés. Drea wondered if she'd ever learn who the real one was, or if she'd even met her yet.

"Nice place. Makes me wonder why you sat in juvie for six weeks. Why couldn't your parents have bailed you out instead of you waiting for your not-quite-a-boyfriend to do it?"

"Because my parents aren't around."

"Where are they?" Drea asked as she examined one of the paintings, disappointed to the find the work hadn't been signed.

"Hell if I know. The day I turned sixteen, I filed the emancipation papers from the mother I hadn't seen in nearly a year. I don't even remember what my father looks like. Whoever came up with the term deadbeat dad must have known mine." Gigi walked over to the painting Drea had been studying and straightened it, though Drea hadn't touched it.

"But this apartment is really nice. I love the print on those throw pillows," Drea said, hoping that would remind Gigi she'd yet to offer her guest a seat. "You must be doing okay."

"I'm very good at making money, but I'm just as bad at saving it."

"Or is it because the boss takes most of your haul?" Drea really did wish she was more subtle, but now wasn't the time to try her hand at charm. She had important business to handle.

"Boss? I don't have a boss." Gigi took a seat in a gray leather club chair and began brushing some unseen dirt from the arm.

Drea took a seat on the sofa when it was clear Gigi wasn't going to offer her one. The girl pretended she wanted Drea gone, but she'd let her into her home and had been honest in telling some very personal stuff about her family. Or at least Drea thought it was the truth. Sometimes, trying to get a read on Gigi was like trying to watch a pixilated video. Drea found it strange—aside from her parents, she'd never had problems reading a liar before. Maybe it was because Gigi was not only a good actor, but being a grifter, she was skilled at hiding lies behind truths.

"One thing I've learned from having a cop in the family— there are no coincidences. You and Xavier arriving at Woodruff at the same time—given your backgrounds and the fact no one is usually admitted after ninth grade—is not a coincidence. And I know the boss likes using kids in his crew."

Gigi took a moment before she answered, probably trying to decide whether to lie. "I was at Woodruff to scam rich kids, of my own accord. Whoever this *boss* is you keep talking about, he wasn't mine."

Drea didn't sense a lie, but Gigi had fooled her before. On the other hand, if she did work for the boss, she wouldn't have all this nice stuff or expensive apartment. He'd have taken it all; her only reward would be freedom, according to Xavier.

"I'm one of the richest at Woodruff. Why didn't you target me?"

"Because I was told"—Gigi paused before explaining—"you don't shit where you eat. Your locker was right next to mine, and I didn't want you in my business."

"Or were you warned off by the boss, because of my parents? Because they were how you and Xavier were able to get into Woodruff in the first place. With all the money they donate to that place, the board does whatever they ask. And my parents did whatever the boss asked of them."

"Oh my God, you can't *possibly* be this naive," Gigi said, exasperated. "Your *parents* hired me to case their party guests."

Drea was stunned, but didn't want Gigi to know it. She had long ago figured out Cray had gotten Gigi one of those Faraday-bankrolled scholarships last fall. It made sense he'd get her parents to do his dirty work by hiring her directly, keeping Gigi in the dark that he was a dirty lawyer. But it must have been at his command. How else would they know Gigi? It wasn't like there's a temp agency for con artists.

"Okay, so you were at Woodruff working for yourself. I don't remember you being all that social at Woodruff, except with the drama club, so how did you pull off scams?"

"There were plenty of good targets in the drama club. And then there were the boys."

"Which boys?" Drea asked.

"*All* of them, of course," Gigi said, throwing her arms up with dramatic flair, like she was doing a morning stretch. "Alas, there were more boys than time."

"I guess that explains all the guys hanging around your locker. There were a few times there I wanted to suggest you get a room," Drea said.

"Jealous much?"

"Yeah . . . no. So you were casing these kids—but you don't break into houses," Drea said, recalling Xavier's explanation of why the boss put him in Woodruff.

"Damn straight I don't. That's so blue-collar—no offense to your boyfriend. I'm more of an *artiste*," Gigi explained. "I got friendly with a target, then with their parents, gained their trust, and made them think my family was *fabulously* wealthy. Then I told them *all* about the investment deal that made my father so rich."

"I guess you weren't telling them about the father you barely remember."

"That just makes it easier to lie about him. He can be whoever I want him to be, instead of the loser he really is," Gigi said. "Look, is that why you're here, to get my family and criminal background? Because I have things to do."

"I'm here because of something you said yesterday that really stood out. You said my brother planted *fake* evidence. You emphasized 'fake.' Actually, you emphasize about ten percent of your words—that's the tell that got you arrested, by the way—but this was a little different. You said 'fake' with a lot of confidence."

Drea didn't mention that she also sensed Gigi's truthfulness about this, but underneath that bit of honesty, she had been hiding something.

"So what?"

"So why was the evidence fake if you really stole that watch?" Drea asked, but didn't wait for an answer. "Because the one found in your locker is not the one you stole. You still have that watch, don't you?"

Gigi said nothing, but Drea sensed the beginning of the lie she was creating.

"I doubt you keep it here, though," Drea said, looking around the room. "Too risky."

"You have a *lot* of nerve coming into *my*—I mean, my house—making accusations. Like I said—I knew for a fact someone set me up. Now that I know it's your skeezy brother, I have nothing to say to you."

Drea expected Gigi to throw her out, but she got up from her chair and suddenly began straightening things around her already spotless apartment, so Drea didn't move, just watched as Gigi opened a cabinet and pulled out a feather duster.

"I'm miserable enough without you coming in here making it worse. I was dumped today. *Again.* I mean, again. Damn it—you're in my head now, criticizing the way I talk."

"Sorry," Drea said, and she meant it.

She came into this girl's house making accusations, but all Gigi seemed to want was someone to talk to, and she had plenty to talk about. She had no real friends at Woodruff, much like Drea, but at least Drea had a few people she liked to think could be real friends if she'd let them. Outside of the drama club and off the stage, Gigi had been almost a nonentity at school. Well, at least with the female student body.

"I meant for it to be helpful. That's how my brother caught you, you know."

"Yeah, he told me he recognized my speech pattern from the last time I was at Justice. I thought it was *bull* . . . shit," she said, going to work dusting the media center, which from Drea's vantage was white-glove clean.

"Nope. It was true. Because my brother doesn't lie. Well, not about something this important." Drea steered the conversation back to the reason for her visit. "You said you were dumped again. I'm assuming this was the same guy you told me about before, the one who said you shouldn't be together."

Gigi confirmed with only a nod.

"So what changed?"

"He was the reason I came back to Woodruff two weeks ago. He posted my bond, for Chrissake. What else was I supposed to think?"

Drea felt a pang of guilt. She told herself she'd done the same thing for Xavier because she felt guilty about him getting caught, but she had to admit she had the same ulterior motives Gigi suspected of her friend.

"So this guy gets you back into Woodruff, but I'm guessing he isn't a student. I remember you flirting with boys, but you never seemed serious about any of them. Don't tell me it was a teacher because that is just—"

"*Please*," Gigi said, apparently giving up on hiding her speech tell. "Do you know how much teachers make, even at Woodruff?"

"So when did he dump you?"

"Last night, after I came home from finding out my cute cop was *your* loser brother. And he didn't come up with a new excuse, just the same ol', same ol': *It's a conflict of interest*, plus the age thing. I say age is nothing but a number, but he says it's nothing but a warrant for his arrest."

"That's an interesting break-up line," Drea said just as bits and pieces of her conversations with Gigi began to form a picture, and it was a crazy one. "Are you telling me your crush is—"

"He says even if he weren't ten years older, he could never be my boyfriend *and* my lawyer."

"—Maddox Cray?"

Gigi turned toward her, losing her interest in dusting almost as quickly as she'd found it.

"How did you know?"

"Oh, I know a lot, and I'm going to tell you all about it. We're going to come back to the fact you committed a felony by stealing a twenty-thousand-dollar watch for your defense attorney, but first let's look at how coincidental it is that your wonderful lawyer dumped you on the same day Xavier's attorney, also named Maddox Cray, dropped him."

"What's that boy got to do with me?"

"On the same day he stopped representing you, Cray announced he was running for juvie court judge against Claiborne, claiming Justice Academy needs to be shut down due to the recent high-recidivism rate of the students, like you and Xavier."

"You're suggesting Maddox set us up just to create this

platform? You must be crazy. Even if he didn't want to date me, he'd never set me up."

"My parents may have hired you, but he put them up to it. He was setting you up even back then, maybe to get you into his debt and onto the boss's payroll. He probably planned to tie you to the heist, or to the scams he knew you'd run on students, whether you worked for him or the boss or yourself. But then you dropped that Rolex in his lap, tied with a bow, giving him a way to take down you *and* Xavier without the risk of opening up the unsolved heist case."

"No. It isn't possible."

"Let's run through the facts we know so far. First, he drops you after you gave him the watch two months ago. No doubt he'd already decided to run against Claiborne, but you gave him the idea for the recidivism platform."

"So far I've only heard one fact. The rest is speculation."

"He pays your bail and uses his connections—my parents—to get you back into Woodruff just in time for that watch to appear in your locker. Then he says he wants nothing to do with you on the same day he announces his campaign."

Gigi sat down again, this time next to Drea on the sofa instead of opposite her in the club chair, still holding the feather duster. Maybe she expected another cleaning attack to come on.

"But why would he want to be a *judge*? He'd be a government employee and they make *no* money."

"He doesn't want it, but he has a client—one who keeps him in those three-thousand-dollar suits—who does. That client will pay him well to become a judge and do his bidding. It's a whole thing, but we can save that story for another time."

"Do you realize how *crazy* you sound?"

"Oh wait, did I not tell you *how* I know the watch my brother found in your locker was not the one you stole? Because that's the best part."

"Well?"

"Because Xavier put it there. He's a very good thief, and his lawyer made him do it since he, I mean, Maddox Cray, has a ton of dirt on Xavier. I'm guessing you told him you got rid of the watch you stole, and he believed you, which is why he had Xavier steal another one just like it and didn't worry there'd be two stolen Rolexes floating around. But you didn't get rid of it, did you?"

Gigi didn't answer, but from her dazed look, Drea was certain she'd guessed right and continued on.

"And you know how your attendance records mysteriously changed to show you weren't in class the second half of the day you stole the watch, when really you'd made sure you were back in school by the end of sixth period? Not my brother's fault, either. Jason's a very good hacker. How do you think he knew your real name?"

"I just can't believe it."

Drea felt sorry for her because she knew this was not an act. The girl was crushed. She felt even worse that she'd have to leave her like this, but Gigi needed some time to absorb all this new information, and she needed to be alone to do it. Drea pulled out her phone, dialed a number, and a second later, heard Gigi's phone ringing somewhere in the apartment.

"Is that you? How'd you get my number?"

"Jason had already hacked your attendance records, so I figured he might as well go back in and pull your entire Woodruff file. Might be something there I could use, like home address, phone number—"

"Jesus. Who are you people?"

"We're the good guys."

"Like *hell* you are."

"Well, maybe not before. But we are now. I know—it's a lot to take in. Just think about it, and when you're good and pissed off at the right person, call me."

"What if I don't believe you? What if I go to Maddox and tell him all this *slander* you've cooked up just to save your brother from an internal-affairs investigation and probably jail?"

"You're a smart girl," Drea said, getting up and moving toward the front door. "I don't think you'll do that. I also get the impression you aren't the kind of girl to let a guy screw you over the way Cray has. You'll call me. But don't wait too long."

Drea saw herself out.

36

Thursday, 12:25 p.m.

The downtown office building was just a few blocks from the justice center, close enough that Xavier should make it back before his fifth-period pass for a fake doctor's appointment expired. He was relieved to see which security guard was on duty. Normally that could be a problem, depending on which type you were dealing with. Some figured they were only making a few dollars more than minimum wage to guard stuff that didn't belong to them and people they couldn't care less about, so any protection they offered stopped at the uniform and whether or not they'd call the police if something looked sketchy.

The other camp would probably make decent cops but for whatever reason couldn't get hired on at the department. Those guys took their job very seriously and could totally jack-up a well-planned con. The man on the desk today was the second kind of guard, but he'd been employed for as long as Xavier had been coming there. And as far as he knew, Xavier was just a kid who came by occasionally to visit his uncle, who had an office on the sixth floor.

"Hey, Jake," Xavier said in his usual friendly way as he entered the double glass doors into the lobby. "How 'bout those Braves last night?"

"Oh man, a no-hitter to sweep the Mets on the road. I know it's only June, but I think this is the year."

"No doubt, got my fingers crossed." Xavier walked past the security desk, holding up his crossed fingers as proof, and headed for the elevators. He didn't have as much hope as Jake, who, like every baseball fan living within three hundred miles of Atlanta, had been saying "this is the year" since the Braves won the World Series in the nineties. But it was a way to connect with strangers (and overzealous security guards)—a shared hope that their baseball team's glory year wasn't a fluke, even if it had been more than two decades ago.

He looked at his watch before hitting the button for the fifth floor. No one he knew his age wore a watch, but his job depended so much on the precise time, and sometimes his hands were too full with tools of the trade—climbing rope, a lock pick, bolt cutters, hand tools—to fool around with digging a phone out of his pocket.

Besides, his father had given him the watch. At first he didn't like wearing it while on a job, as though his father was there and could see what Xavier had become. Eventually he came to see it as a good-luck charm, like his dad was watching over him. Each time he was caught and arrested, he hadn't been wearing the watch. And each time he'd sit in a holding cell, alternately wishing he'd worn the watch for protection and being glad he hadn't because it was one of the few things he had of his father's. He wouldn't want it to go mysteriously missing from his personal effects when the police released him.

At 12:27, Xavier stepped off the elevator, dropped a bug in the potted plant just outside of it so he could hear anyone else getting off of it, and came upon his second set of double glass doors of the day, except these were locked. He could see the receptionist's desk on the other side was unmanned, left neat and tidy with a small lamp still lit, but the overhead lights were turned off. That meant the office was completely empty. If it weren't, Barbara Jean would have left the fluorescents on when she left at precisely noon. Xavier had figured out by now that B.J.— she hated how her boss called her that, but had long ago given up on trying to make him stop—was under-paid and overworked. But her rules regarding the lunch hour were inflexible: She stopped whatever she was doing at noon, she always took the full hour, not a minute less, and she never ate at her desk.

Xavier had never worked a target he'd known personally. He imagined that would normally make a job difficult, but he didn't mind it today. The job was made easier by the fact he didn't have to case the place. He already knew the lock on the doors was an easy pin-and-tumbler. Considering what went on inside those doors, you'd think there would be better security. Since Xavier had pointed this out to his 'uncle' a hundred times, he didn't feel the least bit guilty as he picked the lock. Not that he would have felt guilty even if he hadn't given the warning.

He made quick work of his job once inside, since he knew where everything was kept, but as he was finishing up, thanks to the bug he'd planted in the potted palm out in the hallway, he heard the ding of an arriving elevator car, followed by familiar voices. That was something he had not anticipated. It was Thursday, which meant the office should have been empty for at least another half hour, until Barbara Jean returned from lunch. Xavier was glad he'd locked the door behind him because it gave him a few seconds to get back to the front office and seated in the chair against the same wall the doors were on, out of sight from the hallway. That's where they found him waiting when they walked in, his lawyer and the man who'd helped set him up.

"What the hell?" Maddox Cray said at the same time his man reached into the left side of his jacket, which Xavier knew meant the man's hand was on the grip of a gun.

"Don't get dramatic, Pike. It's just the Kwon kid," Cray said, walking into his office and turning on the lights. Pike and Xavier followed him. "But my original question still stands. I'd ask how you got in here, but I already know the answer."

"Thieves," Pike said, almost spitting out the word.

Xavier approximated the same tone when he said, "Dirty ex-cops."

"So why are you here, Kwon? I told you I can't represent you anymore."

"Yeah, I saw you on the news the other night. You've got big plans."

"So you know I can hardly be seen with one of the very kids I'm planning to stop Justice Academy from putting back on the streets."

Xavier couldn't believe Cray was saying it with a straight face. He wanted to drop him cold, but not only was quick-draw Pike over there seething, he had come to do a job. He'd almost gotten out clean, too. Now he had to develop a contingency plan, and quick.

"I've got plans, too, and they don't include another year in juvie. You're the only lawyer I trust to get me out of this jam. If you do this one last thing for me, I'll return the favor."

"You'll get me out of jail one day?" Cray went around to the other side of his desk and took a seat. Pike didn't move.

"No. I'll give you the name of the girl you asked me about—the one you said the tipster reported seeing with Jason and me that night at Woodruff."

"What girl?"

Liar. He knew damned well what girl.

"The one you said you needed some background on because Pike suspected she traded certain favors to avoid being arrested that night. And Pike, you must have been a helluva cop back in the day to get all of that out of a tipster's report," Xavier said, thinking it was especially true considering the police report never mentioned a girl.

"Oh right, *that* girl. I asked you who she was two weeks ago when you landed in jail and you wouldn't tell me. Why the change of heart?"

"Because I care more about myself than some girl I hired to be the lookout."

"Spoken like a true thief," Pike said. "Always looking out for number one. I thought there was honor among criminals."

"It's an urban legend, just like honor among cops."

Pike scowled at him but went quiet.

"If you won't do it for me, do it for the boss. I've done good work for him. I know he can still use my skills."

Cray laughed. "I have always liked you, kid," he said, as though he were so many years older than Xavier, instead of ten, and only out of law school three of them. "Tell me who the girl is and I'll help you out."

"I could just make him tell you, Boss," the ever-helpful Pike offered.

Xavier ignored his threat. "I'm not stupid. You trained me, remember? You get her name after my trial."

"You'll tell him now."

"Stand down, Pike. Kwon's got me thinking he may be right. He could still be useful. What good would he be as a thief if you break his hands, or any other parts of him? This shows how much I trust you, right, kid?"

They shook hands on their deal and just as Xavier was about to leave, Cray said, "You've been my client for what...going on three years now? You know I always play golf on Thursdays until two o'clock unless I'm in court. Either way, I normally wouldn't be here. So why wait for me?"

"I called Barbara Jean and found out your schedule had changed. She said I'd have to hang out by the elevators until she got back from lunch at one, but I got impatient waiting out there in the hall."

"B.J. told you? Oh, right. Well, I've got a meeting soon. Close that door on the way out, will you? I don't want B.J. to disturb me when she comes back."

He got the feeling Cray hadn't believed him, but it was all Xavier could think to say. It didn't matter now. He'd done what he'd been sent to do, but he listened at the door just to make sure everything else had gone okay.

"That worked out pretty good for you, huh?"

"Yes it did. You see, Pike? I'm going to win this election because people trust me. That's the second client today to come begging for me to take them back because I'm the only one they trust to help them."

"Well, they're both pretty desperate given the evidence against them, and that Garcés girl thinks she's in love with you," Pike said.

Oh, shit.

"Did you hear something?"

"You're getting as paranoid as I am, Boss, and it's my job to be. Anyway, both of those kids made offers you couldn't refuse."

"I can refuse anything I damn well please. And those kids came back because they *trust* me. The feeling is not mutual, however. B.J. didn't know anything about me having to cancel

306

golf today for a meeting I didn't know I was having until a couple of hours ago, and I told her she didn't need to come back after lunch."

"You can always count on a criminal to lie. You want me to go after him?"

"No. I want you to dig up more dirt on my opponent. Let's grab a sandwich from the lunch truck and get back up here before my next meeting. But check the office first, make sure nothing's missing. I never did trust that Kwon kid."

Xavier frowned as he hustled out of there, already punching in the phone number as he took the stairs, two at a time, six flights down.

37

Thursday, 12:57 p.m.

The scent of grilled meat wafting from one of the lunch trucks lined up in front of the office building almost sidetracked Damon, but as good as the food smelled, he had to pass. Not only was he about to be late for his meeting, he knew it was a bad idea to add a greasy meal to an already nervous stomach. He'd pick something up on the way out, assuming his meeting went okay and he was still in the mood for a spicy noodle bowl, or maybe a gyro with extra feta. Or both. It was bad luck the way nervousness made him so hungry.

When Damon entered the lobby, the security guard took notice, getting out of his seat and coming out from behind his desk. He'd hoped by wearing his uniform, the most he'd get from the security desk was a nod and he'd be on his way, but all he did was attract more attention.

"What can I do you for?"

"Nothing, thanks. I've got it. Do I need to sign in?"

"A brother in blue doesn't need to sign in." The guard winked as if Damon's uniform meant they shared an inside joke. "We don't get too many Magnolia police officers in here. If there's something going on in my building, like a theft or an embezzlement case, I should know about it."

"No, it's nothing like that."

"Wait...it isn't some kind of hostage situation or something like that, is it?"

"If it were, there would be a lot more cops here than me. It's just a friendly visit and I just happen to be in uniform, that's all."

"Oh sure, I get it." The guard winked at him. "You're on the job."

Damon just smiled and turned for the elevators, but he should have known it wouldn't be that easy to get away. As he hit the up button, the guard was rounding the corner toward him, leaving the lobby unsecured.

"Say, do you know anybody in human resources at the police department? I've been trying to get in there for a year. Already got my POST certification and everything, just need to make the right contacts."

"I sure don't, but if I hear anything about hiring, I'll let you know," Damon said as the doors slid open. "Gotta go or I'll be late."

"Okay, good talking to you. The name's Jake—"

The elevator doors shut out the security guard's voice. When they opened again on the sixth floor, he followed the

309

signs on the wall to an office at the end of a hall, where he could see Gigi Garcés sitting on the edge of a desk through a set of glass doors. When he pushed through them, Garcés said, "Maddox is running late, but he'll be here soon."

"You said you had information for me, but you should have called a detective. I already arrested the bad guy. My part's done."

"But you came anyway." Garcés's tone suggested they shared a secret. "Look, I don't trust cops, and I don't need another one *all* up in my business. Besides, most cops don't look like you."

"So why did you insist I meet you at your lawyer's office?"

"Because I'm smart. You already set me up once. I won't let it happen again." She looked him over in a way that unnerved him and made him think of the poor, gullible jewelry salesman. "It's too bad you're a cop. But maybe a dirty cop is just a criminal in uniform, and I could make an exception because you're cute."

"I didn't set you up," Damon said in a hushed voice, looking around the office.

"We're alone, no need to whisper."

Damon walked over to the half-opened door of a larger office, which he assumed was the lawyer's, pushed it wide open, and took a look around. Satisfied, he went back out to the reception area.

"Did you find my prints on that watch I *allegedly* put in my locker?"

"No, you're too smart to leave prints. Besides, you were wearing gloves when you stole it."

The girl got up from the desk and walked around to take the chair behind it. She brushed by him as she went.

"You should have a seat. Maddox might be a minute. So tell me, *why* would I steal a man's watch?"

"I don't know. To sell it."

"Even if I did steal a man's watch, wouldn't I have held it at some point? I mean, it's a beautiful piece, and after all that effort to take it."

Damon didn't say anything, but thought about this for a moment.

"If you think I'm so smart," she continued, "maybe a jury will too. Won't they find it hard to believe I'd actually leave the watch *in my locker*? Especially on the last day of school? What if I'd missed the last day for some reason and couldn't *get* to my locker before the custodial staff could do the summer clean-out? Remember those, Officer Faraday, or has it *really* been that long since you were in school? You don't look so old."

Damon finally took the seat she'd offered, the same one Xavier had taken half an hour earlier.

"Are you admitting you stole it?"

"You're missing the point. Look, I won't *lie* to you. You know *way* too much about me. But I'm a con, which means I know a lot about *you*, too. We have very similar jobs. Reading people, understanding what they're about—and I *know* your whole thing is an act."

"What 'whole thing'?"

"The whole Officer Do-Right thing. I know the *real* deal, even if you had Judge Claiborne get it all erased."

"How do you know about that?"

"Oh, I have my ways. I know you have an expunged record, that you spent time in juvie, just like me. And *somehow* you ended up working for a judge and now you're a cop. If you were able to pull all that off, I'd say I'm not the *only* con artist in the room."

"Maybe, but that was a long time ago."

Damon glanced around the office looking for a way out, feeling the odd sensation of being trapped. It was just instinct, from the old days. But he stood up from his chair just the same. Garcés came around to the front of the desk, taking her original position again, sitting on the edge of it, legs crossed.

"Not so long ago. Isn't that other guy just dying to get out? Always having to act like someone you really aren't must get old."

Damon didn't answer, but looked through the door of the lawyer's office as though he expected someone to come through it.

"I told you—no one else is here," Garcés said. "*Aw*, do I make you nervous? I didn't expect that, considering your player rep around town."

"I'm not nervous, just pissed off that your lawyer is late."

"That reputation has followed you to the police force, I hear."

"What?"

"I heard you're willing to make problems go away for the right kind of suspect," Garcés said, standing and moving closer to him. "Am *I* the right kind of suspect?"

"I have no idea what you're talking about," Damon said, stepping back and putting some space between them. "I think I should go. Have your lawyer call me if you really have any information. And tell him I don't appreciate him wasting my time."

Garcés grabbed his arm and said, "Don't play games. You know *exactly* what I'm talking about. I told you...we're all alone. Maddox won't be here for another twenty minutes. I told him one thirty, and told you one o'clock in hopes we could come to our *own* understanding first."

"Do you even have any information for me or not?"

"You *are* all business, aren't you? I guess the rumors were wrong." Garcés sounded disappointed, but left him and went into Cray's office. "Come on. It's in here."

"What's in there?"

"The evidence that's going to get you a big fat promotion."

Damon moved toward the glass doors, as though he was planning to leave, but stopped, trying to keep his breathing easy, a difficult task since his heart was racing like he'd just run a sprint. A former con himself and now one of Magnolia's finest, with the gun on his hip and a badge on his chest to prove it—he felt ridiculous by how unnerved he was. He followed Garcés into the second office, where she ambushed him, pushing him down onto a leather sofa next to the door and falling on top of him, kissing him.

That's when the door of an adjacent office opened, revealing that Maddox Cray had been there all along.

38

Thursday, 1:11 p.m.

"What the hell is going on?" Damon said, although he already knew. Asking the question was just instinct.

"You set me up, and I just returned the favor."

"And what an excellent job you did, Miss Garcés," Maddox said.

"Did you just entrap me?"

"It isn't entrapment when you're the cop, Einstein," the girl said, shaking her head. "What did I ever see in you?"

"Nothing happened between us."

"Of course it did," Garcés said. "You did get it on video, didn't you?"

The man standing next to Cray, who'd been glaring at Damon since he'd walked through the door, turned on a TV monitor. "We certainly did."

"What we have here," Garcés continued, "is a Magnolia

police officer—thanks for being in uniform, by the way, nice touch—kissing a high school girl he once arrested, who will testify you offered to suppress evidence in her case in exchange for . . . well, that."

Damon looked at the TV monitor she pointed to as Cray and the other guy grinned like they'd just checkmated him.

"Very incriminating, wouldn't you say, Officer?" Cray asked. "Salacious, too. When Kwon gives me the identity of the other girl you helped, it will look like a pattern. Voters love salacious, and they'll hate you *and* Claiborne. You're on the hook now."

"On the hook for what?"

Cray laughed. "For whatever the hell I want. What would your boss think if he ever saw this video, saw your reaction to Ms. Garcés's fine performance? If you're lucky, he'll fire you. But I can't be the best defense attorney in town and not know you won't be lucky. You'll go to jail, and you know what happens to cops in there. That's why I'm sure you'll agree to work for me."

"You're using the video to make me quit my job?"

"That's the big question. You are useful to me in so many ways, I'm not sure what to do with you just yet. But I do own you."

"If you're running for judge, why will you need a cop on your payroll?"

"Oh, I'm sure I'll have all kinds of uses for a cop on the take, won't I, Pike? I know you've worked for Claiborne before, so you know your way around a courtroom. And now you have law enforcement ties."

"I'm not working for you."

"Let's just skip the righteous indignation. We're well past that. But I appreciate your confidence in me. You seem to think I've already won the election," Cray said, adding a smile. "And you'd be right about me winning if I decide to use you as the nail in my opponent's coffin. A juvenile delinquent who got a second chance at Justice Academy where he was taken under the wing of Judge Claiborne, who expunged that delinquent's record so he could become his intern and later, a dirty cop. A shining example of recidivism at Justice Academy. So, do I put you to good use at the police department, or do I turn you in? You see my conundrum."

"I just started on the force. I have zero juice."

"That's how I like my employees—young and trainable. In a few years, you'll be a serious asset, but even now, a rookie can be quite useful," Cray said, clearly having thought about his plans for Damon.

"Like how?"

"Don't," Pike warned, but Cray waved him off.

"When you're on patrol, pretend you don't notice drug deals taking place. Make evidence mysteriously disappear when you're called to one of our deals. Better yet, plant evidence on the employees of my client's rival."

Damon moved away from the door and stood in front of the window, staring out at people going about their downtown business. He turned back to Cray, but his eyes were on Pike, who'd never taken his off Damon since the moment he opened that door, but had now intensified his scrutiny. Damon wasn't intimidated. Any nervousness he'd felt earlier when he and Garcés were alone was gone.

"Well, you know which decision I'd rather you make."

"That attitude put points on the board for keeping you on the payroll instead of sending you to jail," Cray said.

"Shut up, Cray," Pike said.

"Did you forget you work for me? Don't tell me—"

"Shut the hell up!"

Cray pulled his gun at the exact moment Damon pulled his.

"Pike, what the hell is happening here?" Cray asked.

"It's a set-up. I wasn't a cop thirty years for nothing." Damon didn't flinch.

"He's wired," Pike said, pulling Garcés to him. "Put the gun down, Rookie. Forget what they trained you in the academy about not surrendering your weapon. I'm not a freaked-out drug dealer or a rookie cop. You won't win."

Damon didn't move. "I'm not wired."

Pike put the gun to Garcés's head. "You think I'm playing around?"

Damon looked at Garcés and saw her fear. It was clear she was now regretting her association with Cray.

"All right, take it easy," Damon said, slowly lowering his weapon and placing it on Cray's desk.

"And the wire?"

Damon opened his shirt. "See, no wire. Let her go, Pike."

"Where's your backup weapon?"

"Don't carry one."

"Pat him down," Pike said, turning the gun back on

Damon. Cray did as he was instructed, apparently having forgotten what he'd said earlier about taking orders from his second. The man with the gun was always in charge.

"I'm telling you the truth."

"Rookie mistake, not carrying a backup."

Damon smirked, looking Pike in the eye. "I never said I didn't have backup. I'm not wired, but they are listening in. You aren't the only one who can plant a bug and camera. In fact, there's a SWAT sniper across the way with a Remington trained on your head at this very minute. If you don't put down your weapon, he's going to kill you."

Cray looked toward the window. "Bullshit."

Pike stared at Damon, never breaking his gaze.

"No, he's telling the truth," Pike said, slowly raising his hands—and the gun—above his head, just seconds before the room filled with Magnolia police officers.

39

Friday, 12:50 p.m.

Drea was waiting in the assistant district attorney's office with her new friends. Well, it was probably a stretch to call them that, but Gigi, Jason, and Xavier—especially Xavier—meant a lot more to her today than they did yesterday. But still she hung back a little, standing just inside Evangeline's doorway rather than joining the rest of them at the small round table across from her desk. Drea blamed it on the fact that the table was only meant for four, even though Jason—yes, Jason—offered to find her a chair.

But really it was because, as close as they'd grown in just twenty-four hours, she didn't feel quite one of them yet. Even after Xavier's kiss, and the way Jason had been in sync with her since they'd joined forces, Gigi seemed to be more at ease with the boys than Drea, and they'd only known her a few days. I guess that's what happened between strangers when one of them had a gun held to her head for the sake of the others. Talk about taking one for the team.

"So, that wraps it up," Evangeline was saying. "Jason and Xavier, your new lawyers have all the paperwork for your immunity from the break-in charges. Gigi, same for you and the watch theft. You're all back to completing your original probation sentences for your prior convictions."

"So why can't I go back to Woodruff in the fall to make up my last semester?" Gigi asked. Whined, really. "Why do I have to go to Justice Academy? Because that is *not* what I had anticipated."

"Woodruff probably won't have you after they find out about all this, even with the immunity," Xavier said.

"And seriously? You stole a twenty-thousand-dollar watch," Jason added. "Even I can't see how you can gripe about going to Justice."

"But I got immunity—"

"And you violated probation for the sweetheart scam," Drea added, startling everyone at the table. She'd been quiet for so long, they must have forgotten she was standing there. She didn't even mention the people she tried to scam at Woodruff. "Just thank the nice lady, Gigi, and be glad you're going home tonight instead of lockup."

"Don't thank me. This was all your fearless leader's idea, guys. She was the one who told me what Cray was up to, who he really was, and offered your help in exchange for immunity. Drea came up with the idea to have Gigi sell Cray on the plan to entrap her brother and to plant audio/video in Cray's office."

Evangeline made a point of looking at Jason and Xavier when she said, "I don't want to know how she made that happen, but if a bug is ever required again—and it had better not—please let the DA's office do the planting, will you?"

"No worries. Won't happen again," Jason said, but Evangeline didn't look convinced.

"So you owe Drea your thanks, not me. And maybe a pizza or something."

"I definitely plan to thank her." Xavier turned around to flash the smile that made Drea weak.

"I have one question," Drea said. "Cray kept mentioning a client when he was revealing his scheme to Damon. Any idea who that client was?"

"Under questioning, Cray admitted there was no client. It was just a scare tactic to keep his crew in line—you know, some big, scary mafia type who would come down hard on the kids, their friends or family, if they got any ideas about informing or leaving," Evangeline explained as she gathered file folders from her desk and shoved them into her briefcase. "Okay guys, I have court in two minutes. You have to go. Any other questions, talk to your lawyers."

Drea didn't ask any more questions, but she knew Cray was lying even without being in the interrogation room to detect it. There really was someone he worked for. That Cray—the smarmiest defense lawyer in the world—hadn't implicated his client in exchange for a lesser charge, meant the boss was even scarier than they'd all imagined. And her parents were still beholden to him.

That's what was missing, the reason Drea was still cling-
ing to the person she was before the B&E, even if that person
wasn't her real self. Maybe she couldn't fully commit to these
people, these friends—no, her crew—because her parents
weren't home yet, and her world wouldn't be right until they
were. But she'd talked to them an hour ago. They'd soon be
boarding a plane home from wherever Cray had sent them.
Their project had been suspended, but only temporarily, and
that was as much as they would say over the phone. She and
Damon were looking forward to hearing that story tonight.
The boss still loomed, but her family would soon be together
again, and she was certain that the Faradays united could take
him on, whoever he was. She felt happier than she had in
weeks.

When they were all out of Evangeline's office and heading
for the main exit, Xavier leaned in close to Drea and whispered, "You don't believe Cray's story about there being no
boss, do you?"

"Not for a minute, but let's not worry about it today," she
whispered back, before adding in a voice they all could hear,
"Since Judge Claiborne gave us the rest of the day off, I'm taking you guys to lunch to celebrate."

Xavier said, "Shouldn't we be treating you?"

"She's rich," Jason said. "Let her treat if she wants."

"I heard that new French place that just opened down the
street has *to-die-for* chateaubriand and—"

"Whoa, Gigi. Let me clarify. I was thinking food from the
taco truck and our table in the park."

"To our fearless leader," Xavier said after they'd bought their food and settled in at their favorite table, popping open a soda and raising it in Drea's direction.

"I'm no leader, I'm just much better at the planning than the execution. You guys did all the work. Gigi, thanks for trusting me and making that phone call."

"It wasn't so much about trust as it was about wanting to take down that asshole Cray. *Nobody* messes with Gigi Garcés like that."

"It's a good thing you hadn't fenced that Rolex yet—" Drea said.

Gigi responded by putting up a hand to stop her. "I didn't *fence* it because I am not a common thief. No offense, Xavier."

"Some taken."

"Okay, to do whatever you were going to do with it," Drea continued. "Having Xavier plant it in Cray's office when he planted that camera was perfect justice, even if totally illegal."

"By the way, it would have been nice if you'd told me before I went to Cray's office that Gigi had agreed to help," Xavier said. "I nearly broke *my* ankle trying to get down the stairs so I could call and warn y'all about her."

"I figured only Damon and Gigi needed to know that part. Plus the DA and the police, of course," Drea explained. "And before any of you ask, it isn't that I don't trust you, because I do. But when it comes to a good con, working on a need-to-know basis means fewer points of failure."

Jason looked at them, shaking his head. "Just my luck I've joined the least tech-savvy crew in the state. You guys do know

I turned on the bug and was listening to the whole thing the minute I watched X go into the building, right? You didn't need to eavesdrop at Cray's door and risk being discovered and possibly killed. I admit it took me a second to figure out what the hell was going on between Damon and Gigi, though."

Just then, a group of lawyer-looking people in suits walked by holding bags from the taco truck, so they all went quiet. They heard the lawyers complaining about the midday heat before they turned back toward the justice center in search of air-conditioning.

"Anyway, now Cray will be charged with making us both steal Rolexes for him—mine to put in your locker to set you up, and yours just because he wanted it," Xavier said. "Not that it matters, considering the long list of charges he was already facing without us playing dirty."

"It isn't dirty when the end justifies the means, right, Drea?" Jason asked.

"It matters to me," Gigi said as she grabbed a taco from the bag and scowled. "That loser deserved it, and technically, I *did* steal mine for him, even if I did it on my own. Fortunately no one will believe him if he disputes it. And to think, my gift is what gave him the whole idea for his recidivism platform. If I hadn't stolen that Rolex and offered it to him, I wouldn't have been involved in all of this."

"Yeah, but then you wouldn't have gotten to know me," Jason said, still looking hopeful and maybe a little lovesick.

Gigi picked up a pack of taco sauce and started to throw it at him but changed her mind, either because she was Gigi and couldn't turn down adoration from any guy, or because maybe Jason was finally wearing her down.

"It all worked out in the end, but I'd best not *ever* discover the name of the skank who claimed she was my friend and told Damon the watch was in my locker."

"She was probably one of Cray's juvie clients," Xavier offered.

"I don't think so. Damon said she sounded older," Drea said.

"Considering who your parents are, you should know better than anyone that people aren't always who they seem." Gigi affected an aristocratic British accent and added, "I can sound like the Queen of England if I want."

"Are you going to miss conning people out of their money as I much as I'll miss hacking them out of it?" Jason asked Gigi.

"So, so much. It's a shame not to use the talents God gave me." Gigi sighed. Jason nodded his agreement.

Xavier moved closer to Drea and ran his hand down her back, just like that first night they had found each other again in the glow of a SecureForce XJ11 alarm keypad, when he'd stolen her phone. He let it linger briefly at the small of her back before he moved it away. She knew he wanted to kiss her, but there would be time for that later, when they were alone. This moment was about their crew. Mostly.

"I think I could like being on the right side of the law, as long as I get to still be a thief," Xavier said. "You have any other ends that need justifying?"

Drea thought of her parents and whatever it was they wouldn't say over the phone. The Cray affair might soon be a closed case in the DA's office, but she was certain that wouldn't be true in the Faraday house.

But that was a problem for another day. Probably tomorrow. But at that moment, Drea realized that these people who had been strangers—enemies even—only two weeks ago might be her first true friends. She hadn't been totally honest with them yet—and still had a few confessions to make—but they knew more about the real Drea than anyone outside her family had ever known, and that seemed like a good start.

"I just might," she said. "Bad guys are everywhere."

Acknowledgments

While a writer sits alone at her desk clicking away at a keyboard, making up characters and stories and worlds, there are so many other people there with her, helping turn all those things into a book she can share with readers.

To Kristin Nelson, my agent and defender, thank you for looking out. To everyone at Lee and Low Books, thank you for your dedication in producing books in which all children have a chance to see themselves. Stacy Whitman, my editor and publisher—I am so grateful you have created Tu Books and appreciate how passionate you are about giving voice to underrepresented stories, and to the people who write and read them. Thank you for helping me become a better writer.